THE CHINTAMANI

BOOK 4 OF THE MAQLÛ

JC HOLMBERG

Library of Congress Control Number: 2023905797

This is a work of fiction and is a product of the author's imagination. Any references to historical events, real people, or real places are used fictitiously.

Learn more about the history and background of this book at: www.JC Holmberg.com

Front cover image by Rebecacovers

PCIP provided by Five Rainbows Cataloging Services

Names: Holmberg, John C., 1956-

Title: The Chintamani / John Holmberg.

Description: Pine Knot, KY: Tist Fiction, 2023. | Series: The Maqlû, bk. 4. | Summary: Alex Scire helps the ghost of William Wallace find his scattered remains so he can move on. | Audience: Grades 5 & up.

Identifiers: LCCN 2023905797 (print) | ISBN 978-1-956342-17-8 (paperback) | ISBN 978-1-956342-18-5 (hardcover) | ISBN 978-1-956342-19-2 (large print/dyslexic friendly) | ISBN 978-1-956342-16-1 (ebook) | ISBN 978-1-956342-15-4 (audiobook)

Subjects: LCSH: Adventure stories. | CYAC: Ghosts--Fiction. | Magic--Fiction. | Fantasy. | Young adult fiction. | Historical fiction. | BISAC: YOUNG ADULT FICTION / Fantasy / Historical. | YOUNG ADULT FICTION / Fantasy / Wizards & Witches. | YOUNG ADULT FICTION / Action & Adventure / General.

Classification: LCC PZ7.1.H65 Ch 2023 (print) | LCC PZ7.1.H65 (ebook) | DDC [Fic]--dc23.

To David,

Who got me writing

CONTENTS

"Life isn't about finding yourself. Life is about creating yourself."

George Bernard Shaw

CHAPTER 1
A CHANGE OF SCENERY

Alex Scire looked back at the ruins of what had been Vlad Dracula's prison and wondered who'd created the mysterious castle. A sudden thump on his shoulders, followed by a nip on his ear, brought him out of his reverie. An instant later, Sadie was sending him images of a path cutting through the dense pine forest on the opposite side of the meadow.

He lifted the little dragon off his shoulder, tucked her into the crook of his arm, and looked for the opening he'd seen in his mind. Spotting it, he headed for the far side of the meadow, with thoughts of Avalon and the Holy Grail bouncing around in his head.

But as he approached the forest, he wondered if his mind was playing tricks on him as he noticed it was dramatically different from when he'd first crossed the Arges River two days earlier. Not only had the trees changed from primarily deciduous to pines, but he also noticed a new sound had intruded into the forest – that of crashing waves.

He'd only gone a short distance down the path when he felt a cold wind blowing through the forest with an odd briny smell. Shivering, Alex stopped, pulled his jacket out of his pack, and put it on, ensuring the Grail stayed safely inside. He was so confused by the altered conditions that he didn't see the trail ending until he came to a ledge and had to flail his arms to stop from falling down a steep, snow-covered hillside.

Gone were the Arges River and Carpathian Mountains of central Romania that he'd expected to see. In their place was a stunningly beautiful fjord with steep snow-covered mountains surrounding it. Shivers raced down his back as he realized that, somehow, he'd traveled to a different place. He turned to look for the path he'd just come from, but the trail had disappeared, replaced by a solid wall of pine trees.

Hoping Sadie could explain the change in his circumstances, he looked around but saw that she'd disappeared too. Alex called out for her, but all he heard was the moaning of the wind and the crashing of the waves.

As he looked for some sign of civilization, a stocky blonde woman in a long, red, woolen dress apparated in front of him and hovered in mid-air a thousand feet above the dark blue-grey waters of the fjord. He was so startled by her sudden appearance that he stumbled backwards and fell. Staring up at the strange ghost, he asked, "Who are you? What do you want?"

"My name is Sigrid Storrada. I'm not here to hurt you; rather, I've come to thank you."

"The name sounds familiar, but I can't place where I've heard it before," Alex replied.

"You helped my most trusted Jarl, Thorfin Karlsefni, destroy the Palantir and move on to Valhalla. And for that, I'll be forever grateful," Storrada said.

"Ah. Now I remember. He told me about you, but you should know he helped me far more than I helped him. He saved my life countless times and helped me fight a tyrannical king to free a bunch of ghost slaves."

Sigrid smiled and said, "Nevertheless, I want to repay you for all you've done. So, I've gathered a dedicated group of men below who will take you wherever you need to go."

Alex looked at Sigrid skeptically. "How'd you know I destroyed the Palantir? And, for that matter, how'd you know I'd be here?" He looked around and said, "Heck, I don't even know where I am. A couple of days ago, I was in Romania. But this place doesn't look anything like there. It all seems too coincidental that you show up right when I get here.

"That's a lot of questions. But I'll answer the easy one first. You're in Norðweg," Sigrid replied.

"Never heard of it," Alex said. "Where's that?"

"Norðweg is what we called our country a thousand years ago. People nowadays call it Norway."

"But that's got to be two thousand miles away from where I was. How could I get here just by walking down a path in the forest?"

"I don't know what to tell you except to say that Odin moves in mysterious ways. It was Niorun, the goddess of dreams, who told me what you've done and to come and help you. We've been here for quite some time awaiting your arrival. More than that, I can't tell you, as I'm just as confused by all this as you are. Right now, though, why don't we get off this mountain top and out of the wind? My friends below are building a fire where you can warm up. But be careful on the way down, as the path is steep and dangerous."

Sigrid headed down without looking back.

Alex patted his pack to ensure the Grail was still there, then followed her down the narrow rocky trail.

As much as he wanted to look at the amazing view, Alex had to focus as the way down was much steeper and more dangerous than the Viking ghost had indicated. At times he had to turn around and crawl down, holding onto trees and bushes to ensure he had a firm handhold. Just when he thought he'd make it down safely, the warm, enticing smell of the campfire wafted over him. Anxious to warm up, he rushed down the last bit of trail but lost his footing and slid down the path, stopping only when he slammed into a tree and got the wind knocked out of him.

Alex lay groaning on the ground for several minutes, trying to catch his breath. When he could finally breathe again, he stood up and stumbled after Sigrid towards the beach.

With only a light jacket to keep out the cold, Alex looked forward to getting next to the fire but paused when he saw twelve burly men standing around the flames. One man with long, dirty blond hair and piercing green eyes turned towards Sigrid and asked, "Is this the lad you were expecting?"

She nodded and looked like she was about to say something but stopped and turned to Alex. "I was so excited to meet the person who destroyed the Palantir that I forgot to ask you your name."

"Alex Scire, Ma'am."

She nodded and said, "This is Leif Erickson. He and his men will take you where you want to go."

Leif walked over to Alex and looked him up and down. "You don't look like you could hold up in a light breeze, much less destroy the object Queen Storrada has been talking about for the last millennia. Did you use magic?"

A shiver wracked his body just then, causing Alex to ignore Leif's question and run to the fire. Shivering from the combined effect of the wind, the cold, and the ghosts' presence, he stuck his hands out to the flames and said, "I'm not prepared for this cold. Yesterday, it was early summer in Romania. And now…," he waved an arm at the surrounding snowy countryside, "I'm here."

A loud whinny caused everybody to look up into the sky. Alex smiled when he saw a woman riding a chestnut-colored horse, winging her way towards the group. With her golden hair streaming out from beneath her helm, the Valkyrie guide for the souls of dead Viking soldiers swooped down, grabbed Queen Storrada's hand, and hauled her up behind her. An instant later, they'd disappeared into the clouds.

"That sight will never get old," Alex murmured.

All the men nodded in agreement.

"I understand that you helped Thorfinn move on to Valhalla," Leif said. "My thanks to you, for he was a good man."

"You knew Thorfinn?" Alex asked.

Leif nodded. "I met him a thousand years ago, right before he followed my path to Vinland." There was a prolonged silence before the Viking added, "We volunteered for this mission, hoping to move on too. Can you help us?"

Wanting to buy time so he could figure out how to reply, Alex rotated so he could warm his backside, flipping his braids over the front of his shoulders to keep them away from the fire. He looked at the double-prowed Viking longship rocking gently in the water – its bright multi-colored shields hanging on the sides over the oar holes, and shivered at the prospect of sailing on it across the North Atlantic. Seeing all the men staring at him intently, he said, "I'm not sure how things work in the afterlife. The only thing I know for sure is that those who die in battle move on, but not necessarily to the same places that people like Sigrid and Thorfinn did."

"Come. You must know more than that," Leif said.

Alex shook his head. "Not really. Sometimes I've seen ghosts move on when they help me, but not always."

"Well then, I guess we'll take our chances with you," Leif said. "How can we help?"

A little embarrassed at how ridiculous it sounded, Alex said, "I need to get to Avalon, wherever it is. Will you take me?"

"If you don't know where it is, how do you expect us to find it?" Leif asked.

"In the legends of King Arthur, it's somewhere in England or Wales. I feel confident I'll find it if you get me close."

"I can deal with that," Leif said, sticking out his hand.

"I'm sorry. I'd shake your hand, but I get really cold when I'm around spirits and freeze when I touch them. And speaking of cold," Alex said, "I don't see any shelter on your ship. I won't make it dressed like I am. And I'll also need something to eat."

"We'll take care of you, lad." Leif turned towards the group's youngest member. "Thorkel, find him some supplies and clothing." To the other men, he said, "As soon as my son returns, we depart. So, pack up."

As Alex watched the Vikings getting their ship ready, second thoughts crept into his mind about setting foot on another ghost ship. He shifted his stance and felt the Grail softly clunk against him. Alex slipped off his pack and reached in to pull out the Grail. As his hand closed around it, he was surprised by its calming effect. Cold, hungry, and lonely, he whispered, "When I get you to where you're supposed to go – that's it. I'm done with all this and will never seek another magical object again."

CHAPTER 2
IF THE EYES HAD NO TEARS

Thorkel returned an hour later and dumped a load of food and clothing into the longship.

"Where did you get all that?" Alex asked.

"I can take it back if you want, but you won't last a day out at sea dressed the way you are," Thorkel replied.

Alex looked at the snow-capped mountains surrounding the fjord and shivered. "I didn't mean to imply you did anything wrong," he said. "And you're right. I wouldn't last long out there. So, thanks for getting those supplies."

Thorkel nodded and headed to the bow of the ship as his father, Leif, turned to the men still ashore and roared, "Everybody aboard. We're heading to sea."

Alex watched the Vikings fly onto the ship and take their places, wondering how he would board.

"Well, are ye coming with us or not?" Leif bellowed.

Seeing no gang plank, Alex shouldered his pack, tightened the chin straps on his Tilley hat, and, grimacing, waded into the frigid waters. He tried climbing in, but his fingers barely touched the gunwale. Alex crouched down and jumped, but before he could grab hold, one of the crewmen reached down and pulled him in.

He cried out in pain when he fell hard onto a bench, bruising the same side he'd hit earlier. But no one seemed to notice. Shivering from being cold, wet, and sore, he crawled over to the supplies Thorkel had stolen for him and changed into warm, dry clothes. When he finished, he saw that most of the Viking ghosts had already sat down and placed their hands on the oars, except for Snorri Karlsefni, who was hoisting the red and white striped sail into position, and Leif, who stood at the stern, gauging the weather – looking from the clouds to the sea and back again.

The Viking leader looked down at Alex and frowned. "If you want us to take you to Avalon, you'll have to earn your way. So, grab an oar."

It wasn't how he'd envisioned getting to Avalon, but Alex reluctantly found an empty bench and sat down. A few seconds later, Leif shouted, "Row. Let's take the *Naglfar* out." A dozen sets of arms simultaneously pulled back on their oars, with Alex being the only one out of sync.

Leif guided the longship out of the fjord and through the islands at the entrance. When they cleared the Norwegian coast, a stiff breeze hit the ship, making the large sail in the center snap tight and sing. With the wind coming out of the northeast, Leif had his men bring in their oars and lock them in place. Soon the Viking ghost ship was cutting through the water at almost eight knots an hour.

Even though his back and arms ached, Alex was grateful for the exercise as it had warmed him up. Wanting to stay that way, he pulled a coat from the pile, then, with his stomach grumbling in protest at its mistreatment, pulled out a piece of dried salmon and began eating.

The rest of the day seemed to fly by, and before he realized it, it was nightfall. Not worrying about what the Viking spirits would say, Alex picked up one of the reindeer pelts Thorkel and brought on board, wrapped the thick warm hide around him, and lay down between two rowing benches. Comforted by the knowledge he was on his way to Avalon, the sounds and scents of the sea soon worked their magic and lulled him to sleep – despite the bawdy jokes and tales the Viking ghosts were telling.

The winds shifted the next day, bringing cold arctic air down on them and making the sea so choppy that Leif changed course and guided the sleek longship ashore on one of the remote Shetland Islands – just as sleet started to fall. As soon as the crew secured the boat, Leif had his men use the sail as a tent to provide cover for Alex and their gear.

Alex woke the next morning to a grey and sullen dawn. As he stared out over the white-capped waves, he wondered how the shallow longship could survive the rough seas and was surprised when Leif decided to launch, despite the conditions.

His worst fears soon came to fruition as a gale roared in out of the Arctic shortly after they'd put to sea. The waves grew higher, forcing the *Naglfar* to claw its way up one wave after another, only to fall away, sending the ship plunging into the next trough. Cascades of water crashed over the boat, soaking Alex and chilling him to the bone. His hands grew numb from bailing water, but the cold didn't bother the Vikings, as they kept singing and laughing as if the storm were nothing.

Near sunset, Alex spotted an island and crawled back to Leif. With teeth chattering so hard he could barely get the words out, he asked, "Can we land on that island ahead? I need to warm up."

"That's the Isle of Lewis in the Outer Hebrides," Leif replied. "Unfortunately, the wind is blowing from the wrong quarter. If we got too close to shore, the surf would pound this ship to pieces. I'm sorry, lad, but we'll have to stay out at sea until this storm passes. And don't worry about bailing. Just wrap yourself up in one of the hides and try to stay warm. When we were alive, we heated the deck with hanging charcoal stoves, but now that we're dead, we don't prepare for the cold since we don't feel it." Leif abruptly cut off the conversation, as a strong gust tried pushing the ship sideways, forcing the Viking to lean hard on the steering oar to keep the ship from broaching.

Halfway through the night, Alex was so miserable that he began wondering if being in an open longship in a North Atlantic gale was even worse than when he'd fallen overboard during a hurricane in the Caribbean. It wasn't until the sky finally lightened the next morning that he had his answer. Unfortunately, it was just as bad and scary, for all he could see was an endless horizon of nothing but grey – from the sky to the seas crashing over their little ship.

By late afternoon of the second day of the storm, the wind finally calmed down to a steady breeze letting the waves subside slightly. A break in the clouds allowed a tiny ray of sunshine to peek through, highlighting a coastline off the starboard side and cheering Alex. He worked his way back to Leif, who never seemed to sleep nor tire, and asked, "What's that island?"

"That's the eastern coast of Ireland. It's a beautiful land, with a magical feel, unlike any other place I've been to."

"Can we land there tonight?" Alex asked. "I don't know how much more I can take of this voyage."

Leif looked down from his perch and saw how wretched Alex looked. "I keep forgetting what it's like to have flesh and bones. Aye, I'll try, but I won't promise you anything. If it looks too dangerous to land, we'll stay out at sea, and you'll have to endure the hardships."

All Alex could do was nod and return to the middle of the ship, where he curled up in his hide.

Luckily, Leif found a small secluded spot where he beached the *Naglfar* a couple of hours after sunset. Half a dozen Vikings jumped into the pounding surf and pulled the shallow-hulled boat onto the beach. To Alex's relief, while most of the crew went about securing the ship, Leif had some men gather driftwood to start a fire. As soon as it was going, Alex headed towards it as a moth to light.

It wasn't until midnight that Alex finally dried out and started warming up. He'd noticed a small stream that emptied into the ocean a short distance from where they'd beached and headed for it, realizing he hadn't had anything to drink in over a day. The cold clear water almost hurt as it went down his parched throat. Remembering his experience on Bimini, he went easy on the water and returned to the fire, where he had his first meal since the storm began. Then he rolled into one of the reindeer hides that had dried out and fell asleep near the fire on the beach.

The wind had quieted, and the waves subsided when he woke the next day. Alex walked over to Leif and said, "I still don't have any idea of how to find Avalon. What do you think we should do?"

Leif shrugged. "I don't know. Some stories place it in the Mediterranean, some in Europe, but as you said, most put it somewhere in England or Wales. I suggest you don't overthink it and follow your instincts."

Alex looked out over the Irish Sea and said, "It's at times like this that I wish my friends were here to help me think through this situation." He lapsed into silence until he suddenly blurted out, "You're right. Let's head towards Wales. Maybe I'll be able to sense it if you get me close."

"Are you in a hurry?" Leif asked.

"Yes and no. I mean, I'm sure there's no rush in finishing my task because it's been delayed for centuries. But my grandfather and friends have got to be worried about my disappearance. Plus, I want to be done with all this." He shivered just then from a gust of wind and asked, "Is it always this cold? I thought it'd be a lot warmer since it's the middle of summer. I'd hate to be doing this in the winter when it's even colder."

"What are you talking about?" Leif replied. "Of course, it's cold now. It's still spring."

"It can't be," Alex said. "I've only been gone a few days, and it was mid-June when we were searching for the…, I mean sightseeing in Romania."

"I don't know what to say except to tell you it's spring here," Leif said.

Alex was about to argue the point but decided he didn't have the energy and dropped the subject. Instead, he asked, "How easy will it be to get to Wales?"

"Not difficult at all. It's just across the Irish Sea. We could head straight east to England, then follow the shoreline to wherever you want to go."

Alex thought for a minute before saying, "Let's do that."

They sighted the western coast of Wales before noon that day. At first, Alex was riveted by the stunning cliffs along the shoreline. But as the hours passed, with no sign of Avalon, his hopes dimmed.

It wasn't until they finally rounded the southwest tip of Wales several hours later and headed up the Bristol Channel that his heart began racing. He felt the ankh, wondering if it was the cause of his heart palpitations, but was surprised to find it lying quietly against his chest. Unsure what was happening, he made his way back to Leif and pointed south. "Can we head over there?" he asked.

Leaf nodded. "Have you spotted something?"

"I'm not sure," Alex replied. "It's just a hunch, but I've learned to trust them."

Alex spotted a castle atop one of the peaks just as the sun started dipping below the horizon. Fearing he might be seeing things, Alex rubbed his eyes and looked again. When he saw it was still there, Alex crawled over the benches to get to Leif, pointed past the bow to the starboard side, and asked, "Can you see that castle up there?"

Leif looked to where Alex was pointing but didn't answer right away. Finally, he said, "I guess my eyesight isn't as good as it used to be, as I don't see anything."

Even though he wasn't entirely confident the castle was real, Alex said, "I need to go ashore here."

"Are you sure?" Leif asked. "There are easier places to land. If we drop you here, you'll have to climb a sea wall to go inland. Then there are marshes on the other side. It'll be tough going just to reach dry ground." When he saw Alex wasn't going to change his mind, Leif said, "At least wait till morning. You'll be crossing dangerous land in the dark."

Alex gulped down the lump of doubt in his throat and shook his head. "No. I need to go now – before I lose my courage."

A few minutes later, Alex saw a dark gap along the rock wall bounding the coast and said, "There. That's where I want to go. I'll grab my stuff and be ready in a minute."

Before the Viking could reply, Alex returned to his seat, slipped his pack on, and scrambled forward. Leaning against the dragon-headed prow, he watched the shoreline grow larger as they approached. A few minutes later, the *Naglfar* ground to a halt. Alex looked back towards Leif and said, "I can't thank you enough for helping me on this journey. I couldn't have done it without you." Then, excited at the prospect of getting rid of his burden and heading home, Alex jumped off the ship before any Vikings could get out. He splashed through the shallow waters, pausing only briefly to wave at the Vikings before heading towards the gap.

As soon as his foot touched the beach, though, the skies opened up, and rain began pelting down. Alex looked up at the now-dark sky and cried out in frustration. Thinking it would be better to wait on board until morning, he turned towards where the Viking ship had been, but to his surprise, it had vanished.

He took comfort in seeing light reflecting off the clouds to his left, knowing it meant he wasn't far from civilization. But the glow didn't give off enough light to keep him from tripping on the rocky beach and falling to his knees. As he stood, he felt a warm trickle of blood going down his leg, but since he couldn't do anything about it right then, he trudged on.

His hopes soared when he passed through the gap in the sea wall and felt it cut off the wind. But it was a short-lived feeling, as a few steps later, he fell into a pool of cold brackish water. Alex waded across the waist-deep water until he found a dense clump of grass a little way in and climbed on top.

He tried staying on the grass from there on, but he couldn't see where he was going and kept plunging into tidal pools every few steps. Even when he was on the grass, it was so marshy that his feet often sank into standing water. His earlier hopes of getting rid of the Grail and going home were soon forgotten as all he could focus on was one step at a time.

After what seemed like forever, he stumbled onto a patch of firm land. He looked down and was barely able to make out a small muddy track cutting perpendicular to the direction he'd been heading. Remembering seeing the castle on the mountainside to his left, he turned in that direction, hoping he'd come across someone's home sooner rather than later.

He stumbled on through the dark and didn't notice the looming dark spot ahead of him until he crashed into a rock wall and fell backwards.

Too miserable to do anything, he sat in the mud for several minutes, letting the rain wash off the muck. Finally, he stood and felt his way forward. Unable to see where he was going, he followed the wall as it headed first to the left and then to the right. His knees almost buckled in relief when he reached a sheltered spot, and the rain suddenly stopped beating on him.

Alex continued feeling his way along the wall until he reached a corner. Unwilling to chance getting wetter, he bent over and was pleasantly surprised when his hand touched dry ground.

But his troubles weren't over. Despite getting out of the wind and rain, Alex was so soaked that he soon started shivering uncontrollably. He sat down and, with trembling fingers, took his shoes and socks off, then squeezed as much water out of them as he could before putting them back on. He felt a bit of relief and briefly thought about doing the same thing to his pants and shirt but decided against it as he was too cold. Hoping to get warm, he stood, then slowly felt along the wall of his shelter until he hit another turn in the wall. Wanting to ensure he didn't get wetter, he turned around and retraced his steps until he hit the far wall again, then turned back, hoping he would warm up with exercise.

Everything that had happened over the last few days finally caught up with him on his third lap, though, as he slipped down to the ground, curled up, and fell asleep.

CHAPTER 3
AVALON

Alex woke just after dawn, shivering in his still-damp clothes. Knowing he had to get moving to get warm, he wearily stood and looked around the small stone barn-like enclosure he'd stumbled into the previous night. Spotting what looked like a path just beyond the opening, he headed towards it.

Greeted by a stiff sea breeze as soon as he stepped beyond the leeward side of the barn, he pulled back and looked around to see where he was. On the other side of the path was a tall berm. He briefly considered climbing over it to get out of the wind but decided against it as he wasn't sure it would make his journey easier. Beyond the berm were some low-lying forested hills. Off to his right, he saw a set of mountains plunging into the sea for as far as he could see. When he turned left, he spotted the castle he'd seen from the ship – sitting high atop the nearby mountain with a ring of clouds below it.

His stomach rumbled, reminding him it wasn't happy with the treatment it had been getting the last few days. Alex considered eating another piece of smoked salmon, but the thought caused his stomach to grumble even louder. So, he tightened the straps on his pack and stepped back into the wind.

Turning left on the path outside his shelter, he found that it led straight towards the base of the mountain. A quarter of a mile on, he came to a crossroads where the path to his right led over a small footbridge, through a row of hedges, and towards what looked like a small town in the distance. He hesitated, thinking how nice it would be to have a hot meal and get warm before climbing the mountain. But wanting to get rid of the Grail as quickly as possible, he sighed and continued along the coastal path.

Half an hour later, with the clouds obscuring his view above, he spotted a trail leading up the mountain towards where he'd last seen the castle. It wasn't until he'd popped through the clouds that he glimpsed the giant stone fortress up close.

When he got to within a hundred yards, he heard a loud creaking sound and saw the drawbridge lowering. As soon as it hit the ground, a young boy in old-fashioned clothing dashed out and ran down the hill towards him.

The boy, who appeared to be only a couple of years younger than Alex, skidded to a stop, bowed, and said, "My Lady told me to tell you that your arrival caught her by surprise and that she is sorry she wasn't here to greet you. She hopes you'll understand and said she'll be out shortly."

"Relax. Whoever you're talking about couldn't have known I was arriving because I'm not even sure I know where I am." Alex looked around and asked, "By the way, where am I?"

"I'm sorry, My Lord, but My Lady asked me not to say anything else. I'm sure she will answer all your questions when she arrives." The boy looked around to make sure no one was near, then said, "I can't believe I'm getting to talk to you. All the other squires will be so jealous when I tell them I was the first to greet you."

Alex was about to ask what the boy meant when horns blew, and a procession began exiting the castle. He watched in fascination as a regal-looking woman with long brunette hair, wearing an ankle-length diaphanous white gown, led the group hurriedly down the mountain. Immediately behind her were seven men in single file. Alex couldn't see their faces clearly, but he could tell that the first three had long white beards and wore white Arabic-styled robes.

The next three men had on white tunics with large red crosses emblazoned on them worn over gleaming suits of armor. The seventh person in the procession wore long blue robes and had an even longer white beard than the others. After the lead group, there were two columns; one composed entirely of women, dressed much like the leader, and one of men, dressed in robes of green and brown.

Hoping he'd arrived at Avalon and could soon get rid of the Grail, Alex resumed his hike up the mountain.

When the procession got within a few feet of Alex, the woman suddenly stopped and knelt. The rest of the group followed her example.

Alex was so astonished that all he could do was stare blankly at the people in front of him. He studied their leader when she rose and saw that she wore a white ankle-length dress with a green belt that made Alex think she was from the Medieval Ages.

The woman lifted her head and said, "I am Lady Niniane, Mistress of Avalon and Lady of the Lake. Welcome. We are sorry we did not greet you properly, but we did not foresee your arrival. May we have the honor of knowing your name, My Lord?"

Uncomfortable with his reception, Alex raised his hands to stop her and said, "I'm no lord. My name is simply Alex Scire."

Lady Niniane nodded and said, "Words alone cannot convey our gratitude to you. From the bottoms of our hearts, thank you."

"But you don't even know why I'm here."

Lady Niniane smiled enigmatically. "I am assuming you are here to deliver the Holy Grail. What is odd is that I have no idea how you managed to hide it from our sight until you were on our doorstep. But you are here, and we are eternally grateful."

She half turned and waved an arm to the men behind her. "Let me introduce you to some of the members of my court." She pointed to a very old man standing right behind her and said, "This is Joseph of Arimathea, who buried Jesus and rescued the Grail in the Holy Land. Behind him is his brother-in-law, Bron, and his son, Alain. The three knights behind them are Sir Bors, Sir Percival, and King Arthur. And behind them is the wizard, Merlin."

She sighed and looked heavenward. "Alas, my dear Anfortas did not live long enough to see this day." Lady Niniane turned her gaze back to Alex and said, "The rest of the people here are some of the many who have tirelessly worked for centuries to preserve and protect the most precious Holy Relics."

Alex was so awestruck at meeting people he'd read about, but didn't think existed, that all he could say was, "Wow." Seeing everyone staring at him, he slipped off his pack, pulled out the Grail, and thrust it towards Lady

Niniane. He heard a collective gasp from the assembled people, but he ignored it and waited for her to take it.

But Lady Niniane shook her head. "Your offer is most gracious, but it is for you alone to put it in its final resting place. Will you honor us by accompanying us back to the castle and finishing your quest?"

Alex hadn't thought about what would happen once he fulfilled his promise to Vlad. He'd always assumed he'd just hand off the Grail and be rid of it, but the Mistress of Avalon had an almost hypnotizing effect on him. He nodded, stuffed the Grail in his pack, and waited for her to lead the way up to the castle. Instead, she made a half-turn and stuck out her elbow. It took Alex a few seconds to realize she was waiting to escort him up the hill. He took a few steps forward and was about to stick his arm through hers when he paused and said, "You don't want to get close to me. I haven't had a shower in, who knows how long, and I stink."

"Then I am even more honored to walk with you into Avalon," Lady Niniane replied. "It indicates the lengths you have gone through to bring the Grail here. Now come," she said, motioning for Alex to come closer.

Reluctantly he slipped his arm through hers. The others in line stepped aside as Lady Niniane and Alex headed up the hill, then, one by one, turned and followed them in the same order that they came down.

Physically and emotionally worn out, with little to eat or drink the previous few days, Alex found the climb more difficult than he expected. More than once, he thought about asking for a breather, but he couldn't bring himself to stop such a solemn procession and forced himself to keep trudging up the mountain.

Sensing his discomfort, Lady Niniane finally raised her hand and halted the group. Turning to Alex, she said, "Please, take your time. If I had thought about it, I would have brought a chair down for you."

"I'll be fine in a minute." While he caught his breath, Alex said, "I thought it would be harder to find this place than it was. Vlad said he looked for years."

"Who are you talking about?" Lady Niniane asked.

"Vlad Tepes." Seeing the quizzical look on her face, Alex said, "He told me his name used to be Sir Galahad."

Lady Niniane's eyes grew hard. "You mean the betrayer? He was always known as a fierce warrior. How did you take it from him?"

"I didn't take it," Alex replied. "He begged me to bring it here. What's strange is that he made it seem like finding this place would be hard. But you're standing out in plain sight."

Lady Niniane smiled. "The castle is an enchanted place that chooses where it wants to go. It is visible only to those who are worthy to find it. Are you ready to resume the climb now?"

Alex nodded and was grateful when they finally reached the top and passed through the gates. In the center of the courtyard was a marble fountain, its splashing water echoing against the stone walls. Straight ahead, at the top of a set of broad steps, stood a classical Greek-style rectangular building, its marbled columns standing like silent sentinels.

Lady Niniane led him up the steps while the rest of the procession stayed in the courtyard. As soon as they reached the top, a pair of enormous brass doors, as if on some silent command, swung open. Alex had been expecting some ornate church-like interior with gold leaf trim, white marble, and paintings everywhere. Instead, he saw a simple rough wood interior that reminded him more of a barn than a church. At the far end was a long cedar table running perpendicular to the building's length. Lady Niniane brought Alex to the table and pointed at a marble pedestal in the middle. As soon as he placed the Grail on the pedestal, he felt the weight of the responsibility lift from him. He stepped back and gazed at the plain-looking cup – in its home for the rest of eternity. Then he followed Lady Niniane outside, glad he'd never see the Grail again.

When they returned to the courtyard, Alex stopped and asked Lady Niniane, "Why me? I'm sure there have been many far more worthy people than me to have brought the Cup here."

Lady Niniane shook her head. "We have prayed for over a thousand years that God would send us the Grail, and he chose you. He must have had great confidence in you, for you are only the fourth person to touch the Holy Grail and not succumb to its powers. The first three were the original owner of the Cup, Mary Magdalene, and Joseph of Arimathea, who you met below."

"It doesn't make sense," Alex said, shaking his head.

"God moves in mysterious ways," she replied. "I am happy he chose you. And now that your quest is complete, would you grace us with your presence for dinner tonight? We rarely get guests here, and it would please me to hear your tale. Besides, it looks like you could use a good meal."

His stomach grumbled loudly just then, causing Lady Niniane to laugh and say, "I will take that as a yes." She motioned to a young girl who nodded and ran off. Then she whispered something to Joseph, who turned to the rest of the procession and dispersed them. In no time, Alex was alone with Lady Niniane, who pointed to a park-like area off to the side and said, "Shall we take a walk through the gardens while they prepare dinner? It's so beautiful there that I never tire of seeing it."

Alex fell in step beside her but didn't say anything until they were among the trees and hedges. He was so deep in thought that Lady Niniane startled him when she asked, "Is everything all right?"

Alex jumped and said, "Yeah. I was just thinking about how I got here. I didn't start this adventure because I wanted to bring the Grail here. I did it because I wanted to help my sister move on."

"It matters not why you started your quest. It matters what you did on it, which leads me to an important question. Because you've born the Grail and shared in the suffering it represents, you have a choice. You can stay with us and live a very long and peaceful life. If you choose that course, though, you can never leave. Or, you can return to your world and live a normal life with all the joy, pain, and struggles associated with it. But know that if you leave here, you are bound to keep the location and existence of the Grail a secret. You are also honor bound to protect Avalon, and the Grail, from any and all threats."

Alex didn't say anything for some time as he stared at the flower beds surrounding him. When he spoke again, it was in a faraway voice. "I don't fit with the people you introduced me to. They're famous. Anybody who's read much knows about them. I've done nothing like what they have."

"But you just told me that you didn't go on your quest for fame or fortune," Niniane said.

"I've seen what happens to celebrities, and I've seen what power does to people. I think I'll be much happier if I'm never famous."

Lady Niniane smiled again and said, "Perhaps, that is why you were chosen. Enough of this talk. Let us get you cleaned up for the banquet."

The boy who'd first greeted Alex appeared and took him to an austere stone bedroom just inside the castle gates. An hour later, Alex emerged feeling remarkably better but slightly embarrassed at the medieval-styled clothes he was wearing. He followed the boy to a large pavilion just outside the castle where everybody he'd seen earlier that day were waiting for him. Alex sat next to Lady Niniane and had difficulty keeping his eyes off the food while she said grace.

It wasn't a fancy meal, but the mutton and vegetable stew warmed him and calmed his stomach's complaints. Lady Niniane kept up a string of small talk, letting Alex eat in silence. The rest of the assembled company seemed content to keep to their own conversations. After three bowls of stew, Alex had a thick slice of bread slathered with butter and honey for dessert. It was messy but so delicious that Alex closed his eyes to savor the taste. He topped off the meal by downing a large tankard of chilled cider. When he finally finished, he patted his belly and leaned back on his chair, saying, "This was a great meal. Thank you."

"It was a pleasure seeing you enjoy our simple fare," Lady Niniane said. "I know you're tired, but I still have something important to discuss before you sleep."

The Lady of the Lake turned her chair and stared at the fire while the others cleared the tables. When everyone had left, Lady Niniane turned to Alex and said, "I have been thinking about our earlier talk. I sense this is not your first such adventure, which leads me to believe you have some other purpose. If I am right, you must persevere against whatever adversities you face. And know that there will always be those who will help you."

"Why is everyone always so cryptic with their advice?" Alex asked.

Lady Niniane smiled and replied, "One of my favorite sayings is that you can lead a horse to water, but you cannot make them drink. In much the same way, I can tell you more, but I doubt you would listen. So, I think you should learn in your own way. But enough for now. It's late. Come, let me walk with you to your bedroom."

Alex was so tired that he was asleep before his head hit the pillow.

CHAPTER 4
KNOW NOT WHAT WE MAY BE

Chrysophylax was so ecstatic at finally finding his mother, Abraxas, that he didn't care about the usual discomfort of traveling through a wormhole. His happiness evaporated, though, the instant he exited the portal on his home planet Berellus, and spotted a half dozen dragons surrounding the opening.

The waiting dragons took off from their perches high atop the mountains surrounding the portal and headed for Chrysophylax and his mother. Worried that she would struggle in the heavier gravity of Berellus after centuries on Earth, Chrysophylax fell back and took up a position immediately above her to prevent the other dragons from attacking her.

Communicating via telepathy, Abraxas said, *"I sense our welcoming party is out for blood. Do not worry about me, my son. Go to your uncle Nabu and ask him for protection."*

"It would be wasted effort, Mother. It appears they've been waiting for me and will follow me wherever I go." Chrysophylax dipped one of his opalescent-colored wings to signal to the fast-closing dragons that he wouldn't challenge them, then said, *"We haven't had a chance to talk, but you should know much has changed since you left. I just hope that the High Council will overlook my transgression once they see you have returned."*

"What do you mean?" Abraxas asked.

"The High Council no longer permits travel to other planets," Chrysophylax replied. *"They've deemed use of the portals a crime."*

A giant grey dragon with scars over his entire body flew close and said, *"You're to come with us. The High Council will judge what to do with you."*

The procession of dragons flew eastward for the next few hours until they entered a large valley surrounded by steep mountains and headed for a huge opening on the far side. A few minutes later, the group flew into the center of an enormous cavern – large enough to house thousands of dragons and landed in front of a ledge that took up one entire wall. Three of the elders were already awaiting them.

Chrysophylax barely had time to fold his wings before a dragon with scarlet and black stripes addressed him.

"You know the punishment for using the portals is exile, right?" Drakon asked. *"Why did you go against our rules and leave the planet?"*

Before Chrysophylax could answer, there was a grunting and shuffling of feet among the assembled dragons. A few seconds later, a golden dragon with spikes sticking out around his neck and twice as big as Chrysophylax pushed through the crowd and stood by Abraxas. He nudged her and said, *"Welcome home, my love. I never thought I'd see you again."*

"Silence!" roared a giant male dragon with two horns poking out of his head and a spiked club at the end of his tail. *"As much as we are pleased with your mate's return, Glaurung, we're not here to celebrate her homecoming. We're here to understand why your*

offspring ignored our decrees on using the portal and left our planet."

Chrysophylax sighed in relief when a reptilian-looking dragon with armor-plate-like scales and a row of spikes pushed through the crowd and took a place beside him. Leaning over, his uncle, Nabu, whispered, *"I'm sorry I couldn't stop all this, but don't worry. I'll get you out of this mess."*

Nabu looked up at the three dragons on the dais and said, *"Please don't punish my nephew. He was only doing my bidding in going to Earth and looking for his mother, who's been missing for centuries. And, as you can see, he was successful."*

Chrysophylax, who'd never known his uncle to lie, looked up in surprise. But he was so afraid of what the High Council would do to him that he stayed silent and let his uncle defend him.

"We put those rules in place to protect our kind from others," Drakon said. *"First, it was the Irkallans, then the humans. We can't afford to trust other species."*

"I agree," Nabu said. *"It's why I sent my nephew to Earth. As you know, his mother, Abraxas, my younger sister, has been missing for over 500 Earth years. I've been worried that humans had harmed her like they've harmed so many others of our kind and couldn't take not knowing any longer."* Nabu looked down at his crippled front leg and added, *"And obviously, I couldn't go. So, I asked my nephew if he would search for her, which he reluctantly did. I've been anxiously awaiting his return ever since and am overjoyed that he found her and brought her back. I realize I should have consulted you beforehand, but he was just a youth*

trying to help me, which is why I ask you to release him."

A murmur of assent from the other dragons caused the three members of the High Council present to look from one to the other. At last, Drakon grumbled loudly and said, *"Fine, but there will be no leniency should he use the portals again. You may go."*

Chrysophylax waited for all the well-wishers to welcome his mother back to Berellus. When the last had left, he flew home with his parents and uncle. It wasn't until they were safely ensconced in their family's cave that Chrysophylax spoke. *"I knew I wasn't supposed to use the portals, but I never imagined an inquisition. What's changed since I left?"*

Nabu shushed him and closed the outside doors before saying, *"Ok. It's safe to talk now. I've had to create noise-proofing charms to prevent anyone from listening in on us because Vermitrax has spies everywhere. I believe he's using our species' xenophobia to generate a climate of fear so he can overthrow the Elders on the High Council and take power for himself."* He turned to Abraxas and said, *"Enough about that. I've missed you, sister, but why were you gone so long?"*

"A human cut out my heart stone which created a time-space anomaly when my ka tried to leave my body," Abraxas said. *"I thought I would be trapped there for eternity, but some boy found me, healed me, then broke me out of my prison. I don't understand how he found me, nor why he helped me."*

All eyes turned to Nabu, who cleared his throat and said, *"I'm not sure, but you know that plan I've been working on for the last few millennia to remediate the problems we caused by introducing the Maqlû to humans?"* Without waiting for an answer, he said, *"When the ankh suddenly stopped working, I asked Chrysophylax to go to Earth and discover what had happened. He discovered that the boy you met was somehow involved and started following him. I don't know how he's done it, but he's already destroyed two of the Maqlû and freed you."*

"What's his motive?" Abraxas asked. *"I tried killing him when he arrived at the castle where I was imprisoned, but he saved my life despite my actions. He reminded me so much of that other human we invited into our weyr long ago that I adopted him."*

"He says he's doing it to help his sister move on in the afterlife," Chrysophylax replied. *"But I think it's something more. I just don't know what."*

Nabu began pacing back and forth across the cavern. At last, he stopped and said, *"Chrysophylax, I'd like you to return to Earth and study the boy. Figure out what he knows and doesn't know about the Maqlû, and figure out what's driving him."*

"You can't ask that of him," Glaurung protested. *"You heard what the High Council said. They'll banish our son if they catch him using the portals again."*

"My husband is right," Abraxas said. *"It's too dangerous. I won't let my only son return to Earth."*

Chrysophylax surprised everyone, including himself, when he said, *"But I want to go back."*

"Why?" his mother asked. *"Just because the boy helped me escape doesn't mean you have to risk your life for him,"*

"It's hard to explain, Mother, but I feel a connection with him. I've seen how he's risked his life repeatedly for others, and I admire that. He makes me want to do something equally important for our planet."

"But...."

"Whatever his destiny is, sister, I believe we should help him." Seeing Abraxas about to protest, Nabu said, *"But I agree that it's too dangerous for Chrysophylax to return to Earth right now. So, I suggest we wait and let the situation calm down before proceeding."*

Abraxas looked to her mate, then her son, before finally replying. *"Fine. I never thought I'd return home, so plotting to subvert the law of our land doesn't seem as odd as it did a hundred years ago. Somehow, it seems like the right thing to do."*

CHAPTER 5
STONEHENGE

Alex woke the morning after the banquet to the sound of crashing waves. Confused, he sat up and rubbed the sleep out of his eyes. But it took him a few seconds to realize that instead of being in a comfortable bed in Avalon, he was on a forested mountain slope overlooking the sea with a blanket of moss to keep him warm. Alex wondered why Lady Niniane had deserted him but decided grumbling about his situation wouldn't help him and shifted his focus to figuring out what to do next.

Seeing that he was on the same mountain he'd climbed the day before, he slipped on his dad's old army pack, settled his Tilley on his head, and headed down the hillside. Half an hour later, Alex reached the bottom, then turned onto a path running between two tall hedgerows and headed inland. A short time later, he spotted the buildings he'd seen the day before and picked up his pace. His excitement at being close to civilization quickly evaporated when he reached the small village and discovered no one was around. Hoping it was because it was too early in the morning for people to be moving about, he headed towards a small park across the street and sat on the only bench.

Alex rummaged around inside his pack, trying to decide what to eat. He pushed aside his last power bar and reluctantly pulled out a strip of smoked cod the Norse spirits had scrounged for him.

After finishing his chewy dry breakfast, he rummaged through his pack to check on money but only saw a few Euro bills and a handful of coins. He grimaced and muttered, "I guess it'll have to do until I find an ATM."

As he started to stand, a van pulled alongside him. A petite, middle-aged woman with honey-colored hair rolled down the window and asked, "Do you need some help?"

Alex briefly worried that it was some sort of trap, but seeing how quiet the village was, he overcame his qualms, walked over to the van, and said, "I'm trying to figure out where I am."

The woman looked askance at Alex and said, "This is Porlock."

"Is that in England?" he asked.

"Are ye daft? Of course, it is."

Trying to cover for his gaffe, Alex said, "What I meant to ask was, what's the best way to get to, uh…, London?"

"Are ye in some sort of trouble?" the woman asked.

"No, I've been traveling a lot and haven't been paying attention to where I was. But now, I want to head home."

She eyed Alex briefly, then said, "Hop in. I can take ye as far as Salisbury, where ye can take a train into the city."

Alex hesitated only a moment before getting in. As soon as he'd buckled up, though, he noticed that she only had stumps for legs.

Seeing him stare, the woman said, "Don't worry. I can drive this with no problems as all the controls are hand-operated. And besides, I've never gotten into an accident."

Embarrassed by his unintentional rudeness, he stammered, "I'm sorry. I shouldn't have stared. I'm Alex, by the way."

"Don't worry about it. I'm used to the stares. At least ye had the honesty to admit ye were shocked." She stuck her hand out and said, "I'm Frida."

They drove silently for a few miles until Frida said, "I have to be honest with ye. This meeting wasn't an accident."

Alex reached for the door handle and was about to jump out when Frida grabbed his arm and said, "I'm not going to hurt ye. I'm one of Lady Niniane's field agents."

"But I thought...."

"Not everyone who's vowed to give their lives to protect the most precious holy relics lives in Avalon. I'm mortal, just like ye."

"How did you become a field agent?" Alex asked.

"I happened to be in the right place at the right time when one of Lady Niniane's recruiters found me and invited me to join their ranks," Frida said. "Since then, my job has been to scour the country for information on unfound relics. Or, in yer case, helping people. So, when I heard what ye'd done, I volunteered to help ye."

"Where did Lady Niniane and the others go?" Alex asked.

"I have no idea," Frida replied. "I've never been blessed to visit Avalon, so I know very little about it."

"Do you know why they left me on a hillside without even saying goodbye?"

"I can't answer that either. But, from what I've heard, everybody in Avalon is still in shock that ye showed up out of the blue with the Grail because they'd all but given up hope that it still existed."

Alex turned to look out the window, trying to sort through his chaotic thoughts. Neither said anything until Alex spotted an ATM and asked her to stop. After replenishing his money, he hopped back in, and they took off.

At first, he was fascinated with the English countryside, especially the large fields of yellow canola blossoms covering the landscape. But without anything else to distract him, he fell asleep and didn't wake up until Frida stopped in Salisbury.

As he was getting out, Frida said, "Know that ye'll never be truly alone. When ye need us, we'll be there for ye. Good luck, Alex Scire."

He watched her drive off and was about to enter the train station when he heard his name called. Alex whirled around, startled that someone would know him in such an unlikely place. A tall, lanky, black man with a big smile and a colorful shirt strode towards him. A few steps behind him was a short, stocky man with dreadlocks. Alex's jaw dropped. "Jean Paul? Francis? Is that really you?"

Jean Paul came up and hugged Alex while Francis hung back.

"What are you guys doing here?" Alex asked.

Jean Paul looked down at his feet, unable to meet Alex's gaze, and said, "In a way, you're the reason we're here. We took that gold bar you gave us, sold our old boat, and bought a new one to travel the world. We both wanted to see Stonehenge, so here we are. By the way, where is your grandmother?" Jean Paul asked. "I heard that she and some of the others of her order are here too."

"I don't know," Alex replied. "I've been gone for a while and, uh, lost touch."

Jean Paul didn't hear the answer as he was studying Alex. At last, he said, "There's something different about you. I just can't put my finger on it."

"Maybe it's because it's been a year since I've seen you, and I've grown a lot."

Jean Paul shook his head. "No, it's been almost two years since we last saw you." The Haitian snapped his fingers and said, "I know what it is. You don't look like you've aged much."

Alex was about to argue the point of when they'd last met but decided against it as it was the second time since he'd appeared in Norway that it sounded like he'd lost time.

Jean Paul waved off the topic and said, "It doesn't matter. But I'm curious. What are you doing here in the middle of England by yourself?" The Haitian's voice tailed off. "Don't tell me you've gotten lost again."

"I'm not lost. I'm, uh, sightseeing. Yeah, you see, I'm on my way to London. Then I was going back home to my grandfather and cousin."

Alex's stomach took that moment to growl. Embarrassed, he said, "Excuse me. I haven't had much to eat the last couple of weeks, and breakfast didn't do it for me."

Jean Paul looked Alex up and down and said, "You're almost as skinny as when we found you in

Georgia, meaning you need some food. We're about to catch the bus to Stonehenge. Why don't you come with us? There's a cafeteria there where we can get some lunch." Then, after Stonehenge, we'll take you to London since we're going there too."

"I can't impose on you," Alex said.

"After what you've done for us, it's the least we can do," Jean Paul said.

"Are you kidding? What I did was nothing compared to how you helped me. I owe you my life."

Jean Paul didn't argue. Instead, he got behind Alex and steered him to a nearby tourist bus. Half an hour later, the three were sitting in the Stonehenge Visitor Center having lunch.

When he finally finished eating, Alex leaned back and said, "I could get used to this – eating hot meals in warm, dry conditions."

"Where have you been that a cafeteria meal is a luxury?" Jean Paul asked.

Alex hastily sat up and said, "Uh…, you know. Here and there."

Francis laid a hand on Jean Paul's arm, shook his head, and said, "Let him be. He's been through enough."

Jean Paul nodded and turned to Alex. "We have a choice on how to get the rest of the way to Stonehenge. We can either take the shuttle bus or walk." Seeing a questioning look cross Alex's face, he said, "The site is a lot more than just the stones you normally associate with it. If we walk, it'll take at least half an hour to get there, but you'll get to see some of the barrows and get a feel for the whole site that you won't get if you take the bus."

"Let's walk then," Alex said as he slipped on his pack and grabbed his hat.

After leaving the museum area, they crossed the road to the monument and entered a pasture with a long slope upwards. The mowed path didn't have a lot of people on it, but the views of the surrounding sheep and cattle pastures and the flowering rapeseed fields were well worth it. The walk felt like a gentle stroll through the countryside rather than the approach to a UNESCO World Heritage site. They passed through a stand of trees, and suddenly Alex could see the outlines of the Cursus, an almost two-mile-long ditch. The famous circle of stones was still so far away, though, that they seemed like little more than a grouping of rocks. A little further on, he noticed the first barrows and couldn't help but imagine Tolkien's barrow wights swooping down on him.

"Thank you for bringing me here and suggesting the walk," Alex said. "I feel sorry for all those people taking the shuttle bus and not getting this experience."

"This choice was by luck," Jean Paul replied. "Despite all our traveling, we're still learning how to tour. Too often, we've treated the places we've visited like something to check off a list versus experiencing the uniqueness of each place,"

After passing through a third animal gate ten minutes later, they finally reached the entrance to the famous part of Stonehenge. Alex was somewhat disappointed, though, as he'd always imagined the ring of stones to be more impressive. The sheep grazing nearby and a busy highway only a hundred yards away made it seem more like a park attraction than a famous archeological site.

He followed the concrete walkway around the stones until he stepped onto the grassy field surrounding the rest of the site and headed towards the backside. Almost immediately, he felt something pulling him towards the monument. He touched the ankh and was surprised it wasn't what was tugging at him. Alex stepped back and began warily circling the stones, unsure what was happening.

Catching a glimpse of motion, he looked closer and saw a handful of ghosts peeking between the gaps in the stones. Alex continued circling the monument and saw the spirits shifting with him, peeking out between the openings, all while the unseen force tugged at him.

When he'd gone halfway around and had put the highway behind him, the sensation flared up, pulling him forcefully towards the stones. He tried fighting it, but the unseen force continued tugging at him until he was against the rope keeping the tourists away.

Just as he felt he was going to fly through the barrier, Jean Paul pulled him back and asked, "Are you okay?"

The tugging sensation immediately disappeared. But for an instant, he thought he saw a dark tunnel with thousands of pinpricks of light inside the center of Stonehenge. Despite being troubled by the experience, Alex shook his head and said, "I'm fine. I guess I'm just tired. Do you mind if we head to the station now?"

CHAPTER 6
TO UNDERSTAND MORE

As he sat on the train heading to London, Alex brooded about what had happened at Stonehenge. The black hole had looked similar to what he'd seen crossing the Arges River in Romania – but it had felt a hundred times more powerful. He was so lost in thought that Francis had to roust him from his seat when they finally reached Waterloo Station in London.

As they walked through the rush hour crowds, Alex was glad that Jean Paul and Francis were there to help him navigate the train station, as he'd never seen so many people in one place before. What was even stranger to him, though, were all the different languages he heard. It felt like every nationality was present.

When they finally got to the relative quiet of the streets, Jean Paul said, "The place where we're staying is just across the river. There's an extra bedroom – so you can stay with us tonight. Then tomorrow, we'll figure out how to get you home."

Halfway across Westminster Bridge, Alex began feeling like a tourist as he stopped to gaze at the Palace of Westminster and Big Ben. Another half hour of walking brought them to a quiet residential street of multi-story grey brick homes with bright white trim.

After getting situated, Jean Paul said, "I'm glad we ran into you again, but I'm curious. How did you get to Stonehenge on your own?"

Alex studied his hosts for a minute before saying, "Let's stop the pretense. You know quite well that I wasn't on vacation. What I can't figure out is how you'd know I'd be in Salisbury when I didn't know I'd be there until an hour before I saw you. What type of game are you guys playing?"

Jean Paul threw his hands into the air and replied, "No games."

"Then how do you explain running into me as you did?" Alex asked.

Neither Francis nor Jean Paul replied. Instead, they looked at each other as if they were figuring out what to say.

The sudden quiet allowed Alex to sense a subtle source of energy permeating the room that he hadn't noticed before. He looked around for its origin and saw Francis wearing the same strange bronze-colored metallic object with flying buttresses joined on each end that he'd seen in Salem. "Is that how you do it?" he asked. "What did you call it before? Shar... something?"

Jean Paul looked from Francis to Alex. "Why would you think that?" he asked.

"I thought we'd agreed to no games," Alex replied.

Francis pulled the object off his belt and handed it to Alex. "It's called Sharur."

Jean Paul gasped and turned to Francis. "What are you doing? You've never told anyone about it," Jean Paul said. "Don't you think it's dangerous to tell him?"

"I've worn it for ages, but he's the only one who's ever been able to see it, much less feel its power. And this is not the first time he's noticed the object," Francis replied. "Face it – somehow, they're linked." He turned to Alex and asked, "So, how did you get to England? We'd heard you'd gone missing in Romania."

Alex debated how much he should tell them and eventually settled on a partial truth. "It's all a bit confusing, but one day I was exploring something odd in the woods of Romania. And the next, I got thrown into a series of events that led me to Minehead the night before last. When I woke up this morning, I started working my way to London so I could go home and just happened to meet you. I mean, what are the odds of that happening?"

"That is the question. Isn't it?" Jean Paul replied. "But we heard you've been missing for nine months. Where have you been all that time."

Alex shook his head. "I don't know where you heard that. I've been wandering around for the last week and haven't been anywhere I could call my grandfather or grandmother. They must be going crazy with worry."

Jean Paul steepled his fingers and studied Alex while rocking back and forth in his chair. At last, he pulled out his cell phone and handed it to Alex. "Francis will take you upstairs to the guest room, where you can call your grandfather in peace. And while you're doing that, I'll get you more modern clothes. I hope I don't offend you, but it looks like you just came out of the medieval age." He stood up and was about to head out when he said, "I'll order some food. Do you like Indian?"

"I take it you don't mean American Indian," Alex said. "I've never tried the other type, but I'm game."

"Then that's settled. You'll get to experience something new. Now relax. And don't worry; you won't be a burden."

CHAPTER 7
THE TRUTH ABOUT YOURSELF

Alex punched in his grandfather's number but hesitated just as he was about to hit the dial button. Even though he'd never known him growing up, his grandfather Ignacio had taken him in, without hesitation, when Alex's parents had died. He was also the only person who understood the issues of wearing the ankh. But Alex was unsure about the reception he'd get after having gone missing again. Taking a deep breath, he hit the dial button.

A young female voice answered. Hesitantly he asked, "Is that you, Chipeta?"

"Yes, who's calling?" A long silence was followed by a gasp and then, "Is that you, Alex?"

Before he could reply, he heard a clunk, followed by a muffled shout, "Grandpa. Hurry. It's Alex."

A few seconds later, his grandfather Ignacio breathlessly asked, "Alex, are you okay?"

"I'm fine, Grandpa. I'm sorry about worrying you, but I ran into some unexpected difficulties in Romania. I'm in London now, but plan to get a flight back to Denver tomorrow."

"I'm so relieved to hear from you," Ignacio said. "Have you called your grandmother to let her know you're safe?"

"No, I haven't had access to a phone for a while and called you first. Besides, she's probably glad to be rid of me."

"That's not fair to her," Ignacio said. "I've talked to your grandmother, and she feels horrible about losing you."

"It's not her fault," Alex replied. "I wandered away and, uh, got lost."

"Well, I think you should find her and apologize about disappearing in person."

"How can I do that? I haven't been gone that long," Alex said. "She's probably still in Romania.

There was a long pause before Ignacio said, "You're in luck. She's in London as we speak. I talked to her a few days ago, and she said she was bringing one of your friends and the girl's mother. I know you two don't get along, but you owe it to her to put her mind at ease."

Ignacio covered the mouthpiece and said to Chipeta, "Excuse me, but I need to talk to your cousin alone. You can talk to him in a few minutes." Ignacio turned back to the phone and said, "I'm back."

Before Ignacio could say anything else, Alex blurted out, "I'm sorry, Grandpa. I didn't mean to worry you by being gone so long. It's just that things happened that I had no control over."

"Relax, I'm not going to lecture you about going missing and not hearing from you. I'm just glad you're safe." There was a long pause before Ignacio asked, "Was your absence due to the ankh?"

"Yes and no."

"What do you mean?"

"It's a long story," Alex said, "and I don't feel comfortable talking about it over the phone. I'll tell you all about it when I get home."

Ignacio paused, then said. "I think you should stay and continue with your quest. No one wants you to come home more than I do, but I believe that if you quit now, you'll regret it. You've got to see this, whatever it is, to the end."

Alex couldn't believe his ears. It took him a moment before he said, "Are you kidding? You, of all people, should know what that necklace can do. I nearly died because it led me off into the woods in Romania. And, now, here I am fifteen hundred miles away. That's not normal."

"My heart aches for what's happening to you," Ignacio said. "You have no idea how many sleepless nights your cousin and I have had since you left for Salem the first time. What I'm trying to say is that you're doing something no one in our family has ever done. You're facing the mysteries of the ankh head-on. I've told you its secrets destroyed my mother's life, your father's, and nearly destroyed mine. But the Great Spirit has seen fit to give you the presence of mind to deal with it."

There was a long silence before Ignacio asked, "Is what you were doing while you were gone important?"

"Yeah, but..."

"Important enough to be gone all this time?"

"Yeah, but I don't know if I can handle it anymore. It's overwhelming at times."

"Since I haven't walked in your shoes, I can't say I understand all you're going through. But I can tell you what my gut is telling me. It's like what Gandalf told Frodo near the start of the Lord of the Rings. He said that sometimes a person doesn't get to decide if they want to be involved in the great events of their time. Their only choice is to decide what to do with the time given to them.

"Chipeta and I have talked about your situation and feel that the Great Spirit has chosen you for a reason and that it's important you finish your journey. Do not shy away from it just because times are hard, or you're tired, or lonely."

There was another long silence until Alex said, "I guess you're right. Can I come back and live with you when all this is over?"

"Of course. Enough of this serious talk, though. Your cousin has been pacing the house, waiting for her turn to talk with you. I love you. Good luck, and be safe."

CHAPTER 8

SINCE HAPPINESS
HEARD YOUR NAME

Alex tossed and turned throughout the night, wondering what to do with his grandfather's advice. Knowing he couldn't get back to sleep, he rose an hour before sunrise and went downstairs. When he walked into the kitchen, he was surprised to see Jean Paul already there, having milk and cookies.

"I see you couldn't sleep either," the Haitian said.

"I'm anxious to get home, but my grandfather said my grandmother is here in London, and I should find her and tell her I'm all right in person. Besides, I forgot to get her number, and there's a seven-hour time difference to my home, so I have to wait to get it."

"How about we do some sightseeing this morning, then call your grandfather later? We could see the Changing of the Guard if you'd like. It's only a forty-five-minute walk from here if we cut through Kensington Gardens and Hyde Park."

"That sounds great."

"Then let's have an early breakfast and go sightseeing," Jean Paul said.

The three headed out shortly after the sun had poked its head over the townhouses in the area. The walk through the parks did wonders to improve Alex's mood, as it was the first time in weeks that he felt he could relax and enjoy the sights.

Spotting a sign to Buckingham Palace, Alex pointed to it and asked, "Isn't that where the Changing of the Guards happens?"

"That's where most tourists go," Jean Paul replied. "But it's only a small part of the whole ceremony. In my opinion, the best way to see the most is to start at St. James Palace, where the ceremony begins. Then, we'll follow the soldiers to Buckingham Palace, where we can watch the rest of the soldiers and horse guard units passing through." He looked at his watch and added, "We better hurry if we want to get good spots at St. James Palace, though."

A little while later, they arrived at an old, rather plain-looking set of two-story brick buildings protected by a tall wall. "Is this really a palace?" Alex asked.

"It's the oldest one in the kingdom at 500 years old," Jean Paul replied.

"Why are we across the street instead of at the gates?" Alex asked. "It doesn't look like we can see much from here with all those people crowding around the entrance."

"Be patient," Jean Paul said. "The police will come and shoo them away soon. Trust me. We're in a good spot."

When soldiers finally started coming out of one of the buildings half an hour later, Alex was surprised to see only a dozen, relatively short, dark-skinned soldiers in green uniforms lined up."

"Where are the red coat soldiers with the big black bearskin hats I've always seen in the pictures?" Alex asked.

"You'll see them and more, but you're getting a special treat today," Jean Paul replied. These men are Gurkhas – Nepalese soldiers who have a reputation for being some of the fiercest soldiers in the world."

About fifteen minutes later, a Gurkha band appeared and took their place in front of the soldiers. Alex was disappointed when nothing happened for another ten minutes. But when the Gurkhas finally exited from the palace gates at a quick march, Alex had to alternate between running and walking to keep up.

They followed the soldiers, stopping when they got to a big plaza just as a troop of red-coated horse guards passed them, going the opposite way. Alex gazed in awe as every soldier rode a black horse and wore a helmet with a plume and breastplate so shiny that he thought they could use them as mirrors. He was disappointed when the Gurkha soldiers soon disappeared behind the tall black iron fence surrounding Buckingham Palace.

His disappointment faded when a few minutes later, a company of red-coated soldiers wearing the tall black fur hats he'd expected, preceded by another band, marched in from the other side of the plaza. After those soldiers disappeared behind the gates, nothing happened for quite some time. Alex grew impatient with the waiting and asked, "Is it over?"

"Not yet," Francis replied. "The changing of the guard actually happens inside the palace gates. Once they're done, the outgoing guards and bands depart and return to their barracks."

Alex stopped listening when he saw a familiar looking person moving through the crowd across the street. "Excuse me," he told Jean Paul. "I think I just saw my grandmother at the base of that monument over there."

Without waiting for a reply, Alex jumped over the barricades, dodged the mounted police officers, and dove into the crowd on the other side of the street. He wove in and out of the mass of people until he spotted his grandmother standing near Sophie and Diana Bennet. Alex tried to get their attention by yelling, "Hey, Grandma, Diana, I'm over here," but they didn't hear him because of the crowd's noise and bands. His heart started racing as he pushed through the crowd. When he finally reached them, he said, "My grandad said you were in town, but I never thought I'd run into you."

All three Druid women looked like they'd seen an apparition until Diana yelled, "How could you do this to me? You disappear for almost a year and then show up thousands of miles away, acting as if nothing had happened. I thought you were dead." She punched Alex on the arm and ran away in tears.

Alex had imagined what it would be like to see Diana again, but he'd never thought she'd be angry at him. He looked from Sophie to his grandmother and said, "What did I say?"

Sophie glared at Elizabeth Adler and said, "This is exactly why you need to make sure we're done with him once and for all when we get to Scotland." She made some disgusted sound, then followed Diana off into the crowd.

Alex flung out his arms and stepped towards his grandmother to hug her but stopped when she grimaced and backed up. "I didn't mean to surprise you, Grandma," he said, "but I ran into those two men who rescued me in Georgia, and they brought me here today."

"How can you be so cavalier after having been gone so long?" Elizabeth demanded.

"I'm sorry," Alex replied. "A lot of weird things happened after I got lost in the woods, and next thing I knew, I wound up here."

Alex wasn't sure whether his grandmother, shaking her head at his disclosure, was in disgust or bewilderment. When she didn't say anything, Alex looked to where Jean Paul and Francis had been standing, but the English band passed by just then, blocking the view.

The crowds soon started scattering, making it even tougher for Alex to spot his Haitian friends. They waited for ten minutes until most of the onlookers had dispersed before Elizabeth snapped, "I'm getting cold standing out here in the wind. Where are they? They must not be that good of friends to bring you here and leave you alone, especially given how young you are."

She turned on Alex and said, "So, what's your story this time, mister? You put Diana and Jane in harm's way yet again, then disappeared for nearly a year without a single call or message. And when you finally show up, you act as if nothing happened."

"I don't get it," Alex said. "I've only been gone for a couple of weeks. Why do you and others make it sound like I've been gone a lot longer?"

Elizabeth looked at him as if he was crazy. "You expect me to answer that?"

He felt horrible about the worry he'd caused everyone, but memories of everything he'd endured to bring the Grail to safety made him want to explode at the seeming injustice of his reception. Knowing his travails weren't his grandmother's fault, he slowly counted to five before he added, "I never meant for any of this to happen. Diana and Jane tried talking me out of going into the woods, but I didn't listen to them, as I intended to come right back. But, as I said, something strange happened, and I've spent every day since then fighting my way back to civilization."

Elizabeth nearly shouted, "Why didn't you call? I've been worried sick about you and berating myself all these months for letting you get into danger on my watch again."

"None of this is your fault. I would've called if I could've, but last night was the first time I've seen a phone since I saw you in Romania," Alex said. "I was planning to go home today, but my grandfather said you were in London and told me I should try and meet up with you to let you know I'm safe."

"Aargh! I don't want anything to do with you and should send you home, but it's impossible right now because of that damned Icelandic volcano erupting again and stopping flights to the States. And since I can't let you traipse all over a foreign country by yourself, I should ground you to the hotel rooms I've got, but I don't trust you, and I won't punish Sophie or Diana by having them watch over you. Since we only have a few more days in London before heading to

Scotland, you're coming with us. But, you're to stay with us at all times and behave. I'll send you home as soon as they allow the planes to start flying again. Got that?"

Relieved that her scolding wasn't as bad as he thought it would be, Alex said, "Yes, Grandma."

CHAPTER 9
IN ALL DISORDER

All of Brother Robert Stafford's dealings with the Bandruí over the centuries had been with Lady Yvaine. After Alex had taken his *Sibylline Book*, Stafford had thought about meeting Elizabeth, but the boy's disturbing habit of showing up in the oddest places and doing the most unexpected things drove him to keep his distance.

Seeing Jean Paul and Francis appear unexpectedly in the crowd surrounding Buckingham Palace hadn't overly worried him at first. But when Alex, who he thought had died the previous year, suddenly darted across the road, the hair on his arms stood up. Seconds later, he gasped when he saw him greet his grandmother.

Stafford thought the odds of all four parties showing up at the same time and place were astronomical. Unsure how to react, he hastily ducked out of sight when he saw Alex pointing towards where he was standing. Making sure to keep people between him and the Druid priestess, he backed further into the crowd, wondering what his next step should be. A nearby conversation, spoken in a language he hadn't heard in over a millennium, drove him to bend over and pretend to tie his shoes.

Stafford surreptitiously looked towards where the familiar voices were coming from and was relieved to see Jean Paul and Francis leaving. When they were safely out of sight, he stood up, looked around for the boy, and was relieved to see him walking away – towards Trafalgar Square with his grandmother, a middle-aged woman, and a curly-haired teenage girl.

Wondering what they were doing, he headed after them, ensuring he always kept tourists between him and the Americans. He followed them into the National Gallery and was pleased to see Elizabeth standing alone when everyone else headed for the bathrooms.

Not wanting to startle her, he maneuvered around until he could approach her straight on. When he was a few feet away, he said, "Excuse me, Elizabeth Bennet?"

He could see the High Priestess of the Salem Grove was surprised, so he quickly added, "My name is Brother Robert Stafford, and I've been friends with Lady Yvaine for a long time. I would like to talk to you about a subject of mutual interest to both of us."

"I'm sorry. Should I know you?" Elizabeth asked.

"No, but I would like to arrange a time to talk with you in private about your grandson. I believe we have common concerns about his…, shall I say, propensity to surprise. Is there a time we could meet?"

Elizabeth stared at him for a few seconds, then opened her purse, pulled out a card, and handed it to Stafford. "Call me at that number after nine tonight. Now go, before anyone sees us talking."

He nodded, then melted into the crowd. Not wanting to risk running into Alex, Stafford returned to his order's London home and called his brother. Unfortunately, the talk didn't go as he'd hoped, as once again, they disagreed on the approach to take towards the boy. So, it was with a bit of frustration that he called Elizabeth later that night.

"I'll get right to it," Stafford said when she answered. "Your grandson is a threat to not only your order's plans but mine as well."

"I'm sorry," Elizabeth said. "I don't know what you're talking about. You'll have to start at the beginning and explain who you are and why you're calling."

"I apologize. I assumed you knew something of us since I've worked with Lady Yvaine for quite some time. I'm the head of the Magos Order, whose goal is the same as your order's – to find and protect the Maqlû."

He could hear her gasp before she said, "How do you know about those objects? That is supposed to be best kept secret."

"A long time ago, Lady Yvaine and I used to work together trying to find and safeguard the Maqlû," Stafford said. "We eventually decided to go our separate ways but agreed that it's best that your order guards the objects while my group takes in suspected warlocks and ensures they don't cause problems. Unfortunately, I fear your grandson is a threat to both of our order's goals."

There was a long silence before Elizabeth said, "Why should I trust you? Aren't you a warlock?"

"Yes," Stafford replied. "But you should know that it was my *Sibylline Book* you used to search for the Palantir in Lamanai. I gave it to your grandson in Salem to help you find the object. Surely that should be enough of a recommendation."

"I wondered about my grandson's story at the time. Why are you telling me all this now? Why not then?" Elizabeth asked.

"I wasn't sure what to do about him back then. Nor was I sure of what type of reception I'd get from you."

"Well, it was a wasted effort," Elizabeth said. "No…, it was an unmitigated disaster. We didn't find a trace of the object, but many of my people got hurt. And what does my grandson do? He disappears into the Caribbean, somehow convincing two of our younger members to go with him."

"I know all about the events that happened and have given it a great deal of thought," Stafford said. "You assume he didn't find the Palantir. But what if he did?"

"I would have known about it."

"Would you? Have you ever held one of the Maqlû?" Stafford asked. "I have. I've seen several of them and even used one of them before. Just being near one leaves a lasting impression on a person. And I believe he's held one. What worries me even more, though, as I'm sure it does Lady Yvaine, is that I suspect your grandson did something with the Palantir and hid it somewhere."

"That's impossible," Elizabeth said.

"Are you sure? Your grandson is dangerous – to both of our order's goals, and therefore we're already working to stop him. But, if that doesn't work, I ask you to use your order's procedures to stop him. Call a conclave. Tell the others in your order what you've seen and what I'm telling you. Lady Yvaine won't listen to me, but I beg you to do this – for both of our orders."

Elizabeth hesitated, then said, "I shouldn't be telling you this, but that's why I'm in England. We've already called for a conclave, even though he's been missing for months. His rather abrupt appearance earlier today has unnerved me and further proves we're heading down the right path. So, be assured – neither of us will have to worry about him much longer."

"It's a relief to hear we're aligned in our concerns," Stafford said. "But neither of us can relax until he's stopped. If he's as powerful as I fear, then who knows what he'll do if he finds out what we're doing and fights back. I have to go now, but thank you for taking the time to talk with me tonight. And if you ever need help, please don't hesitate to contact me."

CHAPTER 10
IF AT FIRST YOU DON'T SUCCEED

Richard Cheney had rarely been surprised at the targets his clients paid him to take out. But the call he'd received a few hours earlier had been a first. And for once, he'd hesitated before taking the job – as his client had asked him to eliminate a teenage boy. Curiosity had gotten the better of him, though, and he'd accepted.

Cheney was sitting in the lobby of the Mandarin Oriental Hotel, pretending to read a paper, when he spotted his target heading out of the hotel with three women. He wasn't worried about being spotted, as his ability to blend in with crowds had served him well in his many assignments. Cheney was of medium height and build, with medium length dark hair and brown eyes. Even his clothes were nondescript, helping him look unremarkable in every way.

He took the time to observe each person closely. The slender elderly lady leading the procession held herself in such a rigid fashion that he guessed she was a driven woman, probably intolerant of anyone who didn't see things her way. He gazed at the attractive thirty-something-year-old woman walking one step behind her and wondered what her occupation was as she dressed as if she was on safari. The girl behind them was an athletic-looking, curly brown-haired girl who, like most teenagers, appeared to want to disassociate herself from the older women. The boy clearly didn't fit in as he hung back from the rest of the group. He was a little shorter than the girl, much darker skinned, and had long black braids hanging down his back.

Cheney never rushed his hits, as he wanted to make them look like accidents or random attacks. So, it didn't bother him to wait across the street while the foursome had dinner in a nearby restaurant. After the meal, he followed them into Hyde Park and along the pathway on the north side of the Serpentine Lake. He couldn't believe his luck when the boy darted across the grass and dove into a tree with long droopy branches that made it look like a natural hut.

Making sure no one was looking, Cheney hustled across the lawn towards the only opening in the tree's canopy and ducked inside. He was momentarily surprised by how dark it was as the leaves blocked almost all the glow from London's lights. Cheney paused and slowly looked around, letting his eyes adapt to the gloom under the tree. He spotted a dark shape moving on the opposite side of the enclosure and slowly withdrew his pistol, with silencer, from his jacket.

Cheney lifted the pistol, sighted along the top of the barrel, and squeezed the trigger. He saw the boy drop to the ground but didn't move as he waited silently to see if he'd finished the job. Cheney swore softly when he saw the boy stand and move towards the entrance. Knowing that underneath the tree canopy was a perfect place to finish his business, he shifted his aim and squeezed the trigger again. He heard the soft thwack of the bullet hitting the tree trunk, followed instantly by the boy cussing softly.

An instant later, he heard a girl's voice calling, "Are you all right, Alex?"

"Yeah, but it's so dark in here that I can't see where I'm going and keep running into things."

A second later, a phone's flashlight shone through the opening. Not wanting anyone to recognize him, Cheney covered his face and brushed past the girl at the entrance.

The miss rankled him, as he'd never missed a target before, especially not one that close. Determined to fix his mistake, Cheney decided to change methods and go with what he felt most comfortable with. He hurried back to his hotel room, locked the door, and pulled out the suitcase he'd stashed in the closet. Opening the hard grey-shelled case, he reverently took out his weapon of choice – a sniper rifle that was deadly accurate up to 1000 yards out. He quickly assembled it while keeping one eye out for the group. When he finished, he attached his bipod assembly, screwed on his customized silencer, then slid a round into the chamber. After he was satisfied everything was ready, he turned out the lights, opened the curtains, and sat by an open window, occasionally looking through his spotting scope, waiting for his next chance.

He was usually very patient and could focus on his objective, but the misses earlier in the night kept bothering him. Every so often, he shook his head and wondered how the kid had twice moved at the exact instant required for Cheney's bullets to miss. He wondered if it was just bad luck or if his client was right – that there was something about the boy that would make this assignment more difficult than he'd anticipated. Knowing they were distractions, Cheney pushed his doubts aside and redoubled his watch on the street below.

It wasn't until well after ten that he spotted the group coming out of the park. He placed the rifle's bipod on the windowsill, glanced through the spotting scope, then quickly got out of his chair and kneeled on the floor. Fitting the rifle butt to his shoulder, he sighted through the scope and zeroed in on the boy, pleased that there were just enough people still out walking for this to look like a random shooting. Cheney moved his left thumb and pushed the safety lever off. His right index finger slipped into the trigger guard and slowly started its deadly curling motion.

Letting out his breath, he squeezed the trigger, then quickly lowered the rifle so he could look through his spotting scope. He watched as his target threw his hand out and fell. Cheney smiled, happy that he'd finally finished his assignment.

He was about to start disassembling his rifle but got a feeling that something was wrong. It took him a minute before he realized that what was bothering him was that the city noises hadn't changed. There should have been screams and crying if his aim had been true. But, for the third time that day, Cheney saw something he'd never experienced – his target stand. Stunned, he zoomed in on his spotting scope and saw blood flowing down the boy's face.

Cheney hastily set up his rifle, settled his cheek against the gunstock, and sighted through the scope. He nearly pulled the trigger a second time, but the older woman shifted her stance and blocked his view of the boy.

He then watched helplessly as Alex crossed the road and disappeared from his sight. Cheney pulled his rifle back in and began pacing the room in a rage. It was some time before he calmed down enough to turn his thoughts to figuring out how the next time would be different. Knowing he wouldn't get another chance that night, he disassembled his rifle, put it back into its case, and began rethinking his plans.

CHAPTER 11
THE TOWER OF LONDON

Alex hoped the frosty reception he'd gotten the previous day would have thawed a bit, but as soon as he arrived at breakfast, he knew it had been wishful thinking. Sophie and his grandmother glared at him while Diana avoided looking at him. He would have begged off if he hadn't been so hungry, but his stomach got the better of his fears, and he sat down with the others. But before he could take a bite, his grandmother launched into him.

"What did I tell you about sticking with us and not causing any problems? I had to send Diana looking for you last night, and then you fell and hurt yourself. Are you trying to make me angry?"

"I'm sorry, Grandma. I saw some kids coming out of that cool-looking tree and had to check it out. I've never seen anything like it. And as for the injury – it was a freak accident. You can't blame me on that one. Some car must have kicked up a rock. But I promise I'll stick with you guys today and not do anything dumb. It's just that London is like a giant candy store – there's so much to see and do that I get distracted."

Elizabeth shook her head in disgust. "Fine, but as I told you, I'm sending you home as soon as the airlines are flying again."

After a quick stop at Sherlock Holmes' legendary residence at 221 B Baker Street, they headed to the Tower of London where, after getting tickets, they passed over the dry moat and into the heart of the complex. They wandered through the different towers and over the walls for the next hour, eventually winding up at the line to the crown jewels just as a light rain began falling.

Seeing the long line waiting to get in, Alex forgot his grandmother's warning and asked, "Can I wander around on the battlements some more? We've already seen a few crowns, and I'm not interested in waiting in line to see more."

Elizabeth clenched her fists and bit down on her top lip. Before she could say anything, Diana intervened. "I'm not that interested in the jewels either, so I wouldn't mind keeping an eye on him. Just call me when you're ready to move on. That way, you can enjoy yourself without him bothering you."

Elizabeth almost looked relieved as she said, "Fine, but don't get in trouble."

"We won't," Diana replied. Before Elizabeth could say anything else, Diana slid her arm through Alex's and led him away.

When they were out of sight, Alex said, "Thanks. I didn't mean to upset her. I guess I wasn't thinking."

"You think!" Diana said. "You disappear for almost a year, then show up acting like everything's okay. I'm so mad at you I could scream."

Alex dropped his head and shuffled his feet. "I didn't mean for any of this to happen." He paused, then asked, "This will sound weird, but I've got to clarify something. Why does everybody keep saying I've been gone for almost a year? It's only been a couple of weeks."

Diana stood with her mouth open before saying, "Hello. You disappeared last June in Romania. It's now May." She stepped closer and studied Alex before asking, "Did you get hurt and lose your memory or something? Is that why you didn't call?"

Alex shook his head. "No. I crossed the creek, and the next thing I knew, I couldn't get back to you and Jane. It was freaky."

Diana threw her hands up and said, "You know what? I don't want to hear anymore. I'm still mad at you, but I'd rather enjoy my time here than hear why you ditched us. Come on."

They'd only gone a few steps when Alex cried out and jumped back.

"What's wrong now?" Diana asked in a huff.

Alex shuddered. "There are a few dozen ghosts up ahead staring at me – some carrying their heads."

"You're not just saying that to scare me. Are you?" Diana asked.

Alex shook his head. "I'm guessing it's the ghosts of some of the prisoners we've read about." He was about to say more but suddenly felt the ankh tugging him back towards the river wall. Without thinking, he pulled Diana along, until they were again in front of the Traitor's Gate.

"What's wrong with you?" Diana asked. "Why did you drag me here?

Alex couldn't reply as he accidentally stumbled on the cobblestones just then and bumped into Diana, knocking her straw hat off and sending it into the river's dirty green water below.

"Now look at what you've done," Diana cried. "I liked that hat."

"I'm sorry. I'll get it for you." Without hesitating, Alex jumped over the low wire mesh fence and ran down the concrete steps leading to the water. He got to the last dry step, bent down, and reached for Diana's hat, floating a couple of feet away.

He almost had it in his grasp when the ankh tugged at him, causing him to fall into the slimy-looking water, where his right arm sank to his elbow in the muck at the bottom of the Thames River.

Diana laughed and said, "That was graceful, but you need to get out of there before you get in trouble."

"Very funny," Alex said. As he pushed himself up, he shifted his hand for better leverage and touched something odd. Forgetting about the muck, he felt around until his fingers grasped the unknown object and pulled it up. Still unsure what it was, he got to his feet, grabbed Diana's hat with his other hand, and climbed back onto the steps, swishing the unknown object in the dirty water for a minute to wash the mud off. When he pulled it out again, he was surprised to find he was holding a human skull.

Not wanting to get in trouble, he tucked it inside Diana's hat, scrambled up the steps, and jumped back over the fence.

"What are you hiding?" Diana asked as she reached for her hat.

Alex turned his shoulder, preventing her from getting it, and said, "Nothing."

She held out her hand and said, "I know you're hiding something because you're acting suspicious again."

Seeing a Beefeater walking towards them, he said, "Not here. And I'm giving you fair warning – you won't like it."

Diana rolled her eyes. "Well, at least let's get out of the rain. You're already wet enough."

They hurried away and found a gate where no one else was around. Alex nodded at Diana and said, "Why don't you get underneath? I'll stand outside and let the rain wash off some of this muck."

Diana crinkled her nose and replied, "Good idea. So, what is this mysterious thing that you've found?"

Alex looked around to ensure no one was in sight and opened her hat, showing her the skull and saying, "I just hope my grandma doesn't find out, or she'll send me away for doing another dumb thing."

Diana didn't hear what he said as she stared at the skull. In her Boston-accented monotone voice, she said, "Oh my god. What is it with you? You've only been here for two days, and you're already getting into trouble. How did you find that?"

"I just happened to feel it when I fell in."

A ghostly head suddenly appeared a few feet in front of Alex and, in a booming voice, said, "Thanks, laddie. I've been dead almost 700 years and am ready to quit this place."

Alex let out a tiny shriek and nearly dropped the skull.

The ghost yelled, "Och, be careful, lad. That's my head you've got in your hands. I've protected it from rocks, logs, and ships bashing it for centuries. I'd hate to see all my work undone by one clumsy boy."

Not knowing how to respond, Alex stuttered, "I'm sorry. Should I put your skull back where I found it?"

The spirit replied, "Are ye daff? You're the first living person I've been able to talk to since I died. Of course, I dinnae want you to put my head back in the muck."

"What's going on, Alex?" Diana asked. "You look like you've seen a ghost."

"I have! The spirit whose skull I found is telling me to keep it."

"You can't do that," Diana said.

"Then what am I supposed to do? I can't just ignore his request and toss his skull back into the river," Alex replied.

The spirit interjected before Diana could reply. "I'd suggest we save this discussion for later. I doubt if it's smart for a person to talk with a skull in public. I'll come talk to you when we have some privacy." With that, he disappeared.

Disregarding Diana's glare, Alex hastily tucked the skull into his pack and handed her hat back, saying, "Let's find grandma and see if they're ready to leave."

CHAPTER 12
THE GUARDIAN OF SCOTLAND

Alex was glad it started raining harder as it washed the River Thames muck off him. By the time he met back up with his grandmother, all four were soaking wet, so they returned to the hotel. He was still blow-drying his clothes, the only ones he had, when he heard a knock at his door. Making sure he secured his bathrobe, he opened the door and was surprised to see Diana.

"Am I supposed to be some place I didn't know about?" he asked.

"Relax. Your grandma asked me to check on you and ensure you don't get in trouble since they have a conference call and will be busy for a while."

When Alex didn't say anything, Diana reached into her khakis' and pulled out her phone, covered by a fluorescent orange safety case. As she flipped through it, Alex asked, "Is that case bright enough?"

She shook it at him. "Just so you know, without you around, my phone has survived for almost a year without a scratch. I'm making sure nothing happens to Kenny, as I've sworn that I won't get another one until it wears out."

"Hey, it's not my fault you've wrecked so many phones. You were the one who jumped into a river to play with crocodiles, tried petting a boa constrictor, and used your phone to try and stop a train."

Diana sputtered as she retorted, "I wouldn't have been in any of those situations if it weren't for you."

Alex grinned and held his hands up. "Peace. I was just messing with you. I didn't mean to rile you up because it's been good seeing you again.

Diana blushed. "As for the case, it's to make sure I don't lose it." She shoved it back in her pocket and said, "You can't last a day without getting into some new mess. What happened today? And don't give me some gibber jabber trying to hide the truth. You know I'll find out what you're up to one way or another."

He scratched his head and said, "I'm not sure. The last thing I wanted today was for something odd to happen. What worries me is that I fear that finding that skull was no accident. My hand sank right to where I found it, as if that spirit, or something, wanted me to find him."

"Who was it?"

"I have no clue. But, since I haven't seen him since then, I'm hoping it was just a ghost playing a prank."

Diana's phone went off, but she didn't answer it.

"Shouldn't you get that?" Alex asked. "Your mom will probably start worrying about you and blame me for corrupting you if you don't."

Diana glanced at it, rolled her eyes, and sighed. "This discussion was just getting interesting. My mom just texted that their meeting ended early, and they want to go to dinner now. So, you better get ready and meet us downstairs in the lobby in ten minutes."

As she pushed her chair back, Diana said, "Sometimes I wish you had my hearing. That way, you wouldn't hear them calling for me." She started walking away, then stopped and pointed a finger at him. "We're not done, bub. I still want to hear the whole story of the skull and your absence later."

After dinner, Alex headed straight to bed, still trying to recover from his recent adventures. As he lay there, with his fingers laced behind his head, he wondered how much he should tell Diana when she cornered him the next time. He didn't get a chance to come up with an answer as cold air suddenly washed over him. Alex jumped and nearly fell out of bed at the sight of a heavily bearded head floating in the middle of the room.

It took him a few seconds before he recognized it was the same head he'd seen at the Tower of London. "Who are you?" Alex asked.

"I'm Sir William Wallace, the first Guardian of Scotland," the ghost replied.

Never having heard of him, Alex shrugged and asked, "Why are you here?"

"Since ye're the first living person I've met who can talk to ghosts, I wanted to ask if ye'd find the rest of my body parts and lay me to rest in my native Scotland, so I can move on."

It took Alex a few seconds to digest what Wallace had said before he responded. "I'm sorry. I just assumed you were choosing not to show all of you. What happened?"

Wallace's head started moving as if he were pacing the floor. Finally, after several turns, his head came to a stop, looking directly at Alex. "I've been dead a long time, so I think it best to tell ye my story so I can convince ye to help me.

"I was born in the year of Our Lord, 1270. At a young age, I went to my uncle's household, where I had a classical education, learning how to read and write in English, Latin, and French, as well as studying the sciences. I also trained to be a soldier, but I was more interested in religious studies. Alas, a series of events, when I was about yer age, sent me down a much different path.

"Alexander, who had been King of Scotland for quite some time, died without an heir, throwing our country into turmoil. The Scottish lords started quarreling among themselves as to who should succeed him. Since they couldn't agree on anyone, they asked King Edward I of England to settle the issue. He settled it all right – at the price of getting the Scottish Lords to swear fealty to him. In one fell swoop, he took control of our country. He eventually selected John Baillol as King and pacified the rest by giving them land and money. That dinnae work for long because Baillol was weak and did whatever Edward told him.

"Things started heating up, and clashes between the occupying English forces and Scottish people became more frequent. Then the English killed my father, and from that point on, I fought to free Scotland from the English.

"Now, I was no saint, for I had a fierce temper, but the point of no return came when an Englishman made fun of me and tried to take my dirk from me. Although ye can't tell by the looks of me now, I was a giant of a man and made short work of him. Soon after, I killed three more Englishmen for trying to take my fish away from me and would've killed two more if they hadn't run off. From then on, I was an outlaw.

"I enlisted a few friends, and we tried ambushing the Sassenachs. It didn't work out too well, as the English promptly caught me and threw me in jail. God works in mysterious ways, though. I got deathly sick while in jail and went into a coma the day before my trial. Instead of hanging me, the English jailers tossed me out onto the trash heap. An old crone rescued me and nursed me back to health."

"Before I left her, she gave me a strange, multi-colored stone and told me to always keep it with me – that it would bring me good luck. That near-death experience drove me to gather another band of men to attack the English. Ironically, our first pitched battle was at the same site where my father died five years earlier, where I killed the English knight who'd killed my father. I soon learned I could defeat the English if I engaged them on my terms and didn't fight them in the open, like the time when we killed a hundred Englishmen and lost only three men. The success of that action brought more Scots to my side, including my most trusted friends Stephen of Ireland and Kerly – may they rest in peace."

"Don't get me wrong, this is all fascinating, but what does it have to do with me?" Alex asked.

"I'm getting to that. Things seemed to be going my way because shortly after that, I met and married Mariod Braidfute, who rewarded me with a darling little girl the next spring."

Wallace's eyes grew hard. "But the cowardly English busted down her door and killed her while I was away. I had my revenge on the men who killed them, though, as I snuck back into town and killed every able-bodied Englishman. It wasn't the end of the atrocities. Shortly after that, the English hung my father-in-law and 360 other Scots in a barn. Those who performed the dastardly deed thought they should celebrate their grisly accomplishment. It was the last thing they ever did. After they got drunk, I locked them in the barn and burned them alive. From then on, it was all-out war against the English."

Alex gasped but didn't take his eyes off Wallace as he'd become engrossed in the Scotsman's story.

"I was so successful at fighting the English that my band of men grew into a small army, as many of my countrymen were tired of the invaders. Late that summer, I joined forces with Sir Andrew de Moray's small army, which had been fighting in the north. Our first joint battle was near Stirling. In their arrogance, the English came out of their castle and crossed their army over a small bridge. We waited until they had about half their army across the river before we attacked from the hills above. Their heavy cavalry got bogged down in the marshes and were ineffective. We trapped the rest of their army along the river, where we slaughtered them like the swine they were.

"We continued our offensive, and shortly after that, we drove the last English forces out of Scotland. To ensure they never returned, I continued with my army and attacked northern England to give them a taste of what we'd been experiencing for years.

"Shortly thereafter, the lords elected me Guardian of Scotland. I tried to reform the feudal and church systems to make them less oppressive, but I went too far, too fast. My changes scared the Scottish nobility because they feared losing their wealth and privilege.

"King Edward didn't take his defeat too kindly either. The following year he gathered an army and invaded Scotland again. Rather than fight them in open battle, I continued harassing them, always staying just out of reach of his army. He kept pursuing me without regard to his supply lines. The English grew weary and hungry as we took all the food ahead of them as they advanced." Wallace paused and asked, "Do ye remember me mentioning my lucky stone earlier?"

"Yes."

"I lost it about then, and with it went my luck. I should have fled when I discovered its loss, but I was too arrogant and stayed the course.

They eventually became so desperate that they attacked my army at Falkirk, trapping us in front of the river Avon, where the English longbowmen mowed my soldiers down from afar.

"The Scottish lords used that defeat to bring down my government. It was the last time I led a large group of men into battle. I felt like I lost my moral compass after that as I drifted, performing errands for a friend of mine, and fighting in petty little wars in France.

"Longshanks, the nickname for the King of England during my life, didn't sit idle while I was in France, though. One by one, he wooed the Scottish Lords by bribing them and threatening their comfortable status. I couldn't take what was happening to my country, so I returned. It was too late. From then on, Edward used the Scottish nobles to hunt me down.

"My friend Kerly and I fled to Sir John de Menteith's castle at Dumbarton to meet up with Robert the Bruce and try to win him back to our movement. I thought we were safe since I was godfather to de Menteith's sons, and I had papers promising Bruce would show up."

His eyes glazed over for a moment before he continued with his story. "I went to the assigned meeting place for eight nights in a row to meet Bruce, but I never saw hide nor hair of that coward. Then, one night, my servant, Jack Short, may he rot in hell, slipped drugs into my drink, and took my weapons. Some sixty Englishmen snuck into the castle, with de Menteith's help, killed Kerly, then pounced on me. Even though I was groggy and without weapons, I still managed to kill two of them before they overwhelmed me.

"After that, they took me to Westminster in London, riding only at night for fear of the populace attacking them. There, they charged me with treason, homicide, spoliation, robbery, and arson. The men who judged me, may they rot in hell, weren't interested in what I had to say. The only words I spoke were to deny the charge of sedition because I never swore fealty to Edward."

Even though he had no body, Wallace seemed to shudder. "I can't believe they called themselves Christians, for my execution was barbaric. I was drug through the streets, hung till I was nearly dead, stretched, then drawn, quartered, and beheaded."

It took Wallace a few moments before he quietly said, "That's why I'd like yer help in finding the rest of my body and giving me a decent burial. Will ye help me?"

"My sister asked me to help her move on," Alex said. "But I haven't been successful yet. I can't imagine I'll be any more effective with you. Besides, my grandmother won't let me wander around by myself."

"I've been stuck in this condition for 700 years, laddie. Ye've been here for two days and have already found my head. To me, that's progress. I understand ye might not find all of me, but will ye at least try? Otherwise, I fear I'll be stuck here for eternity."

"Do you know where your other body parts are?" Alex asked.

"I don't know if my bones are still intact or if they've turned to dust," Wallace replied. "The reason ye found my skull in such good shape was because they tarred my head to ensure it lasted a long time hanging on the old London Bridge. As for the rest of me, the Sassenach displayed my right arm in Newcastle, my right leg in Berwick, my left arm in Stirling, and my left leg in Perth. It's not much to go on, but it's all I've got. So, will ye do it? Will ye try to find the rest of me?"

Alex sat for a long time in silence. At last, he said, I've been through so much trying to help my sister and other spirits move on that I don't know if I have it in me to take up another request."

Wallace looked down at the floor and then out the window. "I understand. It was a lot to ask of ye, so I'll take my leave of ye for now. But I'll check back to see if ye change yer mind."

Alex reached out to try to stop Wallace, but he was too late. Wallace's head had disappeared.

CHAPTER 13
AN OVERDUE EXPLANATION

At breakfast the next morning, Alex was surprised when Elizabeth looked to Diana and asked, "Do you think you can keep a close eye on him for one day? Your mother and I have some work we need to do and don't have time for exploring."

Diana glanced at Alex and said, "I'll make sure he doesn't get into trouble."

Alex heard Sophie mutter, "That'll be the day," but ignored it as he was too excited about being free of their supervision.

Diana motioned for him to hurry up and eat, and within half an hour, they were standing outside the hotel. Before he could ask where they were going, Diana said, "Do you mind if we go to Kew Gardens? It's a UNESCO site with the most diverse collection of plants on Earth."

Alex rolled his eyes, thinking there had to be more interesting places to see. But, having promised his grandmother he'd behave, he said, "You're in charge."

Diana pulled out her phone and said, "Good. Now, give me your credit card again."

"What for?" Alex asked.

"Remember us doing this in Spain last year? I'll put your information on my phone, which will make buying things easier. Besides, this is the least you could do for deserting us in Romania."

"It's nice having you do all the organizing, but what happens when you destroy Kenny again? We're still going to need cash."

"It won't be a problem because I won't let you get us into any crazy situation again," Diana replied.

Alex mumbled, "Good luck with that," then followed her across the street to the metro station.

The gardens far surpassed Alex's expectations, however. He saw giant redwood and sequoia trees for the first time in his life, plants that looked like stone, a greater variety of cacti than he thought could exist, and plants that looked like they'd come from outer space. His favorite part, though, was Rhododendron Dell, which was in full bloom. He'd seen lots of rhododendrons in New England, but they paled in comparison to the variety and quantities he saw in Kew Gardens. The only downsides to the visit were Diana's discomfort with the height of the Treetop Walkway and having to leave all too soon.

They arrived back at Knightsbridge Station in the late afternoon, but not wanting to go to the hotel yet, Diana convinced Alex to walk through Hyde Park to see it in daylight. With no particular destination in mind, they soon found themselves on the Serpentine Bridge. Alex found a spot near a life preserver, leaned onto the stone railing, and stared over the Long Water Lake in Kensington Gardens.

Diana, who was watching a pair of swans swimming along the north shoreline, leaned back against the railing and looked towards Alex. "What's with that long face? Is it because you're trying to decide how to tell me why you disappeared for so long?"

When he didn't respond, she said, "You can trust me. I won't tell anyone. Well, except for Jane."

Alex shifted to look at Diana and asked, "But can I trust you? No offense, but isn't your first duty to your Druid Order?"

Diana glared at Alex. "You have no idea how many times Jane and I have lied to my mom and your grandmother for you. We care what happens to you – so much so that we both went a little crazy last summer, blaming ourselves for thinking we had caused your death. So, why won't you trust me?"

Alex stuck his hands in his pockets and shrugged. "I'm sorry about what I just said. I'm stressed out from all that's happened, and my mind's in a whirl."

"You want to tell me about it?"

"I can't tell you much," Alex replied.

"Can't or won't?" Diana asked.

"A little of both, but I can tell you I didn't do anything wrong." Seeing Diana lift one eyebrow in disbelief, he added, "Well, at least I was working on a great cause. But you have to believe me that I don't understand everything that happened. For instance, you and others have said I've been gone for almost a year. But it's been less than two weeks for me. I was trapped inside a castle for a couple of days and spent the rest of the time getting here. So, I don't understand the time discrepancy."

"We had search and rescue teams scouring the area for days. But the only castle in the area was Poenari," Diana said.

"I wasn't in Poenari," Alex responded. "What can I say? The castle is just another part of the mystery."

"At least your explanation partially explains why you hardly look a day older than when you disappeared. Put aside the time issue. What were you doing while you were gone? Did you leave death and destruction in your wake, like you normally do?"

"I didn't start it. I was only trying to survive."

Diana's eyes grew wide as his words sunk in. "So, that's a yes." She stepped closer and said, "You found it. Didn't you? What was the Grail like?"

"I didn't say I found it," Alex replied.

"Is this something you can't tell anyone about?" When she didn't get an answer, Diana asked, "Can you at least tell me how you ended up here in England?"

"When I finally escaped that castle, I headed back the way I came but somehow wound up in Norway."

"How can that be?" Diana asked.

"That's the point. One minute, I was in Romania. And the next, I was overlooking a fjord in Norway."

"So, how did you get to England?"

"Do you remember me telling you about Thorfinn?" Without waiting for her reply, he said, "Well, the queen he'd been trying to help showed up and arranged for Leif Erickson and his men to give me a ride to England on their ship."

"No way. What was he like?" Diana asked.

"Crazy. We sailed across the North Atlantic in an open ship, and he and his crew were having a great time while I was wet, cold, thirsty, and hungry. And by the way, I apologize for not understanding your seasickness before. I was never more miserable in my life."

"Well, I'm sorry for having wished you'd get seasick, but then what happened?"

"They dropped me off near Porlock, which is across the Bristol Channel from Wales, and I worked my way here only to find that skull by accident."

"And what happened with that ghost?" Diana asked.

"He showed up last night. It was William Wallace, and he made it sound like he used to be a big thing in Scotland."

"He's only their national hero," Diana replied. "What did he want?"

Alex grimaced. "He wants me to help him find his missing body parts."

"You said yes, right? What's your plan?" Diana eagerly asked.

"I didn't agree to help him," Alex replied. For one thing, he's probably just a bunch of dust by now. And secondly, since you've known me, when have things ever gone smoothly when I go off on some crazy adventure?"

Diana laid a hand on his arm to calm him and said, "I don't know all you've been through in the last year, but I know it wasn't a walk in the park. When I first saw you two days ago, you looked like death warmed over. But, it's like Jane keeps saying – there must be a reason that these things happen to you."

She took a deep breath and added, "I know you might not want to hear it right now, but you're only focusing on the negatives. What about all the good things that have come out of your adventures? I bet just about anything that you did something good on your latest escapade. Am I right?"

When Alex started hemming and hawing, Diana waved his non-response aside and said, "I'll take that for another yes. You know, my fifteenth birthday is coming up soon, and I hadn't been looking forward to it since Elizabeth and my mom are so focused on the conclave they're going to in Stormhold, but...."

"In case I forget, or am gone, happy birthday," Alex said.

Diana shook her head and grinned. "You're not getting off that easy. As I was about to say before you cut me off, I know what you can get me."

"Uh, oh. I don't like the sound of that."

Diana ignored his half-hearted protest. "For my birthday, I want to go on another adventure with you. I want to help you find William Wallace's body parts. It will be epic – my best birthday ever."

She rubbed her hands in glee and added, "I can't wait to tell Jane about this."

For the first time in days, Alex laughed.

"I'm glad you finally have a smile on your face. So, what are we going to do about Wallace?" Diana asked.

"I don't know. For one thing, how would we get around England and Scotland to search for him?"

"Let me think about that. Getting around the country with my mom and your grandma will present a problem, but it's not insurmountable," Diana said. "We won't have much time to look for him, so I'll research Wallace's death, then find out more about your grandma's agenda."

"I don't understand," Alex said. "After everything you've been through, why would you go on another adventure?"

Diana turned away, unwilling to let Alex see the emotions crossing her face. In a somewhat husky voice, she said, "My mom has planned out my life for me, and I never really questioned it until I met you. Don't get me wrong. I love being a Druid, doing all the magic stuff, and looking for magical objects, but most of the time, it's boring. The older members of our order look like they're just going through the motions. I don't want to end up like that."

Alex turned to look at the London skyline and said, "What about all the danger we'll probably encounter?"

Diana scoffed. "Danger? I've already endured sacrificial altars, cave-ins, hurricanes, pirates, thugs, and more. It can't get any worse than that. Besides, no magical objects are involved. And who would get upset if we search for the bones of a 700-year-old ghost."

"I wish there was some wood I could knock on because those sound like famous last words." Alex pulled a blue velvet bag out of his pocket and handed it to her. "By the way, these are for you."

Diana held back and asked, "What are they?"

"They're compensation for all the trouble I've caused you."

Diana hesitantly took the bag and shook it. Hearing clicking sounds, she loosened the drawstrings, looked inside, and gasped. "Are these real?"

"I believe so. I thought you could use them for your college fund."

Alex could see tears welling in Diana's eyes. Wanting to avoid the hug he thought she was about to give him, he walked over to the end of the bridge to get a closer look at swans that had climbed onto the bank.

Suddenly, he felt the ankh thumping against his chest. The next instant, his feet slipped out from under him. As he fell, a tiny wisp of air blew over his head. Laying on his back, too stunned to move, he noticed a middle-aged man in a grey suit with a funny-looking pipe protruding from his mouth hurriedly walking away. He instantly forgot about the man as the pain from the fall set in.

Diana ran up and asked, "Are you okay?"

Alex sat up and pointed to a banana peel. "Except for a couple of new aches I'm going to feel tonight, I'm fine. I can't believe I fell for the old banana peel gag, though."

Diana frowned. "I've noticed you've been unusually klutzy recently. Since it's probably because you're tired from all that adventuring you've been doing, let's head back to the hotel so you can rest."

Wincing, Alex pushed himself off the ground and headed after Diana.

CHAPTER 14

A DAY AT THE MUSEUM

Diana kept looking over at Alex as they strolled along the Serpentine. When she couldn't take the suspense any longer, she raised the bag of gemstones and said, "These are magnificent. If they're real, as I think they are, then this bag could be worth millions. There are some huge blood-red rubies, a large red diamond, plus smaller diamonds, sapphires, and emeralds. How did you get these?"

"Believe it or not, I picked them up off the ground because nobody wanted them," Alex replied. "I thought they might help me return to civilization, but now that I'm here, I don't want them. They're yours. Besides, you have a bigger need for them than I do."

"There's got to be more to it than – you just picked 'em up."

"There is, but I can't tell you about the rest of the story."

"By now, you should know that you can't just go around finding and giving away treasures," Diana said. "You'll get in trouble someday because someone will think you stole them."

"It's the least of my worries right now," Alex replied.

"You're unbelievable. You know that, don't you?"

Alex ignored Diana's comment and said, "I'd suggest you get a lockbox and put the lockbox in the hotel safe every place you go until you get to

Stormhold. If they're worth what you think they are, you can't be too safe."

"Why do you keep making it sound like you're leaving?" Diana asked.

"You heard my grandma. She's sending me home as soon as the skies clear over the North Atlantic. And even though my grandpa thinks I should stay and see this out, I'm not sure how I can live in a foreign country on my own."

Diana held up the bag of stones and said, "You could always have Jane fence these for you."

Alex shook his head. "Money's not what I'm worried about. It's being alone a long ways from home with no plan on what to do."

"But you've been in that situation before," Diana said.

"In the cases you're talking about, I was trying to get home, or help my sister move on. This is different."

"Jane and I would be willing to help you out."

"Thanks, but no thanks," Alex replied. "Let's just drop it. Just talking about it stresses me out."

Diana stuffed the stones into her hip bag and didn't say anything for the rest of the walk back.

The following day was foggy, so the foursome headed to the British Museum. But the line to get in at the main entrance was so long that the security guards sent them around to the Montague Place entrance on the other side of the building. Alex had heard Diana talking about how big the museum was, but it didn't sink in until they were still walking ten minutes later. Once in, they circled the huge Great Court Shop heading for the Rosetta Stone exhibit. The crowds there were so large, though, that they couldn't get close to the famous stone. Not having the patience to wait, Alex and Diana decided to go off on their own.

Diana led Alex to the right, into the Ancient Egyptian Hall wing. He was so excited to finally see mummies that he left Diana behind as he sped through the statues, sarcophagi, and other artifacts. His euphoria quickly turned to disappointment when he didn't see a single mummy in the room. He waited till Diana caught up to begin a slower weave through the exhibits. But there was so much to see that it soon became overwhelming.

By the time they got to the Egyptian Life and Death rooms on the upper floor, he was on sensory overload. He grew even more numb when he saw all the mummies on exhibit. What came next didn't surprise him. Cold air started washing over him, followed immediately by a multitude of spirits emerging from their resting places. Hoping they wouldn't follow, he looked for the nearest exit and headed for it, unaware of the ankh beating rapidly on his chest.

He was in such a rush to get out that he barely noticed an English gentleman wearing a tweed sports coat rapidly walking towards him while pulling a shiny golden cigarette-like case out of his pocket. From the corner of his eye, Alex saw the man flip the case open, pull the catch back with one finger, and grope for a button on the bottom side of the case.

The ankh's insistent beating finally broke through his awareness. But it was pounding so hard that Alex grew dizzy, lost his balance, and tripped. Trying to break his fall, he thrust out his arm, but instead of hitting the floor, he accidentally hit the English gentleman, knocking him over and landing on top of him. He looked at who he'd fallen on and hazily recognized him as the same person he'd seen near the Serpentine Bridge the day before. He apologized and pushed himself up.

As a crowd gathered around, the man angrily brushed aside Alex's apology and rushed out of the room.

When Alex's vision cleared, he noticed a well-dressed man lying nearby in obvious pain. A beautiful young woman knelt beside him, holding his hand and calling his name. Seconds later, the man started convulsing.

A guard pushed his way through the crowd, took one look at the man jerking around on the floor, frothing at the mouth, and called for help on his radio. But by the time the guard knelt, the man on the floor had grown quiet. The guard felt his pulse and leaned over to listen for any breathing. Not detecting any signs of breathing, he started performing CPR.

Alex stood up and backed away, bumping into Diana, who guided him to a nearby bench. "Are you all right?" she asked. "You look really pale."

"I'll be fine. I suddenly felt dizzy and knocked some man down right before that guy over there started convulsing."

Diana groaned. "Oh, please don't say you were the cause of all this hubbub. I promised your grandmother I'd keep you out of trouble."

"It was an accident. Besides, I didn't touch that guy on the ground."

More museum personnel poured into the room and shooed out the public. One guard came over to ask them to leave but let them stay when Diana said, "My friend here was part of that accident and isn't feeling well. He needs to rest."

The woman looked from Diana to Alex and replied, "Okay, but stay out of the way."

As the medics whisked the stricken man out of the room on a gurney minutes later, a tall man in his thirties wearing a blue pin-striped suit with a yellow pastel tie broke off from the group of officials and walked towards Alex and Diana. When he was standing in front of them, he asked, "Which one of you was involved in what happened here today?"

Alex raised his hand. "I am."

"I'm Inspector Forrester." The officer showed his badge, flipped open a small notepad, and asked, "What happened?"

"I was feeling dizzy, bumped into some man, and accidentally knocked him down. I didn't see what happened to the man who got sick. He was already on the floor twitching when my head cleared enough that I could stand. Then one of the guards came and started doing CPR on him. That's all I know."

"It might be a coincidence that three people end up on the floor simultaneously, but it doesn't look good for the man they just carted out of here. I'll need your name, phone number, and address if I have more questions. We'll call you if we need anything else."

"Am I in trouble?" Alex asked.

"No. This is just normal routine for these types of situations," the inspector replied.

Diana rolled her eyes and mumbled, "You're always getting into trouble."

The Inspector heard her grumbling and asked, "Do you have something else to add, Miss?"

Alex was about to say something when Diana interjected, "No. I was just talking to myself because I know he's worried about getting in more trouble with his grandmother."

After getting their contact information, Inspector Forrester flipped his pad closed. "If we need anything else, I'll get in contact," he said. "You can go now." As the Inspector turned around, he noticed the cigarette case. He pulled out a baggie, scooped it up, and asked, "Do either of you know who this belonged to?"

"Yeah," Alex replied. "That guy I bumped into was carrying it."

The Inspector closed the baggie over the case, slipped it into his pocket, and left.

Alex and Diana searched the museum until they found Elizabeth and Sophie, then spent another couple of hours touring the rest of the museum before heading out for a late lunch. When they returned to the hotel that evening, they were surprised to see several uniformed police officers and two men in suits waiting in the lobby.

***

One of the men broke from the group of officers and came over to Elizabeth. He showed her his badge and said, "I'm Inspector Forrester from Scotland Yard. Could we talk in private?"

Elizabeth motioned for the others to head towards the elevators and asked, "What's going on?"

"I'm sorry to inconvenience you, ma'am, but I'm looking for evidence connected to a murder that happened earlier today. Unfortunately, it's a bit of a sticky situation. You see, the victim was a rather well-known Minister of Parliament in the middle of pushing an aggressive deficit reduction plan. A young lady…," he cleared his throat and added, "who wasn't his wife, happened to be accompanying him. We are investigating whether this case might be an assassination to stop that legislation from passing. I'd like to…."

Elizabeth cut him off and called over her shoulder, "Alex. Get over here." Addressing the Inspector, she said, "I'm sorry to hear about it. The kids told me what happened, but I thought the man just went into convulsions from something like a heart attack. I'm Elizabeth Adler, the boy's grandmother and guardian. I must ask. Are you charging my grandson with anything? If you are, I insist on a lawyer being present before you talk to him."

"Why do you assume we're interested in the lad?" the inspector asked.

Elizabeth snorted. "I've been around my grandson enough to know when he's caused some problem."

The inspector smiled. "His friend said the same thing. Rest easy. We don't suspect him of anything. We just want to find out if he saw anything unusual and would like your permission to talk with him. Can we go someplace that's a little more private?"

A few minutes later, Alex and his grandmother were sitting in her room across a table from the inspector. The interview didn't last long because Alex told the inspector the same things he'd told him earlier.

"I was hoping you could tell us more," the inspector said. "But it doesn't sound like there was much to see. Think hard; was there anything unusual that you saw?"

Alex started shaking his head, then suddenly stopped. "Well, there was one thing that I thought strange. I thought I'd seen the man I knocked over before."

Forrester sat up eagerly. "Where and when?"

"My friend Diana and I were on the Serpentine Bridge yesterday. I had slipped on a banana peel, and as I was getting up, I saw him walking away from the bridge. I remember him because he looked like a stereotypical Englishmen – you know, wearing a little bowler hat, a tweed jacket, and smoking a pipe. Of course, it could be just a coincidence. I mean we were doing the touristy things that everybody does. Do you need anything else from me?"

The inspector shook his head and told Alex he could leave. When the door closed, Elizabeth asked, "What's going on?"

Inspector Forrester drummed his fingers on the table for a few seconds before saying, "What your grandson said about seeing the man yesterday and today is disconcerting. I came here tonight thinking that your grandson happened to be in the wrong place at the wrong time. We've done a background check, and you came up squeaky clean, although there are some odd things in your grandson's file – specifically his disappearances." The inspector went silent again and resumed drumming his fingers. He finally seemed to make up his mind about some problem and said, "You have to keep what I'm about to say in the strictest confidence. I'm sharing it in the hopes you can give me some insight into the situation."

"Of course," Elizabeth replied.

"The minister didn't die from a natural heart attack," the inspector said. "Our forensic pathologist found a fast-acting poison dart in him. We've done some preliminary checks and have found a few other well-known, unsolved murders caused by a similar type of weapon. We checked with Interpol, and they think this might be the work of an assassin they have been trying to find for over twenty years. It seems possible that the man your grandson accidentally bumped into might be this assassin. If he is, then we might have our first real lead into someone MI6 calls The Quiet Man."

"That sounds like something straight out of a James Bond movie," Elizabeth said.

"You're not far off. Interpol thinks he got his start as a hired assassin for the Russians. Later, he became a free agent and began selling his services to the highest bidder. The only reason we believe he exists is a trail of near-perfect assassinations. He has always stayed one step ahead of us by staying non-descript, being very professional, and constantly changing his operating method. We've never known him to slip up before.

"But when your grandson ran into The Quiet Man today, he must have knocked his weapon out too. I picked up a small cigarette case off the museum floor near where your grandson fell and discovered it had a special compartment for a poison dart. That's when I knew we were onto something big. Amazingly, this man has been operating in complete anonymity for two decades. But because of your grandson's clumsiness, we now have our first description of him, the murder weapon, and potentially his fingerprints."

Elizabeth rolled her eyes. "That's because your assassin never met my grandson. Let me tell you, I doubt if this was chance."

"I don't understand," the inspector said. "He's a teenager who doesn't even shave yet. Are you saying he knew about The Quiet Man and intentionally attacked him?"

"Of course not, but there's almost nothing you can say about my grandson that would surprise me."

"I don't understand," Forrester said.

"I don't either." A hard glint showed in Elizabeth's eyes. "But someday, I'll find out."

The inspector sat silent for a minute. "I'll have to reevaluate everything we've been assuming on the case. We've been proceeding as if the minister was the target. But based on what your grandson said about seeing him before and what you're telling me, I'm not so sure now."

"Is my grandson in any type of danger?"

Forrester hesitated. "Normally, I wouldn't think so because what possible motive could the world's most successful assassin have for killing your grandson?"

Elizabeth shook her head. "He might be annoying and disturbing, but I've never seen him do anything illegal. And yet, he's done so many strange things that I wouldn't rule it out."

"My guess is the Quiet Man will most likely try to leave the country as soon as possible to cover his tracks.

We've got a lookout for him at all the country's ports, railway stations, and airports. But since he's so slippery, I'd suggest you leave London immediately – just in case he tries to double back and eliminate witnesses."

"Thank you for your candidness, Inspector," Elizabeth said. "We'll leave first thing tomorrow morning. Now, if you'll excuse me, I have to make some travel arrangements."

CHAPTER 15

A RIDDLE WRAPPED IN A MYSTERY

Diana hit the speed dial number and waited for Jane Roland's freckled face to appear on her screen.

"I was wondering when ye were going to call," Jane said with her slight Scottish accent.

Diana lowered her voice and said, "I don't have much time because my mother and Elizabeth will be back anytime now from their meeting with the police."

Before Diana could say anything else, Jane asked, "What has he done this time?"

"Wait. You know Alex has returned?"

"The whole order knows it," Jane replied. "Elizabeth called Lady Yvaine the same day he reappeared and has been giving her regular updates about his activities. But I haven't heard anything today. Is all quiet on the western front?"

"Of course not. Alex has gotten involved in something serious because Elizabeth looks shaken while my mom is positively glowing."

"Do ye know what it's about? Is he in some sort of danger?" Jane asked.

"I don't know. We were in the British Museum when I saw Alex accidentally bump into a man he thought he saw yesterday in the park. An instant later, a third man fell to the ground and died a short time later, foaming at the mouth."

Diana noticed the faraway look Jane often got when she was deep in thought. "What are you thinking?"

"Has anything else out of the ordinary happened?"

Diana tried answering, but all she could say was, "Uh…."

"I take it that's a yes. Ye said Alex thought he'd seen the man he bumped into yesterday. What were ye two doing?"

Diana blushed. "Nothing much. He'd just given me a bag of gems he'd found at some castle in Romania right before he slipped on a banana peel."

"I'll get to the gemstones in a minute, but what's this about a banana peel?" Jane asked. "It sounds – off."

"He was just being klutzy. Why do you ask?"

"Haven't ye noticed that he's pretty graceful most of the time?" Jane asked.

"I don't understand what you're getting at," Diana replied.

"Don't ye think it's funny how he's only klutzy at times – usually right before, or during, something bad happening? I have a feeling that something causes his mishaps – almost as if someone, or something, is trying to keep him safe. Crazy, huh?"

Diana thought for a bit, then shook her head. "Actually, no. It explains some of his more bizarre actions. What are you thinking?"

"My guess is that Alex has gotten involved in some serious stuff. But I have no clue what, why, or how. I'm looking forward to the day I figure him out. But, what's this thing about gemstones ye mentioned earlier?"

"He said he found them lying on the ground in Romania. And they're not just ordinary stones. I think they could be worth a fortune."

"What makes ye say that?" Jane asked.

"First of all, they're dazzling! I've never seen anything like them."

"They could be fakes," Jane said.

Diana shook her head. "I don't think so. Alex told me they're to help me pay for college. He wouldn't have said that if he didn't think they were valuable. Besides, he suggested I get you to help me fence them."

"Unbelievable. Right now, though, I want to know what else ye're hiding. Ye're bouncing around like ye can't wait to spill a secret."

"You'll never believe who Alex met," Diana said. When Jane motioned for her to continue, Diana blurted out, "William Wallace. Or at least his head. Alex found his skull in the river at the Tower of London, and Wallace asked him to find the rest of his body parts. Just think how cool it will be to search for The Guardian of Scotland."

"Has he committed to helping him?"

Diana's shoulders slumped. "No, but I think he should.

"I've never seen ye excited to go on one of Alex's misadventures. What's changed?"

"Maybe it's because I'm becoming more like you, which scares me because his antics never seem to faze you. What's up with that? Can you read his mind or something?"

Jane blushed and looked away from her phone. "What makes ye say that?"

Diana misunderstood Jane's reaction and said, "I didn't mean anything by that comment. But it's like I've said before, you seem to know what people are thinking better than anybody I know."

Jane visibly relaxed. "Except for him. Alex is a riddle, wrapped in a mystery, inside an enigma." Both were silent for a minute before Jane said, "I think ye should somehow make it convenient for Alex to get involved in this search for Wallace's body parts."

"That seems like an out-of-the-blue idea. Why do you say that?"

"Even though he keeps getting involved in a bizarre set of random occurrences, I think they're all linked together somehow. I jest have no idea how they're linked."

"What do you suggest I do?" Diana asked.

"When do ye think ye'll arrive in Stormhold?"

"I don't know what the plan is. Why?"

"Both ye and yer mom love exploring. So, as ye come north, try to convince yer mom and Elizabeth to see some historical places, working in the places where Wallace's body parts were scattered. If nothing else, use yer passion for touring UNESCO places as an excuse. But get him to help Wallace."

"I love that idea," Diana said. "But what is that going to accomplish?"

"Ye've heard Alex say many a time that he doesn't have a plan when he sets out on one of his adventures. Yet he always achieves his goal. I'd bet jest about anything that something will come of it. I jest hope nobody gets hurt in the process. And I'll talk to Lady Yvaine and see if I can join ye on yer journey."

"I'd better go," Diana said. "I don't want my mom finding out we've been talking because she'll guess it's about Alex." Diana had just enough time to end the call when the door opened.

CHAPTER 16
TO WEIGH THE ENEMY

News of Alex's sudden reappearance unnerved Pythia, as she'd assumed the boy had died, along with the ghosts she'd sent after him. Wondering how he'd survived yet another attempt on his life, Pythia considered shifting from using spirits and magic to eliminate the boy to more conventional tactics. But she'd learned Brother Stafford's plans to use professional assassins had been equally unsuccessful. She found herself wishing her former partner, Gilgamesh, was still around to advise her on next steps, but his aggressiveness had made him too many enemies, and he'd disappeared centuries earlier.

She sighed and slipped back into the hidden mountainside grotto above Delphi she called home. Sitting down on her tall three-legged stool, she stuck her index finger into the silvery liquid of her magical cup, Jamshid, and chanted,

"By the power of Aether
I call on thee to slow the stream of time
What was past, and what will be
Show me now what I need to see."

Pythia felt relieved when the waters began swirling in their usual colorful pattern. A few seconds later, they stopped and turned into an image of the boy talking to a body-less spirit. She listened intently in on their conversation but was disappointed when it ended without the boy making any plans.

She got up and went to her computer, searching for information on the ghost the boy had been talking to. After reading all she could find on William Wallace, she began pacing the grotto's stone floor. It was some time before she came up with a new plan to get rid of the boy.

Hoping the spirit she was thinking about hadn't moved on, she sat back down on her stool and called the cup's waters back to life. A tall man wearing a loose, long-sleeved red silk tunic that hung to his knees appeared in the waters and called out, "Who summoned me?"

Despite a droopy left eyelid, Pythia was surprised at the fury radiating from the ghost's eyes. "Are you Edward I, the former King of England?" she asked.

"I am. Who are you, and why did you call me here, woman?" the spirit asked.

Pythia swallowed the anger rising inside her at the man's misogynistic attitude and said, "I've summoned you because I believe we can help each other. I want a boy killed."

"Why should I care what you want?" Edward growled.

"I've already unsuccessfully tried killing him three times and have concluded that someone who's highly motivated will be more successful than the random killers I've chosen before," Pythia replied.

"The boy means nothing to me," Edward said.

"Ah, but what you aren't aware of is that the boy has recently discovered the whereabouts of your longtime nemesis – William Wallace. And he's promised to find

Wallace's body parts to help him move on. Do you want him to help your enemy move on before you do?"

"What! That scoundrel Wallace isn't in hell yet?" Edward screamed. "He was the bane of my existence. Even after he died, his memory kept the embers of rebellion in the Scots alive. How could he still be here on earth?"

"I don't know," Pythia replied. "But unless you stop him, I would bet almost anything that the boy will find your archenemy's body parts and help him move on. Are you interested in thwarting your old enemy?"

"This doesn't sound like much of a challenge," Edward said.

"Don't underestimate him. I have given powerful magical objects to your predecessors, but none have returned, and the boy is still alive."

Edward scoffed. "That's because they took your objects and ran. Why should they do your bidding when they already had their reward?"

"Those objects were inconsequential," Pythia said. "Their main incentive was my promise to resurrect them were they successful."

"No one can do that," Edward said.

"Summoning you was a simpleton's task. I have magical powers at my beck and call that are beyond your comprehension."

Edward stared at the translucent head floating in front of him. "So, you'll resurrect me if I kill the boy? You said you gave your previous hires magical objects. What about me?"

Pythia studied the English spirit for a minute before saying, "I'll give you Xtheni's Talon if you accept this mission."

"What's that?" asked Edward.

"It's a powerful sword made of energy – not steel," Pythia replied, deciding not to warn the former English monarch that it would eventually possess him. "But I should warn you, brute force alone won't get the job done. You have to be cunning to outwit the boy. But if you kill him, Wallace won't be an issue."

"It sounds like you're not telling me everything," Edward said. "What are you hiding?"

Pythia took a deep breath. "The boy has a knack for finding powerful magical objects which, I believe, he uses to defeat his foes. I'm guessing that he'll lead you to one of the Maqlû, possibly the object Wallace used to defeat your forces – the Chintamani."

"What is it?"

"It's a small, brightly-colored, oval stone, but don't be fooled by its size. It's an extremely powerful magical object, much stronger than anything I have."

"It can't be that powerful because I killed Wallace," Edward said.

"He lost the stone right before the battle of Falkirk. I've often wondered how things would have turned out if he'd retained it."

Edward paled. It took him a few seconds before he regained his composure and asked, "What is it that you really want? – the boy dead, or the object?

"Both, because I believe they are linked. If I'm right, the boy will eventually learn about the Chintamani and search for it to help your foe," Pythia said. "Again, I warn you not to underestimate him. If I were you, I'd let the boy lead you to the Chintamani, then snatch it from him and use it against him and Wallace."

"You sound like you're scared of this boy."

"No, I'm cautious," Pythia replied. "And I'd suggest you be cautious too. Study him before you attack. Learn his strengths and weaknesses and use them to your advantage."

"If you're so intent on killing him, why don't you do it?"

"I am an extremely old woman and have no interest in chasing after him and fighting battles. I'm much better at incentivizing someone else to do that type of work. So, will you do it?"

Edward didn't respond right away. At last, he nodded and said, "I will. Where can I find them?"

"They're in London right now, but you'll have no problem finding him," Pythia said. "All you have to do is follow the strongest aura you can sense."

"And how will I get this sword you mentioned?"

"I'll bring it to you in two days. And don't worry about a meeting place. I'll come to England and summon you."

CHAPTER 17
AND LEAD US INTO TEMPTATION

Diana looked up as Elizabeth and Sophie entered the room. "What's going on?" she asked. "You look like something bad has happened."

"There's been a change in plans," Elizabeth replied. "You two are leaving for Stormhold tomorrow morning."

"Why the sudden change?" Sophie asked. "Wait. Don't tell me. It's your grandson, isn't it? What's he done this time?"

"It doesn't matter," Elizabeth replied coldly. "We're leaving, and that's that."

"Since we were supposed to be in London a couple more days, could we instead use those days to see things on our way north?" Diana asked.

Elizabeth balled her hands into fists but didn't say anything until she had her emotions in control. "Fine. You have three days to get to Stirling, but you must leave London tomorrow morning."

"What about Alex?" Diana asked. "Is he coming with us?"

Elizabeth made a sound of disgust. "I forgot about him because I'd been hoping that flights would resume. He'll go with you two for now. I'll make arrangements to send him home when he gets to Stirling. Until then, you're responsible for him, including telling him of the change in plans. I have to pack now because I'm taking the night train." She held up her hand to stop Sophie's protest. "Deal with it," she said and headed to her room.

After Elizabeth left, Sophie sat at the desk and drummed her fingers, staring moodily out the window.

Trying to distract her mother, Diana asked, "Where do you think we should go?"

Ignoring her daughter's question, Sophie growled, "Like always, that boy is messing things up for us."

"Mom, you can't say it's his fault this time," Diana said. "He was just in the wrong place at the wrong time."

"Oh, can't I? He shows up out of the blue and forces his grandmother to watch over him. Except I'm the one who's stuck with him."

Diana wracked her brain for some way to calm her mother and help Wallace. She reviewed all the cities where the English had taken Wallace's body parts and said, "You know of my fixation on UNESCO sites. Since we only have three days, I thought we should skip the peak and lake districts and stick to the sites on the train route north to Edinburgh. That way, we could see Hadrian's Wall and Durham. Oh, and I'd like to stop in Berwick upon Tweed too, since it looks like it has a cool fortress town right on the water. Then, on the third day, we could hop a couple of trains to get to Stirling with plenty of daylight left. What do you think?"

"I'm too angry to think about it now," Sophie replied. "Since you have such strong preferences, you can make the train and hotel reservations."

Diana practically ran to Alex's room to tell him the news.

Their rail car was nearly empty the next morning, so Alex and Diana sat several seats away from Sophie to talk without her mother hearing them. As soon as the train pulled out of the station, Diana asked, "Where should we start looking for Wallace's right arm when we get to Newcastle?"

"What are you talking about?" Alex asked.

"Are you serious? I can't believe you haven't thought about Wallace's request. Were you just going to ignore him?"

"Hey, I never agreed to help him," Alex replied.

"How can you ignore his plea for help? That's not like you."

"I didn't know we were going to Newcastle until this morning at the train station," Alex said. "And anyway, why are you so interested in searching for him? His bones have probably all turned to dust by now."

"Wallace's skull didn't," Diana said.

"Even if I agreed, I still wouldn't know where to start."

"That's never stopped you before. Why are you being so hesitant? Did something happen in Romania that has turned you off of adventure?"

"You can say that," Alex replied. "And anyway, why are you so interested in doing this? If the past is any sort of indication, it's probably going to be dangerous."

"It's hard to explain," Diana said. "I know I've grumbled in the past about your extra-curricular activities, but when you were gone this last year, I felt empty. That's when I realized I feel more alive and useful when I'm on one of your adventures than when I'm living my normal life. And besides. It's for a good cause."

Diana looked on expectantly as Alex turned and stared out the window. At last, he said, "Fine. But I'm not promising anything because I don't see how this can work.

"I understand. To be honest, even though I'm excited to search for him, I think there's a low probability of us being successful," Diana said. "Nevertheless, I spent a couple of hours last night searching the internet for potential hiding spots for his arm in Newcastle but only came up with three possibilities. The city is big and new, and it looks like they didn't protect many of the old buildings and castles as they did in London and Edinburgh. The best idea I came up with is someone might have tried to bury his bones on the north side of Hadrian's Wall, west of the city. The problems with that idea are that it would have been dangerous for Wallace's supporters to steal his bones and hide them and that most of the wall is gone."

To her surprise, Alex fixated on only one part of what she'd said. "What is Hadrian's Wall?" he asked.

"You know Rome used to rule most of England. Well, a little after 100 CE, the Emperor Hadrian ordered a wall built to keep the tribes in Scotland from attacking England. It started in Newcastle in the east and stretched across Britain until it ended at the Irish Sea coast west of Carlisle. It represents an old dividing line between Scotland and England which is why I could see some Scottish patriots burying Wallace's remains on the north side of the wall in a symbolic gesture. I did find out something eerie about this part of him, though. Legend has it that as Wallace's right arm dried on the stake, it turned to the north and pointed to Scotland.

"Cool. What else did you find?" Alex asked.

"Not much. The only other structures I found that date back to the same period were an old building near the train station called Castle Keep, which is the city of Newcastle's namesake. Across the street from the castle is the Black Gate. But they've remodeled it so often that even if his remains are still there, they're probably buried now."

Alex nodded and said, "Since we'll be right there, don't you think we should rule out the castle first? Besides, you and your mom love history. How can you pass up something called the Black Gate?"

"Good point," Diana said.

"The bigger question, though, is how are we going to ditch your mom to conduct our search?"

"Since she doesn't like you, I don't think it'll be that hard to go off on our own from time to time," Diana replied.

The talk drifted on to other subjects, and they didn't return to Wallace for the rest of the trip.

Once they got to Newcastle, it was only a five-minute walk from the train station to Castle Keep. Looking up at the tall, rectangular stone building, Diana felt a tinge of disappointment in its plainness. "Is that all there is?" she asked. "I thought it would be like a real castle."

She turned to Alex and whispered, "I just hope Hadrian's Wall is more promising than this because I feel we might be on a fool's errand."

CHAPTER 18
CASTLE KEEP

Sophie, Diana, and Alex wandered around the Black Gate for a few minutes before making their way inside. After buying admission tickets, they headed for the castle.

The first thing that struck Alex once he was inside were the stone stairs lining each of the walls that went off in all different directions. The second thing he noticed was how cold it was, even though one of the employees had warned them about it.

Alex was grateful when they headed up one of the stairs, as the activity kept him warm. But he hadn't gone very far when a ghost wearing a long white tunic underneath mesh armor passed through the castle walls, and stopped a few feet before him. A second later, Wallace apparated next to Alex and growled, "Sir John de Seagrave. What are you doing here?"

Alex cried out and stumbled backwards into Diana, nearly knocking her down.

Sophie, who was leading them up the stone stairs, turned and asked, "What's wrong now?"

Diana blushed and said, "Nothing, Mother. He just stumbled."

Sophie shook her head and continued up.

Diana helped him stand and under her breath, asked, "It was an accident, wasn't it?"

Alex shook his head, grabbed her hand, and pointed to the two spirits hovering near them.

Diana gasped when she saw the two ghosts suddenly materialize in front of her. It had been so long since she'd last seen a ghost, that she'd almost forgotten that by touching Alex she could see and hear ghosts.

Seagrave wasn't much taller than Alex but was much more muscular and had a full beard and mustache that covered the lower half of his face.

"Don't trust this man," Wallace said. "He's the scoundrel who used bribery, drugs, and deceit to bring me down. Once he'd captured me, he fed me scraps, had his men beat me, and marched me to London at night because he was a coward. He was also one of the judges that sentenced me to death in that farce of a trial. And it was he who read the sentence that subjected me to my horrendous execution and the scattering of my body parts."

Seagrave looked up at Wallace's floating head. "I was following the orders of my liege lord King Edward I."

"Hah. I respected ye as a soldier, but what ye did to me was not honorable. And all so ye could gain favor with Longshanks."

Seagrave lifted his chin in an attempt to look defiant and said, "Everything was perfectly legal."

"Then ye were blind. The feudal system ye paid allegiance to was corrupt. It enabled power-hungry clergymen and nobles to trample on people's rights to gain land and power. Change always starts with one person willing to do the right but usually unpopular thing. Ye deserve yer punishment of haunting this earth with no reprieve," argued Wallace.

Alex jumped when Sophie called down, "Why are two just standing there? Is everything all right?"

"Can you keep your mom busy while I sort through this?" Alex whispered.

Diana nodded, passed him on the stairs, and called out, "Hey, Mom, I'd like to go back to the Great Hall and Chapel to look around some more because going up and down these stairs isn't that interesting. Why don't we let Alex run up to the ramparts and burn off some of his energy."

"Oh no, you don't," Sophie said. "Every time he goes off on his own, he disappears."

"I promise I won't wander away, Miss Bennet," Alex said. "Besides, where could I go on the roof?"

Sophie looked at Alex and muttered, "All right. But don't you dare wander off."

After the two Druids disappeared, Alex headed for the roof. When he got there, Wallace and Seagrave were already waiting for him.

"So, why are ye lurking around here?" Wallace demanded of Seagrave.

"I've had seven centuries to ponder that question but still have no answer," Seagrave replied. "I appeared in this castle as soon as I died and have tried leaving countless times, but I've always failed. I'm stuck here in the Entrance to the Afterlife and have no idea why."

"Ye got yer just deserts. Now begone," Wallace said.

Seagrave ignored the command and floated closer to Alex. "Who are you?" he asked.

"It's none of yer business," Wallace replied.

"Maybe it is," Seagrave said. "It can't be coincidence that he's the first living person I've been able to talk to."

"Bah," Wallace said. "I cannae forgive ye for what ye did and never will."

"Maybe there's a way of helping me make amends for your barbaric death," Seagraves said, "I know someone who says she knows where your bones are, Sir William. Unfortunately, I cannot verify the truth of her statement, for she is shy and reluctant to confide in anyone. She and I are the only ghosts who are permanent residents here. Everyone else comes and goes when they please."

"Who are you talking about?" Alex asked.

"I don't know her real name, but her nickname is 'The Poppy Girl.' You'll have a hard time getting her to talk, though. It took me nearly a century before she spoke to me. Her story is a sad one and understandably caused her to fear others. She was an orphan who sold flowers to eke out a living, but the authorities threw her into this castle when it was a prison because she owed some people money. Unfortunately, one of the other inmates murdered her soon after she arrived, and she's been roaming the castle ever since."

"How could they do such a horrible thing?" Alex asked.

"Sometimes it's the way of the world," Seagrave said. "But that's beside the point. A couple of weeks ago, she told me, 'They're coming.' When I asked her what she meant, she said she didn't know, but she seemed very excited – the first time I've ever seen her happy."

"I can't see how she can help us," Alex said. "She was born centuries after both of you died. How could she know where Sir William's bones are?"

"I'm not sure," Seagrave replied. "You should ask her. She always appears around nine in the evening."

"That's after this place closes," Alex said. Assuming I can even sneak away, how will I get in?"

"Don't worry. I'll take care of that," Seagrave replied.

Seconds later, the two ghosts disappeared, leaving Alex alone on the roof. In a pensive mood, he went searching for Sophie and Diana, and soon after, they left the castle.

Alex didn't get a chance to tell Diana what had occurred until Sophie went to the restroom during lunch. After a quick recap, he asked, "What do we do now?"

Diana scratched her head and thought for a minute before saying, "It sounds like we can't do anything until tonight, so let's just enjoy the rest of the day."

After lunch, they took a bus to Segudunum – an old Roman fort and the easternmost point on Hadrian's Wall. Before they'd even passed through the gates, Diana stopped and wailed, "This is a UNESCO site? There's nothing here except some gravel pathways and rocks outlining where buildings used to be."

"I'll admit I was hoping for more, too," Sophie said. "Maybe the museum here will be interesting."

"We only have a couple of days to see the sights. Instead of spending more time here, why don't we go to Durham? It's not that far away," Diana pleaded. "We can return to Newcastle tonight, then leave tomorrow for Berwick."

"Very well," Sophie said. "But you'll need to make all the arrangements."

Diana led them to a nearby metro stop, where they hopped a train back to the heart of Newcastle. There they switched trains and were in Durham less than an hour later.

After crossing the River Wear, they strolled through the historic downtown of Durham. For only the second time since he'd waded ashore in Porlock, Alex felt like he was in an authentic English city. However, Diana kept pushing them, saying they didn't have much time to see the cathedral and castle before catching a train back to Newcastle.

As he walked across Palace Green, a young dark-haired woman appeared, seemingly out of nowhere, grabbed Alex's arm, and begged, "Please help me, sir."

Alex yelped from the ghost's icy touch.

Diana, who was walking with her mother a few feet ahead, turned and glared at him, silently pleading for him not to make a scene.

Alex pointed at the spirit and mouthed, "I can't help it."

Diana picked up on his silent warning and hooked her arm into Sophie's, saying, "Hey, Mom. Could we go back to the museum shop? I saw some things there when we got our tickets for the castle tour that I was interested in getting." She then turned to Alex and asked, "Do you want to come with us or wait out here?"

Grateful for Diana's quick uptake of the situation, Alex said, "It's so nice today that I'd prefer to stay out here in the sunshine."

He waited until they were out of earshot before he turned to the ghost and asked, "What do you want?"

The young woman swallowed to work up her courage and said, "I need your help."

"You already said that. Why do you think I can help?"

"Your aura gave me hope. You see, my boyfriend continues to blame himself for my death, and I can't move on until he forgives himself."

Feeling guilty that he'd been so crotchety earlier, Alex softened his tone and said, "I'm not sure I can help, but I'll do what I can. Unfortunately, I have to leave pretty soon."

"All I want you to do is give my boyfriend a letter that explains what happened that night," the woman said.

"Where is he?"

The woman pointed to the castle where Diana had been leading them and said, "He's in the study hall right now. I can show you who he is."

"Do you have a letter I can give him?" Alex asked.

The young woman shook her head. "Would you write what I tell you?"

Alex rolled his eyes and said, "Wait here. I'll be right back."

He ran to the museum shop and asked Diana for a pen and paper. With both in hand, he ran back out and sat on one of the benches around the green and proceeded to write down what she dictated. He'd just finished when Sophie and Diana came out of the shop.

When Diana gave him a questioning look, he stood up, folded the paper, and returned her pen, saying, "I'm ready. Let's go."

Since the castle was an active university, they had to wait for their tour group to form before heading in. Alex kept looking at his ghostly companion, wondering how he was supposed to hand off her message. When they got to the Great Hall, she grabbed his arm, pulled him away from the other tourists, and led him to a student in his early twenties. The young man was sitting by himself at one of the dining tables, staring into space with his books and papers spread out before him.

Alex cleared his throat and asked, "Are you, Winston?"

The young man blankly looked up at Alex, nodded, and returned to staring into nothingness.

Before he lost his nerve, Alex thrust the note he'd written in front of Winston and said, "Julia asked me to give this to you. She's upset that you're not moving on with your life and told me to tell you that it wasn't your fault. It was an accident, and she says you need to forgive yourself."

It took a few seconds for Winston to register what Alex had said. When he did, he jumped out of his chair, advancing on Alex until he was only inches away. "How dare you. Is this your idea of some twisted joke? Who put you up to this?" He looked around the dining hall and saw everyone staring at him because of his outburst. "I don't know who you are, but you better leave before I knock your block off."

Alex backed up a step, held up his hands, and said, "This is no prank. I can see ghosts, and your girlfriend approached me outside and asked if I'd give you this letter. She said it'd explain everything. So, please calm down and read the letter before you do anything rash."

Winston grabbed the letter and unfolded it. He'd only read a few lines when he staggered back and fell onto his chair. He read the letter twice, running his hands ruthlessly through his hair, before he finally looked up, tears in his eyes. "Can you really talk to her?"

Alex nodded. "Ghosts often approach me and ask for help in moving on. I believe your girlfriend is stuck in the afterlife because of your grief and guilt. She said you didn't cause her death."

"Where is she now?" Winston asked, tears flowing even more freely down his face.

"She's standing right beside…." Alex's jaw dropped as he saw Julia suddenly swallowed by a blinding flash of light. A second later, she was gone.

Seeing the shocked look on Alex's face, Winston asked frantically, "What's happened?"

It took Alex a few seconds before he recovered and let a smile spread across his face.

"Tell me what's happened," Winston said, grabbing Alex by the arm and shaking him.

"She's at peace now and has moved on," Alex replied. Seeing Diana running towards him, he said, "I've got to go now, but don't disappoint her. Live your life to the fullest."

Before Winston could say anything else, Diana grabbed his arm and hissed, "Come on. You're in trouble again for wandering off." When Alex seemed reluctant to go, she asked, "What did I miss?"

"You just helped a couple get over a tragic loss. I wish you could see when ghosts happily move on because you'd get some repayment for all the troubles you go through because of me. Believe me, sometimes the heartache on our part is worth it."

"You can tell me more about it on the train ride back," Diana replied.

But it wasn't until they got to their hotel later that evening that he could fill Diana in on what had happened in Durham and Castle Keep. As she peppered him with questions about both events, he kept looking at the clock and, at last, cut her short.

"I need to get going if I'm going to help Wallace." He picked up his pack, slipped it on, and was heading for the door when Diana said, "Hey. Aren't you forgetting something?"

Alex stopped and patted down his pockets before looking around the room. Unable to figure out what she was referring to, he asked, "What?"

Diana smiled and rose from the bed where she'd been sitting. "Me. I'm coming with you. And no arguments. I've already told my mom we were going to wander around because I figured you'd gotten yourself involved in something, so let's go."

They left the hotel and reached Castle Keep a few minutes before nine. Diana looked up at the brightly lit, silent castle and asked, "How are we going to get in?"

"I don't know. The Seagrave ghost said he'd...." Alex's words tailed off as a sweet floral smell wafted over him. A moment later a petite young ghost wearing a tattered gray smock appeared before him. Her soulful brown eyes peered out of her shoulder-length, heavily matted hair, causing the hair on Alex's arm to stand up.

The young girl looked up at Alex and asked, "Are you the one?"

CHAPTER 19
THE POPPY GIRL

"Am I the one what?" Alex asked.

"The one I've been waiting for," the girl replied.

Alex felt Diana slip her hand into his and said, "I don't know what you're talking about. Why don't we start with introductions. I'm Alex, and this is my friend Diana. What's your name?"

The girl dropped her head and, in a shy voice that Alex could barely hear, replied, "Mary."

"Hi, Mary. Now, why don't you explain what your question is."

"I used to have a friend here, a kindly priest who was the first person who ever seemed to care about me," Mary replied. "We would take walks in the castle every night and talk about all sorts of things. It was the only time in my life that I was happy. Then, one night, he said he wanted to share a secret with me. He said that only a special person could do the job, and that was why he picked me. I was excited because no one had ever told me I was special before. He led me up to the unfinished stairs and told me that since he wouldn't be around forever, I needed to know that he and some other monks had placed something special at the end of the stairwell.

"I thought he was just telling me a story to entertain me. Regretfully, I didn't pay attention as I was listening to his magical voice. I remember, all too well, what happened next. After he finished talking, I opened my eyes and saw him shimmering. He was radiating happiness and love and was more peaceful than I'd ever seen him. Then he smiled and was gone. I've never seen him since, and that was over a hundred years ago." Mary looked at the night sky and said, "The stars are so beautiful and peaceful tonight. Do you think that's where my friend went?

Alex swallowed a lump in his throat and said, "I'm sure he's in heaven and that it's just as beautiful and wonderful as the stars are."

Mary sighed and said, "I miss him terribly. I wish I were good enough to go there. Then I could talk to him every night." After a pause, she added, "I heard his voice again a few days ago – asking me to help a person who would come to see me soon. I believe it's you."

Feeling left out of the conversation, Diana said, "Since we don't have much time to find Wallace's bones, we need to figure out how to get inside without the police catching us."

Before Alex could reply, Wallace apparated, followed a second later by Seagrave. "Does she know where my bones are?" Wallace asked.

"Possibly," Alex replied. "A friend told her there was some secret in the unfinished stairs area."

Seagrave furrowed his brow in thought for a few seconds, then lit up and said, "Ah, the priest. He started visiting the keep soon after Mary arrived. It was as if he had been waiting for her. Then, one day, he just disappeared. I haven't seen him since.

"Now, let's get you two off the street. And don't worry about getting in. I've already cut the feed to the security alarms and monitors." He then led the group to the castle's front doors and passed through. Seconds later, one of the heavy outer wooden doors slowly swung open.

Alex followed Diana in and closed the door.

Even though there were security lights inside, it was dim enough that Diana conjured a ball of flames to light their way.

Seagrave led them up a flight of steps, then turned left to a smaller door. After he'd opened the door to the inner part of Castle Keep, he stepped aside and let Mary lead them across the Great Hall, up a flight of stairs that turned right at a small landing and dead-ended five steps later.

Mary pointed to a small, rough opening and said, "This is where the priest told me the secret was."

Alex turned to Diana and asked, "Could you use your magic to move them?"

"I could, but I might destroy this place as I don't have the control to move things so precisely. Besides, I don't know which stone to move."

Frustrated at hitting a dead end after having come so far, Alex paced around the small landing for a minute before bending over and crawling up to get a closer look. He stopped at the second to last step and looked around, but it was so dark that he had to pull out his small Maglite to look closely at the stones.

A few seconds later, Diana crawled up and said, "Scoot over." Alex shifted as far as he could, allowing Diana to wedge herself between him and the inside wall. "Have you found anything yet?" she asked.

"Nothing. This looks like a waste of time."

Diana didn't respond, as she was intent on running her fingers along the inside creases in the steps. At last, she said, "Don't give up just yet. I might be able to use magic after all. I felt a tiny gap between the top and the second step." She pointed down the stairs and said, "I need you to go around the corner while I work because I don't want to hurt you if something goes wrong."

"What about you?" Alex asked. "Will you be safe?"

"Since the magic is coming from me, it should deflect any debris flying around. Now go."

Alex headed down to the next flight of steps and leaned against the outer wall, hoping Diana's efforts would be successful. He heard her chanting something under her breath. A few seconds later, a low rumbling reverberated through the cramped stairwell, followed by a fine mist of dust. He called up, "Are you all right?"

Diana didn't immediately answer. Instead, he heard some grating sounds, followed by a thud, then silence. He let the dust settle down, then crawled back up the stairs, where he saw a rock had fallen onto the top step. Looking up at Diana, he asked, "What do you see?"

"Nothing yet. It's too dusty. Since this is your quest, do you want to do the honors?"

"Nope," he replied. "You've earned this."

"Oh, great. Reaching my hand into some dark space is something I always look forward to." Diana crawled back onto the last step and reached into the hole. A moment later, she pulled a soiled canvas bag out and backed down to where Alex was. She untied the bag, stuck her hand in, and pulled out a couple of bones with a skeletal hand at the end. "There are more bones in here," she said. "It looks like some ribs, a shoulder blade...."

A yelp from Wallace caused Alex to look at the Scottish spirit. Transfixed by what he was seeing, he stuck out his hand and said, "You've got to see this, Diana. The right side of Sir William's torso is growing out of his head – arm and all. You did it."

Wallace was so excited that he let out a yell that deafened the other ghosts and Alex. Holding up his newly formed right hand, he examined it closely, then flew over to Alex, extended his right hand, and said, "Lad, I'd like you to be the first to shake my hand in centuries." Then, Wallace began singing an ancient Scottish song that Alex couldn't understand. It was some time before he calmed down and said, "I never thought this day would come. Thank you all, but I beg your forgiveness, for I must leave before my emotions betray me."

Noticing she still held the bag of bones, Diana handed the sack to Alex and said, "You keep these. They're your responsibility. I need to put the rock back, and then I want to get out of here before we get in trouble."

Replacing the step was much easier than pulling it out. A couple of minutes later, Seagrave led the group silently back to the main entrance, where he paused and stuck his head through the heavy wooden doors to see if the way was clear. After what seemed like an eternity, he pulled his head and one arm back in and motioned them forwards.

As soon as the door started opening, Diana squeezed through. Alex followed Diana seconds later, relieved to be outside the Keep again.

"Go on," he said to Diana. "I'll be right behind you. I need to thank Mary and Sir John for helping us tonight."

"I'm not going anywhere without you," she said, grabbing his hand to ensure she didn't miss anything.

Alex turned back to the two ghosts hovering near the doors, nodded to Sir John, and said, "Thank you. I know this must have been tough on you, but without your help, we would never have found Sir William's remains. I hope you get to move on. I would offer our help, but I don't think we'll ever come back here, so it would be a promise I couldn't keep."

Seagrave shook his head. "Tis I who should be thanking you. It feels wonderful to make some small amends for what I did to Sir William. He was a worthy foe and far more principled than I …." Before Sir John could finish his sentence, he started slowly becoming more transparent. Realizing he was finally moving on, Sir John called out to Mary, "Farewell, my little friend. I know that one day, you'll move on to a far better place than I am going. I wish I had gotten to know you better, for you are a kind and generous soul."

Seconds later, Sir John de Seagrave had moved on.

Even though he'd seen it before, Alex couldn't swallow the lump in his throat. The lump grew larger when he looked at Mary and saw tears streaming from the corners of her eyes. "I know this is small consolation, Mary, but thank you for your help. Without you, we would never have found Sir William's bones. I'm sure you've made your priest friend proud of you."

Alex stopped talking as her shoulders shook from the sobs escaping her petite frame. He was about to say something to comfort her when a bright light appeared along with a small, thin man wearing a black cassock.

The ghost radiated a peacefulness Alex had never experienced. "The boy is right, Mary. I am proud of you. Tonight, I finally saw the Mary I always knew was there." He held his hand out towards her and said, "Come, it's time for us to go."

Mary ran towards her friend with her arms outstretched. As she stepped into the light surrounding the priest, she stopped and hugged him. The light grew softer and started glowing with all the colors of the rainbow. Mary, the Poppy Girl, began ascending into the clear, starry night along with her friend. The disparate pair of ghosts grew smaller and smaller until they disappeared into a tiny point of light.

In a voice thick with emotion, Diana said, "Thank you for sharing your gift. I felt a love unlike anything I've ever experienced radiating through this square. I envy you, Alex Scire. I know you've been through hell and back, but if this is your reward, it's well worth it."

CHAPTER 20
A LITTLE GRAVE ROBBING

After boarding the train to Berwick-upon-Tweed the next morning, Alex couldn't get The Poppy Girl out of his thoughts. It wasn't long before Diana elbowed him and said, "You've been quiet ever since we left Castle Keep last night. What's wrong?"

"Nothing. It's just I've been thinking about everything that's happened in the last few days, and I can't help but wonder what's next?"

"You've been in some tough situations before and thrived," she replied. "I'm confident you'll be fine."

He turned to look at the countryside rolling by and let his thoughts drift. Comforted by Diana's presence, he closed his eyes and leaned against the window. The gentle rocking of the train soon lulled him to sleep, and he stayed that way until Diana shook him awake when they got to Berwick.

With only his dad's Army backpack for luggage, he took Sophie's suitcase and followed her from the train station down into Castle Vale to a B&B overlooking the river Tweed. After checking in, they stowed their luggage and headed back outside.

For a small town, Alex was amazed that it took them nearly the whole day to wander along the river, through the city, over the Elizabethan Walls, and out onto the seawall to listen to the crashing waves of the North Sea. But at the end of the day, Alex felt no closer to figuring out where he could find the next set of Wallace's bones than when he'd arrived.

He went straight to his room after dinner and had just closed the door when a soft light passed through the window and hovered in front of the windowsill. Perplexed, Alex walked towards the light and immediately jumped back, shivering from the unexpected cold. Wondering if this was some new spectral being he'd never encountered, he worked up the courage to ask, "What are you? Are you some sort of ghost?"

A deep voice with a heavy Scottish brogue answered from the light still hovering in the room. "Ye can see me?"

Waving his hands around to approximate the misty cloud, Alex replied, "Not really. All I see is a small, shapeless cloud with a dim glow. I've never seen a ghost with a shape like yours."

A moment later, the mist materialized into a short, burly man with long, wild, red hair and a pair of intense green eyes peering out of a craggy-looking face. What caught Alex's attention, though, was the dark stains on his threadbare clothes. "What manner of man be ye that I can talk to ye? Are ye the one I'm looking for?"

"I don't know. Who are you?"

"I'm Kerly of Cruggleton. I was William Wallace's aide during our fight for Scottish Independence and was with him the night the English captured him. I've been wandering the borders of Scotland ever since, waiting for him to return. Then, tonight, I felt a strange presence and came to investigate. And here be ye."

"Sir William must have mentioned you because your name sounds familiar."

The Scotsman grabbed Alex by the shoulders and shook him. "Ye've met William?"

With his teeth chattering from being shaken so hard, Alex managed to stutter out, "If...if...you...could...could...let...let...me...go...go ...I...could...tell...tell...you."

"Sorry about that, laddie, but I've been waiting so long for news of him that I'd jest about given up."

Before Alex could reply, another blast of cold air swept into the room, and Wallace appeared. Kerly took one look at Wallace and eagerly rushed towards him but stopped mid-stride, stunned and dismayed by the dreadful fate of his longtime friend.

Undeterred by his appearance, Wallace flew to Kerly and gave him a one-armed bear hug. "Kerly, it's been too long. I've missed ye."

Kerly dropped his head to hide his emotions at seeing his friend again. "I've missed ye too. I've waited for 700 years to tell ye how sorry I am for falling asleep that last night. I should have known something was amiss at dinner. De Menteith and his wife were too anxious to please us, and I let my guard down. They must have put something in my drink."

Wallace shook Kerly by the shoulder and said, "It wasn't your fault. Once the Scottish nobles turned against us to save their bony little arses, it was only a matter of time before the English caught us. Cheer up, though. This young lad and his friend are helping me find my bones. So, what are ye doing here?"

"After I died, I found myself here in Berwick, unable to leave. I realized what happened to ye when I saw the Sassenach hang yer leg on a stake near the river. It stayed there, rotting away, until a couple of brave lads, about the same age as this one, took yer leg down and buried it. I've made sure no one has dug in that spot since then, hoping ye'd come back one day. Now, here ye are."

Alex interrupted, saying, "I'm sorry, but if we're going to find his leg, we need to take advantage of what little time I have left here – because I'm leaving in the morning."

Wallace motioned with his arm for Alex to lead the way. Alex picked up his pack and quietly opened his door before leading the pair of ghosts down the hall. He hesitated briefly at Diana's door and thought about knocking but decided he didn't want to get her in trouble and lowered his hand. Alex was about to take another step when Diana opened her door and whispered, "Are you going somewhere?"

"Were you listening for me?" he whispered back.

"I'm hard of hearing, not deaf. That floorboard outside my room creaks and groans every time someone walks past. Besides, I figured you'd be sneaking off tonight, so I was ready for you. So, have you figured out where it is?"

Instead of answering, he lifted a finger to his lips and waved for her to follow him. When they were outside, he grabbed her hand so she could see the ghosts and said, "Sir William's friend Kerly showed up and said he knows where one of Wallace's legs is buried." He turned to Kerly and asked, "Where are we going?"

Kerly grinned. "We're going to do a little grave robbing," he said.

Alex wasn't surprised when Diana groaned and, in a resigned voice, said, "I can't believe I'm going along with this. But it's what we've got to do, so let's get it over with."

Fog began swirling in off the North Sea as soon as they reached the earthen walls surrounding the town. Kerly halted the group near the start of the Bronze Bastion, pointed to a stone wall below, and said, "William's bones are down there. It's steep, and the grass is probably slick with dew, so be careful going down." Both ghosts flew down, leaving Alex and Diana alone on top, with the city lights reflecting off the fog, providing enough light for them to see the cemetery below.

Diana broke the silence, saying, "In my wildest imagination, I never dreamed I'd be robbing graves one day. But what's even more bizarre, is that I'm totally stoked about it."

"I long ago gave up wondering about the crazy things I do. I'm just sorry I have to keep involving you," Alex replied.

"I'm not. But, if we're going to do this, I'd prefer we have some light so we don't break an ankle getting down. And I don't think conjuring up a ball of flames is the best thing to do out here in the open."

Alex grunted and pulled out his Maglite. He turned sideways and took a few steps down before looking up and saying, "Let me get down, then I'll shine a light up, so you…." He didn't finish his sentence, as his legs went out from under him, and he slid down the hill. It took him a few seconds to recover once he hit bottom and turned on his flashlight for Diana.

"I think I'll pass on your way down," Diana said. "I saw a little grassy ramp a short way back, so I'm going to take the easy way." Before he could object, she retraced their steps until she reached the entrance to a gently sloping ramp, then turned and came down. When she got to where Alex and the ghosts were waiting for her by a metal gate, she asked, "Where are we?"

"We're at the back of the cemetery of the Church of the Holy Trinity and Saint Mary, more commonly known as the Berwick Parish Church," Kerly replied. "His bones are right inside."

Alex shook on the gate, but it didn't budge. Shining his light around, he discovered the iron bars and frame were bolted into the stone wall. He shook it half-heartedly, knowing it wouldn't budge, then turned to Diana and said, "I guess we're going to need your magic to take this gate down."

"No need to do that," Kerly said. Before Diana could say anything, the ghost had flown her over the wall.

Diana screamed but was back on the ground so fast that she was laughing a moment later.

Alex had no time to shush her before Kerly whisked him over the wall. As soon as his feet hit the ground, Diana said, "Sorry, I couldn't help it. That was so much cooler than the first time I flew."

Alex made it hard for Diana to keep contact with him and see the spirits as he beat his arms and hopped around to warm up from being touched by ghosts. Seeing Kerly searching for the grave site off to their left, he asked, "Did you forget where he's buried?"

"Give me some time, laddie. It's been 700 years," Kerly replied.

"We've got to hurry up and get out of here before someone sees us."

Kerly cut off their conversation, exclaiming, "Hold on. I think I've found it." He bent over and pushed some weeds and grass aside. Finding the mark he was looking for, he shouted, "This is it."

Alex shone his light to where Kerly was pointing but didn't see anything until Diana exclaimed, "I see it!" She let go of Alex, kneeled on the grass, and pointed at the letter W cut into the base of the stonewall.

"Are you sure they're still there?" Wallace asked.

"At least what's left of them," Kerly replied. "The original marker was a simple stone over the spot, but they built the church and this wall several hundred years later, helping preserve yer burial site. The original plans called for the wall to go over yer gravesite, but I managed to persuade the workers to move their work a bit – if ye know what I mean. I've been guarding it ever since and can tell ye that nobody has disturbed the site."

Alex looked around the darkened cemetery and asked Kerly, "How far down are his bones because I didn't bring anything to dig with?"

Diana sniffed. "It's amazing how helpless you can be at times." She walked off, found a flat rock with a pointed end, and came back."

"I could have done that," Alex said. "Why don't you use your magic instead?"

"It seems sacrilegious to use magic in a cemetery."

Alex took his backpack off and got down on his knees. "I'll dig then. That way, you can deny involvement if someone catches us."

"Oh, great. Now you think of the consequences," Diana said laughingly.

Alex grinned and started to scrape away the dirt at the base of the rock wall. He'd only been at it a short time when ghosts started appearing, looking on at the midnight grave digging. Kerly shooed them away, but a minute later, a young, wiry-looking ghost appeared and began lustily singing,

"With knot and muscle and heart and brain
He is lost to Scotland; he is lost in vain
So listen, and you can hear
The sounds that echo through the ages
The creak of the burial cart...."

Kerly tried shooing the boy away, but he flew into a nearby tree and taunted the elderly ghost, saying,

"Nah, Nah,
Can't catch me."

"Billy, I don't have time for your pranks. I'm busy, so go away and leave us be," Kerly shouted.

The young ghost hopped down and cackled, "Well, I'll tell you what I'm going to do." Then he lifted one leg, let out a loud fart, and scampered away.

Kerly turned back to the others and said, "Ye'll have to forgive the lad. He's still adjusting to being dead, so he likes to joke around both here in the cemetery and among the living."

Alex resumed digging. When he had dug a hole a couple of feet in diameter and a couple of feet deep,

Kerly said, "Be careful. Ye should be coming across his remains any time now."

As if on cue, Alex's rock struck something hard. He set it aside and started digging with his hands. Minutes later, Alex spotted some material. When he'd exposed the outline of it, he grabbed one end and yanked. It came out so easily that he found himself lying on his back, holding a dirty, rotting canvas bag with several hard objects inside.

He sat up and was so excited at the discovery that he didn't mind Kerly and Wallace leaning over his shoulder to see what was inside. His hands shook as he tried untying the hardened leather thong sealing the canvas. He quickly gave up and ripped the knot off. The canvas wrapping fell away, revealing a collection of small and large bones. A yell of joy from Wallace caused Alex to look up just in time to see Wallace's right leg grow out of his torso. Seconds later, Wallace was hopping around on one leg with all the excitement of a kid winning a potato sack race.

"Kerly, I cannae thank ye enough," Wallace said. "I'm in yer everlasting debt."

The burly Scotsman dropped his head and blushed from the praise of his friend.

Wallace turned to Alex and said, "Thankee, lad. Tell yer friend that ye two are restoring my faith in humanity. In my lifetime, I never experienced people from other countries coming to the aid of strangers without expecting a reward. I'm glad ye were the one who found me. I bid ye adieu, for I grow weary after all this excitement. Come Kerly. We've got a lot of catching up to do."

The two ghosts disappeared, leaving Alex and Diana to walk back alone. When they got to the door of the B&B, Alex said, "You have no idea how much you coming along means to me. Thank you." He blushed, then rushed inside, not caring about the squeaky floorboards. Minutes later, he was sound asleep.

CHAPTER 21
CONCLAVE

Elizabeth wondered if she was betraying her dead daughter's trust by calling for a conclave on her grandson. She looked around at the other grove's high priestesses sitting at the order's octagon-shaped table and reviewed what she knew of each one. It would be easy to convince most of them to declare her grandson a warlock. The hardest one would be Lady Yvaine, but Elizabeth figured that if she got the other priestesses on her side, Yvaine would have to agree.

She had sat through the morning's discussion, hardly listening as the others gave updates on their progress to find and protect magical objects. Elizabeth had provided her updates on Sophie's work to find the Palantir in Belize but let Senora de Leon, the High Priestess of the Spanish grove, update the others on the failed search for the Sangreal in Romania.

Elizabeth became even more nervous when the conclave moved onto the main topic. After Lady Yvaine gave her the floor, Elizabeth took a deep breath and stood, placing her hands on the great oaken table, and looking at each of the other high priestesses.

They all knew what was coming as it had been the main topic of conversation within the order for the last two years. She let the rustle of excitement die before saying, "First of all, I apologize for acting so slowly against my grandson, but I wanted to have all the facts before I came here to discuss his situation.

"As most of you know, I was as surprised as you were to discover that my daughter Jessica secretly had a son against our rules. As a mother, I forgave her because I loved her. But I can't condone her choice, as we all know what happens when we stray from the vows we took when we joined this order. Maybe this wouldn't have been much of an issue if she had been a squib, but my daughter was far more proficient in mastering the five elements than I will ever be. More gifted, dare I say, than all of you, except for Lady Yvaine. To make matters worse, my grandson's father also had magical abilities. I fear their combined magical genes have given my grandson powers I'm scared to think about.

"I give you that background to reinforce how worrisome his actions are. You know he found and opened the *Palantir Sibylline* book. You've heard how he broke into my study and used my scrying dish to listen to your conversations. You also know he has lured two of our members on dangerous excursions, not once, not twice, but three times. I could go on with all the unnatural things he's done, but you have the full documentation of his activities in the file before you."

Elizabeth drummed her fingers on the table for several minutes while she allowed the other attendees to leaf through the file. A shiver ran down her spine when she noticed Yvaine did not bother opening her packet and was staring at her instead.

Fatima Soghra, the High Priestess of the Istanbul grove, asked, "Why bring this up now? I understood he's dead or at least has been missing for the last year."

Elizabeth shook her head. "I assumed he was dead too, but he appeared out of nowhere a few days ago in London. His latest actions have reinforced my belief that he's a serious threat to us. I called this conclave to ask you to declare my grandson a warlock and deal with him according to our order's rules."

Everyone but Lady Yvaine immediately started talking. Elizabeth smiled at the buzz in the room, pleased that her words had the intended effect.

Meritamun, the leader of the Alexandria grove, raised Alex's file and asked, "How has he done all this? What type of magic does he use because none of us can do these things?"

"That's the most troubling aspect," Elizabeth replied. "I don't know. It's unlike any magic I've ever seen."

Lady Yvaine interrupted, saying, "It's something I'm investigating. I have tasked Jane Roland to learn as much about him as possible. She's gotten close to him and tells me she doesn't think he has magical abilities – as we know them."

"She's not one of us, so how can we trust her?" Señora de Leon asked. "Besides, her statement doesn't make any sense. If he doesn't have any abilities, how can he do the things on the list?"

"I can't answer your question, but I trust her implicitly," Lady Yvaine replied.

"I hear Diana Bennet thinks that much of what happens around Elizabeth's grandson is dumb luck," Meritamun said. "But it seems to me that all his bumbling might be due to him trying to master his magical powers. Besides, I don't need to remind you of the age at which most warlocks start coming into their powers – it's much later than for girls."

There was a murmur of assent. When it died down, Fatima asked, "Where has he been for the last year?"

"He was in Romania for some of the time," Elizabeth replied, "but he was very vague about where he spent most of the time. Strangely, he seemed convinced he'd only been gone for a couple of weeks – not ten months."

"He was just lying to throw you off kilter," Señora de Leon said.

Elizabeth was surprised at herself when she shook her head. "That's what I keep trying to tell myself, but I got the distinct impression he wasn't trying to deceive me about the time differential."

"So, how does that tie to this topic?" Fatima asked.

"Just that he's full of contradictions," Elizabeth replied. "I would be remiss, though, if I didn't point out that he seems to be a kind soul. He has willingly given over information of significance to our order. And he has saved Sophie and Diana Bennet's lives numerous times while risking his own."

"But none of those things change the facts," Fatima said.

"You're right, which is why I ask you to support me in declaring my grandson, Alexander Graham Scire, a warlock and a grave threat to this order." Elizabeth sat down, wanting to feel like she'd thrown off a great burden but feeling so uncomfortable about what she'd done that she barely heard Lady Yvaine banging her gavel to restore order.

When all was calm, Lady Yvaine looked around the room and said, "This is a serious charge. I appreciate

Elizabeth's concerns and applaud her for having the courage to bring this important topic to our attention, despite him being her blood relative. We all know the painful parts of our order's history concerning our male progeny. However, I'd like to remind you that well less than half of the males born to our members have become warlocks. Most have tended to be simple, sweet boys who never quite become men and are completely harmless to society. I would hate to rush to judgment and punish him when he has shown no overt tendencies of becoming a warlock. I'll admit the evidence looks peculiar, but I have done some research and have not heard one complaint about the boy harming anyone. As you heard Elizabeth say, it's quite the contrary. He's saved people's lives and, in a limited way, has helped our order accomplish its mission of finding and protecting the Maqlû. I don't want us to fear that which we do not understand, and ask that you remain patient. Let us find out more about him before we rush to judgment."

Ester Jochebed from Jerusalem rose from her seat and said, "I don't like the coincidences. I've talked with Sister Elizabeth and think the boy's actions are too suspicious to trust him. I agree with her and believe we must declare him a warlock and carry out the designated sentence for our safety."

Everyone in the room started talking agitatedly when Ester sat down. The high priestesses spent the rest of the day discussing Elizabeth's charges in detail.

Long after midnight, when it was clear everyone else had made up their minds, Lady Yvaine rose and said, "I have listened to your concerns, but I cannot condemn the boy to death because of your fears. Per our rules, our vote must be unanimous before we punish anyone. We've done that throughout the ages because of the severity of the punishment. It's a protection we built to prevent us from succumbing to the same types of hysteria we have dealt with through the centuries.

"Yes, he's different, but before we condemn him, I want to understand better how he can get into our studies, use our scrying dishes, and find information we cannot. Those are abilities that not even the most powerful warlocks have shown. I want to know where he goes and how he survives in his absences, but all we have are garbled explanations by Diana and Jane, who know him better than anyone and are his defenders."

"They're girls whose hormones have gotten the better of them," Fatima said.

"Maybe, but I want to know for sure if he's a warlock," Yvaine replied. "I can tell that all of you think I'm making a mistake, which is why I will accept responsibility for overseeing his activities."

A low rumbling discontent spread throughout the room. Yvaine banged on her gavel until there was silence again. "I also agree to hold an emergency conclave at any time should the facts warrant a change in my vote."

The room quieted down. Yvaine banged her gavel again and said, "It's been a long day. We'll convene again at noon."

CHAPTER 22

DAVID'S TOWER

Diana was so tired that she slept for most of the trip to Edinburgh the next day. She opened her eyes just once and saw a WWII pillbox looking out over the North Sea.

When they got to the capital of Scotland, she was surprised to see Jane, with her signature ginger-colored hair and floral dress, waiting for them. Sophie looked as perplexed as Diana and asked, "What are you doing here?"

Jane handed a letter to Sophie and said, "Elizabeth asked me to give this to ye."

"Why didn't she just call?" Sophie asked.

"She wanted me to stay with yer daughter and Alex while ye go on ahead to Stirling. She thinks it will be better for all if Alex stays away from Stormhold. I've already booked three rooms in town overlooking Arthur's Seat and Salisbury Crags and have money to pay for our expenses."

Sophie didn't listen to the last few words as she was already reading Lady Yvaine's missive. After reading it a second time, she looked towards Diana and said, "There's a change of plans. You three are to stay here while I go on to Stormhold. You can see whatever you want, just as long as you're back before dusk." She looked at Jane and added, "You're responsible for keeping an eye on Alex and making sure he stays out of trouble."

"What's going on?" Diana asked.

"Everything's fine," Sophie replied. "It's just that Elizabeth has called me to Stirling to work on something with her and the Council of Elders, and they don't want any of you in the way. So, make sure you stay out of trouble."

Diana nodded and said, "We'll be fine."

After Sophie had left to get her ticket, Jane motioned for Alex and Diana to follow her.

As they walked to the apartment, Diana said, "You know what this means?"

"Yeah, your mom and my grandmother don't want me near your school. I got that," Alex said.

"Stop being so negative and look at the positive. This means freedom. We can go anywhere, do anything, and no adults are supervising us."

Jane chuckled and said, "Ye sound like a kid with money in a candy store. I'm jest happy we're together again. As for me, I'm willing to follow yer lead because I'm sure ye already know what ye want to do."

"What about you?" Diana asked, turning to Alex.

When he didn't respond, Jane said, "Ye're wool-gathering. What's going on in that head of yers?"

"I'm sorry. I keep thinking about this time difference everyone keeps talking about. Diana, you say you're almost sixteen, but I won't be that age until Halloween, and you're eight months younger than me. How could that happen?"

"I've been doing some research and have come up with three possible explanations," Diana replied. "One, you're lying about losing time." Seeing Alex was about to protest, she held up her hand and said, "I don't think you are. Two, you got seriously injured or had amnesia and were out of it almost the whole time. But that doesn't make sense either because you'd probably have wound up in some hospital, and they would've notified your grandfather. So, that leaves only the most bizarre explanation. And as your Sherlock Holmes said, 'when you have eliminated the impossible, whatever remains, however improbable, must be the truth.'"

"And that would be?"

"Time dilation," Diana replied. Seeing he was about to ask what it meant, she added, "It's like when you get in a spaceship and fly away from Earth really fast. The faster and farther you go, the bigger the difference in elapsed time between the spaceship and Earth. I don't know how you did it, but I believe you were involved in option three."

"That kind of makes sense. When I went into the woods in Romania, it felt like I flew through some long dark tunnel with thousands of pinpricks of light," Alex said. "The same thing happened on the way out of the woods. It was a bizarre experience."

They reached the Airbnb just then, and after Jane retrieved the keys from a locked mailbox, they headed inside. But before they could even stow their bags, Diana said. "I've been thinking. Since we're so close, why don't we climb Calton Hill first. Even though I've been to Edinburgh many times, I've never been there because most of the girls I've gone with want to go shopping on the Royal Mile. After that, I thought we could go to Edinburgh Castle. I think you'll like the views and its history." She grinned and added, "And, if you're keeping track, you'll get to add another UNESCO site to your count today."

Jane and Alex agreed to her plan, and in no time, they were back on the streets of Edinburgh.

Instead of the usual dreich Scottish weather, Diana was surprised when the day turned out to be sunny and pleasant, with the gorse on the surrounding hills in full bloom. Even though it was only in the '50s, she saw people walking around or lying in the parks wearing short-sleeved shirts, shorts, and flip-flops. She was also pleased with having Alex and Jane as her companions, as neither complained about going to places she had wanted to see on previous trips but couldn't get her friends to go.

To Diana, Edinburgh, felt like a city straight out of a fairy tale. What gave it a magical twist was how close she felt to nature despite being in a big city. The brilliant blue waters of the Firth of Forth were visible from every high point, along with the desolate-looking Arthur's Seat and the Salisbury Crag. And then there was Edinburgh Castle sitting on what seemed like the biggest rock she'd ever seen.

They reached the castle by mid-afternoon and wandered around for hours, reading up on its history and admiring the fantastic views of the city from the ramparts. Diana was thinking it was the best day she'd ever spent in Scotland when Alex pointed to a sign that said David's Tower and said, "I need to check something in there."

With a sense of misgiving, Diana said, "We need to hurry. The place is about to close."

"It'll only take a minute," Alex replied.

She barely had time to put her phone away when Alex disappeared inside. Knowing her pleasant, uneventful day had just ended, she ducked and followed him into the former royal residence.

CHAPTER 23
THE PSALTER

As they neared the Forewall Battery on their way out of the castle, Alex felt a wave of cold air wash over him. With a sickening feeling in his stomach, he turned just in time to see a ghost fly into a small opening in the outer wall. He called to Diana, then headed into David's Tower, without looking back to see if either girl was following him.

He paused and waited for his eyes to adjust to the gloominess inside. Jane came alongside and asked, "Is everything all right?"

"I'm not sure. I saw a ghost duck in here and followed him."

"Why should ye worry about it?" Jane asked. "Ye see them all the time."

"Not acting so secretively," he replied. Spotting movement in the room below him, he ran down the steps, and saw a ghost over six feet tall, tugging at a brick in the wall. Alex quietly watched him wriggle the stone free, reach into the opening, and pull out a small leather-bound book.

"What are you doing?" Alex asked.

The spirit spun around and stared at Alex. "You can see me? That's not possible," he said.

"Well, I can. Besides, I'd still be able to see the book you have in your hand."

Diana caught up with him and grabbed his arm so she could see what was going on. "What have I missed?" she asked, just as Jane was grabbing his other arm.

"Nothing yet. I saw that ghost come in here and thought I'd follow him because something felt wrong. Apparently, he was retrieving that book."

Before Alex could respond, a blast of cold air washed over him, and Wallace appeared. Even though the unknown ghost was over six feet tall, Wallace stood several inches taller. The Scottish spirit balled his only hand into a fist and yelled, "I should have known ye were the one who stole my psalter. Give it back, Longshanks."

"How dare you accuse me of stealing. I am your Liege Lord, Edward, King of all England, Wales, and Scotland. I determine what you have or do not have at my leisure, you traitorous scum."

"Ye must not have heard me when ye charged me with treason the first time. I'm not a traitor, for I never swore fealty to ye," Wallace replied.

Alex backed up, pushing the girls behind him.

Edward's cheeks turned red as he glared at Wallace and Alex. "You always had more in common with the peasants than your superiors and I see nothing has changed. Now you're getting the living to do your dirty work."

Wallace sneered at Longshanks. "Ye're one to talk. Ye spent yer whole life trying to kill yer fellow human beings. In the name of Christianity, ye borrowed heavily and taxed yer people so ye could go on a Crusade to kill Muslims. But that wasn't enough for ye. As soon as ye came back, ye went to war with the Welsh, then Scotland, using the nobles' greed to enrich yourself. If only they could have seen ye for who ye really are – only caring about yerself. At least ye're paying for that choice by being stuck here in the afterlife."

Edward sneered at Wallace and said, "Of course I took advantage of that squabbling rabble of noblemen. Besides, that bit of rock and dirt you call Scotland needed good English law and order."

"Hah. Ye call what yer officers did in my country law and order? Ye pushed us into rebellion because ye pillaged our country and subjugated our people."

The ghost king was so mad that sparks seemed to fly out of his eyes. "Everything I did was to help my country. I brought peace to our land. Look what I did for the common people. I instituted the House of Commons to bring them into the process of helping govern the country. And I helped clean up the mess about property ownership. But, of course, you would know nothing of what a real government is. You and your rabble lived in the woods and acted like animals."

"We might have been poor, but we lived righteously, while ye arbitrarily chose who got the benefits. Just look at what ye did with the Jews. Ye expelled them from England and took all their property to finance yer wars and lifestyle. It might have made ye popular with the people who owed them money, but that was another shining example of yer bigotry. Ye even threatened the Church with being outlaws until they gave in and paid more taxes. Tax, spend, and go to war. That's all ye ever did."

Edward's transparent skin turned a bright shade of red. "You Scots are all vermin, and you are the worst of the lot. You thought of yourself as a freedom fighter, but you destroyed your people. If it weren't for you, many a peasant would have been able to live out their lives in peace. Instead, you caused them to rebel against me, and consequently, many died on the battlefield rather than in their beds from old age. You didn't feel remorse when you lived, and it's obvious you don't feel it now. I can't believe I've been stuck here on earth for 700 years because I rightly punished you."

Wallace lunged for the book, but Edward was too quick and flew towards the exit, Psalter in hand.

Without thinking, Alex lunged at the former English King, knocking him to the ground. The book skidded across the floor to within a couple of feet of Jane, who scooped it up.

The ankh came to Alex's defense as soon as Edward started beating on him. Shocked by the necklace's energy surge, the former king jumped up and shook his hands in obvious pain. "What are you – the devil himself?" he screamed. "I should have listened when Pythia warned me about you. But don't worry. I will be better prepared when I come back. And it won't go well for you next time." Then, holding his injured hands to his chest, he disappeared.

As Alex got up and dusted himself off, Diana said, "What did we miss?"

Alex winced and looked at his skinned-up elbows. "Only that Pythia woman is still after me for some reason, because she warned him about me." He took the small black leather-bound book with a golden cross inscribed in the center of it from Jane and held it out to Wallace. "I take it this is yours. But what is it?"

"It's called a Psalter. It's the Book of Psalms from the Bible," Wallace replied. "It's small enough that I could keep it in my pocket and read it whenever I needed inspiration." Wallace's eyes got puffy, and he couldn't respond for a few seconds. "But ye hold on to it. It'll be safer with ye," Wallace said.

"Is it okay to put it in my pack with your bones?"

Wallace dipped his head and disappeared.

"They're gone," Alex said as he tucked the book into his pack.

Diana rolled her eyes. "You know if you take this out of here, you're stealing, don't you?"

"The way I see it, we're not stealing. We're just helping someone recover what was rightfully theirs. Now, we better hurry. I just heard the loudspeaker telling people they're closing in a few minutes."

CHAPTER 24
TRY, TRY, AGAIN

Embarrassed and frustrated after missing the boy so many times in London, Cheney hadn't looked forward to giving his employer an update, as there was something about the man who'd employed him that was different than any other person he'd ever worked for – and far scarier. The call went as badly as he'd feared.

But, armed with new information that the boy was heading towards Stirling, Cheney quickly checked out of his hotel, got in his rented Range Rover, and headed north. He grew more agitated the further he drove as he couldn't help but dwell on his failed assignment – something he'd never done before. He'd been so efficient over the past two decades that he now commanded multiple six-figure payments for every hit. It hurt his pride to see everything he'd worked so hard to achieve unraveling because of a kid with a knack for being klutzy at the wrong times. Cheney vowed that his next call would be a wrap-up report.

He arrived in Stirling and waited at the train station for two days, looking for his target. His hopes temporarily rose when he spotted Sophie, but there was no sign of the boy. Worried that he'd missed him, Cheney followed Sophie out of the train station, where he was surprised to see the boy's grandmother waiting.

He snuck closer and overheard the younger woman saying, "Relax, Elizabeth. All they're planning to do today is some sightseeing around Edinburgh. If you need more time to convince Lady Yvaine, I can always have Diana take him a little further afield, perhaps even to Loch Ness on one of those day trips. There's no shortage of things to see."

Cheney didn't bother listening to the rest of their conversation as he got back into his Rover and headed to Edinburgh. Having visited the Scottish capital several times, he was familiar with all the top tourist spots and mentally sorted through them to identify the best location to kill the boy without being seen. He eventually decided to target the *Britannia* since he knew he could rent an apartment overlooking the royal yacht. Cheney stopped in Falkirk to arrange for the apartment, then hurried on to Edinburgh.

Not knowing when, or even if, the boy would tour the yacht, he got up early the next day and started his surveillance. He kept watch all day, except for short breaks to clear his head and ensure he stayed ready. As the hours passed, he began wondering if he'd been wrong to pick a fixed location to wait.

But, late in the afternoon, Cheney spotted the boy's signature Tilley Hat. He watched Alex closely and couldn't believe his luck when the boy moved towards the stern and stepped up on a capstan, giving him a clear target. He opened his window a few more inches, then shifted his attention from his spotting scope to his rifle scope while lifting the butt of his silenced sniper rifle to his shoulder. Cheney sighted, took a deep breath, then slowly let it out. He was about to squeeze the trigger when he saw the boy stumble. Cheney quickly adjusted and aimed slightly right and down from where Alex's head had been the second before. The gun's kick told him he hadn't been able to stop from pulling the trigger.

Cheney switched to his spotting scope and saw the boy lurch forward and tumble over the railing. He chambered a second round and re-aimed his rifle towards the water rippling out below the stern of the big yacht, watching for the boy.

When several minutes had elapsed without Alex returning to the surface, Cheney lowered his rifle and picked up the spotting scope to continue surveying the ship. Seeing no sign of activity, he permitted himself a smile for finally accomplishing his task.

He kept the window open to get the gunpowder smell out, then quickly cleaned up the room, making sure he left no evidence behind that he'd ever been there. A short time later, he packed his gear into his Rover and started driving east, wanting to be long gone when the ambulance and police came.

The next day, while waiting for the ferry to Ireland and his next job in Damascus, he eagerly scanned the Edinburgh newspaper, looking for news of the boy's death. He was a little worried when he got to the back of the paper and didn't see a single article on his hit. Cheney quickly turned back to the front page and went through the newspaper more slowly, looking closely for even a tiny blurb of information on his kill. By the time he finished perusing the paper for the third time, without finding a single sentence on the boy's death, he figured his target had, somehow, escaped again.

Slamming down his paper, Cheney stormed out of the terminal to make the long trip back to Edinburgh.

CHAPTER 25
LIFE IS NOT SEPARATE

Except for the disturbance in David's Tower, Alex was pleased he'd stayed out of trouble for an entire week. The previous day's walk up into the hills overlooking the city had done much to restore his peace of mind. With the sun shining brightly and a light breeze blowing off the Firth of Forth, he stepped up on one of the capstans of the *Britannia's* stern to get a better look over the rail. As he gazed over the water, Alex felt the ankh suddenly tugging him downward. A second later, something hit the side of his head.

The intense pain caused him to lose his balance, tumble overboard, and hit the water headfirst. Stunned by the impact, he slowly sank below the surface. With his life flashing before him, he thought it odd that all he could think about was how cold the water was – even colder than the high mountain lakes of his youth in Colorado. The last thing he remembered before blacking out was a glowing, greenish-grey thing shooting through the water towards him.

Alex didn't know how long he'd been out, but when he woke, he felt like he was lying on the most uncomfortable bed in the world. He opened his eyes, wondering what all the bright lights above him were for, and started to sit up. But sharp pains shot through his head. Everything turned dark, and he passed out again.

When he awoke the second time, he was warm and comfortable. A slow throbbing had replaced the sharp pain in his head from earlier. He tried opening his eyes and was surprised at how much effort it took. When he finally managed that simple act, he immediately regretted it, as the lights in the room were too bright and painful to look at. He tried sitting up, but the pain in his head immediately went from a dull throb to a sharp pain, forcing him to lay back down and return to blissful sleep.

The next time he opened his eyes, he noticed daylight flooding the room. He looked around but didn't recognize where he was. Forgetting the pain he'd experienced the night before, he attempted to sit up. Although not as bad, it was enough to cause him to give up the attempt. As he sank back into the bed, a familiar face appeared above him, but it took him a few seconds before he realized it was his sister, Deborah. He started opening his mouth, but she held a finger up to her lips and said, "Shh, you'll wake up Jane, and I need to tell you something."

"Where've you been?" Alex whispered. "I was beginning to hope you'd moved on."

"Nope, you're still stuck with me. I'm sorry for not being here sooner, but I looked for you in Romania for weeks. I eventually gave up, returned home, and only found out you were still alive a few days ago. I've been racing here to see you, but the Atlantic is a pretty big body of water. And, of course, the moment I track you down, I find you've gotten into some serious trouble."

"What do you mean?"

"Somebody just tried to kill you," Deborah said.

"What!"

Jane shifted in her chair but didn't wake up.

Deborah held her finger to her lips again and said, "I'd just arrived in Edinburgh and was flying towards you when I saw a flash and heard a muffled sound coming out of one of the apartments across the way from the *Britannia*. I flew towards where I thought the shot had come from and saw a man aiming a rifle at the ship. Given your history, I put two and two together and realized you were in trouble. I saw you falling but was too far away to stop you. I worried he would shoot you again, so I pulled you to safety underwater, making him think he'd gotten you.

"You were unconscious but still breathing when I dragged you ashore. So, I left you to check on the assassin but found him packing up, getting ready to leave. By the time I got back to help you, someone had spotted you on the beach and called for help."

Jane woke up and almost fell out of the chair as she scrambled to get to Alex's bedside. Seeing his eyes open, she smiled wanly and said in her light Scottish brogue, "I was worried about ye. How do ye feel?"

Alex was still woozy, so it took him a while before he responded, "My head is killing me."

"Do ye need something?" Jane asked, seeing him look around.

"No, but my sister was here a minute ago, but I don't see her now."

"I can't help ye there," Jane said. "What happened to ye? One minute, ye were walking around the Britannia, and the next, ye'd disappeared. We looked everywhere on board for ye and had jest about given up when I got a phone call saying they had ye in a hospital. I'm glad I taped my number inside your hat because I would've never guessed where ye'd gone."

Not wanting to worry her, Alex decided not to tell Jane what Deborah had told him about the assassin and instead said, "I was being stupid and climbed up on one of the capstans, lost my balance, and fell overboard. Deborah happened to come looking for me just then and pulled me from the drink. Since you can't communicate with her, it was chance that someone else found me and called for help."

"Thank Gaia, she was there for ye. Otherwise, ye'd never have made it to shore alive. It might not seem like it to ye, but yer living a charmed life to have survived so many accidents. The doctors think ye hit your head on something as ye have a big scrape all along yer head."

Alex grimaced, causing Jane to reach out to him and say, "Are ye sure I can't do something for ye?"

"No, really. I'll be fine. What about my grandmother? Did she get mad at me when she heard about my latest scrape?"

Jane looked uncomfortable. In a faint voice, she said, "About that. She doesn't know anything yet. Both Diana and I like the freedom we've had the last couple of days and don't want ye to get into more trouble, so we lied and said everything's fine to ensure Sophie stayed in Stirling."

"How are we going to keep hiding the fact that I'm in a hospital? They'll eventually find out," Alex said.

"Not if ye tell the doctors here that ye feel fine and ask to get released," Jane replied. "And don't worry about the bills. I went through yer pack, gave the hospital yer insurance card, and called yer grandfather to alert him to the situation. I have to say that I was surprised at how laid back he is. I thought he would be all panicky, but he's cool about all this, although he did ask what ye were searching for."

"What did you tell him?"

"The truth – that ye're searching for Wallace's body parts. The way he asked the question, I figured he knows yer secrets."

"Some of them," Alex replied. "He thinks all this is the destiny the Great Spirit has chosen for me."

"Interesting," Jane said. "Anyway, he says to get well soon and stay with yer quest."

Alex suddenly thought about the ankh and patted his chest. When he didn't feel anything, he started panicking.

"Relax," Jane said. "I've got it. I know ye don't like anybody to know about it, so as soon as I arrived, I took it. Right now, though, we need to get ye out of here. I don't want to still be here when Sophie arrives, and we have to explain what happened."

"You and me both," Alex said. "By the way, where's Diana?"

"She's back at the apartment getting some rest. She was here most of the night, and left only a couple of hours ago."

Deborah reappeared and said, "I wanted you two to have a little privacy, so I ducked out for a bit. Has Jane mentioned what's happening at Stormhold?"

"What's happening?" Alex asked.

"She's jest resting," Jane replied.

"That's not what I was asking about. Deborah just returned and asked if you'd told me about what's happening in Stormhold. What's she talking about?"

Jane's face turned crimson. She looked away and, in a low voice, said, "All the high priestesses are meeting to determine what to do with ye."

"What she means is they want to get rid of you," Deborah said.

"What do you mean get rid of me?"

Jane grabbed Alex's hand so she could see and hear his sister. "They're not going to do anything to ye," she replied. "Lady Yvaine has assured me that she won't allow them to. At most, they'll ban ye from going on the grounds of any of the groves in the future. But it means ye won't be able to visit yer grandmother again."

"I wasn't planning to, so that's no loss," Alex replied.

"I suggest you go home where you'll be safe and away from our order," Deborah said.

"But I've promised to help William Wallace move on and am making good progress. I'm hoping that this type of stuff will eventually help me figure out how to help you move on."

"Don't worry about me," Deborah replied. "I've accepted the fact that I'm stuck here. Besides, it's not all bad. I'm getting to know you better. I get to hang around my best friend, Jane, and you guys do a lot of cool things. I'm living a productive life compared to the ghosts I know."

Alex didn't know how to respond.

"The choice is up to ye," Jane said. "Selfishly speaking, I'd prefer ye stay, and I'm pretty sure Diana feels the same way. And don't worry about our order. Lady Yvaine will handle them. Now, if ye think ye're up to it, I think it best if we get ye out of here. I can take care of yer wound jest as good, if not better, than this hospital can."

It only took a couple of hours, but with Jane's help, Alex managed to bluster his way through all the personnel and paperwork to get his release. But as soon as they were outside and he tried to stand, a dizzy spell hit him forcing him to grab onto a handrail to stop from falling. Diana and Jane each grabbed an arm and helped him into the waiting cab. By the time they returned to the apartment, he was so exhausted that he slid into bed and said, "I'm sorry about ruining your free time, but I appreciate everything you two are doing for me. You should go out and have some fun while I take a nap. I'm sure being a nursemaid is the last thing you guys want to do."

"Too bad. I'm staying here because I'm tired as I didn't sleep well last night," Diana said. "Hospital chairs aren't the most comfortable things, you know, so I'll take it easy and catch up on some reading. And Jane hasn't slept much either, so you're stuck with us. Besides, with a head injury, someone needs to keep an eye on you. Now, get some rest. I'm going to watch over you while Jane takes a nap." She then opened the book on her lap, signaling their talk was at an end.

When Alex woke, Jane was bending over him, feeling his pulse. Letting go of his wrist, she smiled and said, "Good. Ye're awake. I need ye to scoot up so I can change the bandage on your head."

Alex sat up, then closed his eyes as she gently unwrapped the gauze around his head. When the last wrap came off, Jane gave a long, low whistle and said, "The doctor who bandaged you must not have looked closely, or he doesn't know much about head wounds. You didn't bump your head. Something grazed your skull. This might sound crazy, but it looks like a bullet wound. If I'm right, you're lucky to be alive because an inch to the right, and you'd be in the morgue now. So, what really happened yesterday? If we don't know, we can't help you."

"I'm not entirely sure. I was looking over the railing, and the next thing I knew, my ankh was pulling me overboard. That's when something hit me in the head. Deb said she saw some guy with a rifle shooting at me from a nearby building. I've been gone for so long. How could anyone know I'm here?" He gently touched the side of his head and asked, "Did I get any stitches?"

"No, but ye'll have a scar there for the rest of yer life. As long as ye don't have any latent concussion symptoms, though, ye should be fine in a couple of days. So, how did yer sister show up jest in time to save ye?"

"She's been looking for me since Romania and only picked up on my aura recently."

Jane scratched her head and said, "I wonder if there is a linkage between a couple of feuding ghosts, this bullet wound, and what happened in London."

Before she could say anything else, Diana came in. "How's he doing?" she asked.

"He'll be fine. He just needs to take it easy for the next few days," Jane replied.

"I'm not sure that's going to work well. While you were napping, my mom called and said there's been a change of plans. She expects they'll finish their business tomorrow and want us in Stirling the day after. So, I was hoping he'd feel up to visiting Falkirk, where Wallace lost and resigned as Guardian of Scotland. It's only twenty miles west of here, and we might get some information to help us find the rest of Wallace there."

Jane frowned when Alex said, "I'll be fine if I take it easy. But for now, how about some food?"

Jane smiled and said, "That we can do."

CHAPTER 26
FALKIRK

Alex felt much better the next morning and tried convincing Jane that he felt good enough to travel.

After much cajoling, Jane caved in, saying, "On one condition. We're supposed to arrive at Stormhold tonight, so we hire a driver to take us there." Seeing Alex was about to protest, she held up her hand and said, "I expect ye to take it easy, which means limited walking and no carrying your bags around. Head injuries can be a little dicey, so we need to keep a close eye on ye."

"I'm still nervous about going to Stormhold after what Deborah told me. Will it be safe?" Alex asked.

"Lady Yvaine gave her word ye would be. And, as Diana can attest, she always keeps her promises. So, let's get ready and go."

When they got to Falkirk, Diana asked the driver, "Can you take us to the battleground?"

"I'm sorry, Miss. Unfortunately, no one knows exactly where the battleground was. Perhaps ye'd like to see Callendar House. It's a 14th-century French chateau-styled house with part of the Antonine Wall on its grounds, which makes it a UNESCO site. Or ye might want to see the Kelpies or the Falkirk Wheel."

Diana looked at Jane and Alex. "Are you guys okay if we go see Callendar Park? I could add another UNESCO site to my list."

They agreed, and a short time later, they were looking up at the magnificent house dominating the grounds.

As they headed towards the entrance, Alex said, "I'm not up for walking around, so you two go on ahead. I'll just go down to the lake and enjoy the sunshine."

"I think that's wise. Relaxing in the fresh air will be better for ye than traipsing around inside," Jane said. "But we'll walk ye down there and ensure ye're settled in."

By the time they got to the lake, Alex's head had started pounding. He found a comfortable spot in the shade and sat down. Looking up at Jane, he forced a grin onto his face and said, "See, I'm being good. Now you two go and enjoy the place. I'll be perfectly happy here."

"Don't wander off," Jane said, casting one more glance back before heading to the chateau with Diana.

He watched the two girls walk away, then laced his hands behind his head and lay back against the cool green grass. Alex watched the clouds scud by and was starting to drift off when a wave of cold air washed over him, and a one-arm, one-legged Wallace appeared, followed by Kerly.

"We came to see how ye're doing," Wallace said.

Alex sat up too quickly and had to steady himself as the world spun crazily around him. When the dizziness passed, he started to answer their question but stopped when he saw another spirit appear in the distance and watched as a middle-aged ghost with scraggly red hair flew towards them.

Wallace didn't notice him until the man knelt at his feet, dropped his head, and said, "Forgive me, Sir William."

The former Guardian of Scotland hopped around and turned beet red when he saw who'd spoken. Even with only one leg and arm, he almost overpowered Kerly to get at the man as he shouted, "Ye filthy, traitorous scum. How dare ye come here and ask forgiveness."

"Calm down, William," Kerly said. "Remember why ye're here. Don't let this poor excuse of a man distract ye."

Wallace reluctantly backed away.

"What's wrong?" Alex asked.

Wallace glared at the newcomer and said, "His name is John Comyn, or as he was known in my day, the Red Comyn. He was a duplicitous traitor who did whatever he could to gain more power and wealth in Scotland, including fighting for the English. He wasn't at Stirling Bridge. Nor did he help when my army invaded England and sacked York. The only time he showed up was here at Falkirk, and even then, he didn't stay long, choosing to retire from the field before the battle even started."

"Why did you fight here?" Alex asked.

Wallace grimaced and said, "My invasion of England got Edward's attention. He stopped warring with France, returned to England, assembled an army, and promptly invaded Scotland again.

"My plan was to draw the English deep into our countryside while destroying everything in their path so they would run short of supplies. It was working until the English made a forced march to catch my army here.

The English had a vastly superior force, which is why I wanted to continue retreating, but the other Scottish nobles argued against my plan. So, we turned and fought. But when the English charged, this traitorous scum took the Scottish cavalry and left the field without striking a single blow. The English cavalry slaughtered our archers. So, in his cowardly retreat, he took away two of the most valuable assets of our army. If Comyn had held his ground, we would have carried the day and stopped the English threat once and for all."

The Red Comyn, who was still kneeling, said, "I feel horrible about my actions that day, and I'm still paying the price for that decision. But in my defense, I was scared by the size of their force. Their heavy cavalry vastly outnumbered our light cavalry, so I pulled my men to fight another day. I apologize again, Sir William. There has not been a day that has gone by since then that I did not regret my actions. I paid for it twice. First, with my life when Robert the Bruce slew me at Greyfriars. And second, by my continued presence here on earth. I've been waiting for yer return, here at the site of my ignominious retreat, to serve ye in any way I can."

Alex cleared his throat and said, "Excuse me, Sir William. I don't know all you've been through, but I have learned a little about regrets and what's important. He's paid for his disservice many times over. Give the man a chance at redemption and take him up on his offer. Maybe he can help you move on."

Wallace dropped his head, unable to look into Alex's eyes. In a voice so soft that Alex could barely hear him, he said, "As ye wish." He looked down at Comyn and was about to say something when Edward and a half dozen phantoms armed with swords apparated.

Pulling his sword out of his scabbard, Edward pointed it at Alex and said, "Kill the boy."

Alex jumped up and started running towards the chateau, figuring there was nothing the ankh could do against real swords. Out of the corner of his eye, he saw Wallace, despite having only half his body, strangling a much smaller man with his hand while both Comyn and Kerly were fighting the attackers. Suddenly, Alex felt a searing pain in his shoulder. Afraid to stop, he kept running until his legs collapsed underneath him, and he fell, face first, to the ground.

CHAPTER 27
STORMHOLD

Everybody at school knew Jane had an uncanny knack for sensing people's thoughts. But Diana was slow to react when Jane abruptly ran out of Callendar House, shouting over her shoulder, "Alex is in danger!" Diana followed her friend out of the chateau and onto the lawns but froze mid-stride when she saw Alex lying face down on the grass, a knife sticking out of his back.

The next hour went by in a blur. Jane stayed unnaturally calm throughout the ordeal, ordering Diana to fetch the driver and a dozen other tasks while they raced to Stormhold Manor, located deep in the Menteith Hills. While Jane was tending to Alex's wound, Diana called ahead and alerted her mom of the situation.

Ms. Inglis, the school nurse, was waiting for them when they arrived and helped Jane get him out of the van, onto the gurney, and into the manor house before Diana had finished paying their driver. After lugging their bags inside, Diana decided to wander around outside, as she was still shocked by what had happened. She'd only been walking for a short time when she saw her mother approaching. Taking a deep breath, she quickly rehearsed her explanation one more time before heading towards her mom, grateful that she wouldn't have to explain his head wound.

"How did this happen?" Sophie demanded as she stormed up to Diana.

"We don't know. Alex stayed outside while Jane and I toured Callendar Park. We were inside for only half an hour when Jane suddenly got one of her premonitions and rushed out. By the time I got there, all I saw was Alex lying face-down in the grass with a knife in his back. Jane thought we should come here rather than go to a hospital, figuring he was in better hands with her and Ms. Inglis. That's all I know."

"Unbelievable. How could he find trouble in such a peaceful place?" Sophie took a deep breath as if she was girding herself for an unpleasant task, then said, "I forbid you from helping in his recovery in any way whatsoever. Do you understand me?"

"But, Mom!"

Sophie held her hand up to stop Diana's outburst and said, "You have to promise you won't tell another soul what I'm about to tell you."

Shocked but intrigued, Diana said, "Okay."

"We're here because Elizabeth called for a conclave to declare Alex a warlock." She rushed on despite Diana's gasp. "You know how many strange things have happened around him and what our rules are. We can't ignore the facts any longer."

It took Diana a couple of moments for the turmoil in her head to die down before she could say, "Is that what you've been working on the last few days? You've been trying to figure out an approved way to kill Alex."

Sophie's eyes flashed. "I know he's ensnared you, which is why we must do this. So, I'm warning you – stay away from him. Let the Council of Elders work this out."

"I hate you!" Diana shouted before running away.

With her thoughts in turmoil, Diana wandered out to her favorite spot at Stormhold to clear her mind and calm down. She lost all track of time as she watched the creek tumble into the lake below the manor and didn't notice it was growing dark until her stomach protested the absence of lunch and dinner.

Despite her mother's warnings, worries about Alex drove her to ask where they were keeping him. Discovering his location, she went upstairs and gazed at the closed door at the end of the hallway. When she saw the latch moving, she turned and was about to head down the steps, when she heard her name. Looking back, she saw Lady Yvaine coming towards her. With her mother's warning still ringing in her head, she tried covering her presence there by saying, "I was just heading down to get a late dinner."

"Don't worry. You're not in trouble. Why don't you come with me and I'll have some dinner sent to my study. I haven't eaten since I heard about the attack and am famished."

Diana was surprised by the invitation, as Jane was the only other girl in school to have ever been in the high priestess's study.

Lady Yvaine led Diana down to the kitchen, made arrangements for their dinner, then headed to her study. It was nothing like what she'd imagined. Instead of a formal English library, it was more like a museum of priceless artifacts from around the world.

Diana spent most of the time they were eating, studying the older woman. Lady Yvaine looked like she was in her early 40s, but Diana knew she had to be much older, as she'd been the school's headmistress for as long as anyone could remember. She had dark-olive-colored skin, piercing grey eyes, and shoulder-length brunette hair exposing a high forehead, full cheeks, and a firm chin.

Diana jumped when Lady Yvaine broke the silence, saying, "I suppose you're wondering why I called you here."

"Yes, ma'am."

"I wanted to know what you think about Alex. You're probably closer to him than everyone except his grandfather and cousin. Do you think he's a threat to our order?"

Diana had often wondered the same question but had never thought the head of the order would ask her opinion. She hesitated long enough that Yvaine said, "You can speak freely here. You haven't done anything wrong, at least, that I'm aware of."

The unexpected teasing put Diana at ease. She surprised herself when she replied, "No, ma'am. I don't think he's a danger to us. Different – definitely. Like everybody else, I haven't figured him out yet, but I can tell you he's got a good heart. And you know he's saved my life multiple times, for which I'll always be grateful."

"But he's also led you and Jane into scrape after scrape," Yvaine said. "For that matter, I still don't understand why you went with him into the Caribbean. You had to know how dangerous it was. It's amazing you're still alive."

"Don't blame him for that," Diana said. "He tried talking us out of coming with him, but we ignored him."

"But why?" Yvaine asked. "What type of hold does he have on you that you keep following him into danger?"

Diana didn't answer right away. Instead, she stared at a bizarre-looking Mayan mask on one of her shelves. At last, she said, "At first, it was because I didn't trust him and was spying on him. But now, it just feels right."

Lady Yvaine studied her for some time before asking, "Why does danger follow him around?"

"That's a good question. Jane and I have discussed it often but have come to no conclusion. But…,"

"Go on," Yvaine said. "This is a private discussion. The only other person I will talk about this with is Jane."

"Jane has put more thought into this than I have, but I have two theories," Diana said. "The simplistic one is that he's so different that he unnerves people. But that doesn't explain things like what happened in Romania. My other theory is that, for some strange reason, Gaia has chosen him to do her work. And here you all are trying to determine whether to kill him or not."

Yvaine startled Diana when she abruptly asked, "Has he found any of the Maqlû?"

Diana hesitated. "My answer hasn't changed from what I've told my mother and Elizabeth. I have not seen him with any magical object." For a second, she thought she had committed an unpardonable sin by avoiding the question. She was surprised when Yvaine smiled.

"You know most people would interpret your answer as a yes. Since I see I'm making you uncomfortable, I'll drop the subject for now. But you should know that you will hear a lot of unfavorable talk about him while you're here."

"I still don't understand why you're allowing his grandmother to call a conclave. He's done nothing to hurt us," Diana said.

"Our rules have been in place for centuries with good reasons for them all," Yvaine replied. "Elizabeth had every right to call a conclave because it's extremely rare that any of our members have boys. Plus, as you noted, Alex's behaviors are so odd that they make people fearful. I promise you, though, he's safe as long as he's in my house."

"Is he all right?" Diana asked.

"Let's hope so," Yvaine replied. "But I suggest you do as your mother wishes and stay away from him for now."

CHAPTER 28
NOT ALL ANGELS HAVE WINGS

Lady Yvaine quietly opened the door and slipped in. Seeing Jane lying on a cot near Alex's bed, she went over to a chair in the corner and sat down, looking fondly at the girl she regarded as the daughter she'd never had. Jane seemed to sense Yvaine's presence and got up. She sat in a chair next to Yvaine and turned on a reading light.

"It's three in the morning," Yvaine whispered. "You need to get some rest and let Ms. Inglis or myself look after him."

Jane brushed some stray hair strands off her face and said, "I'm fine. Elise was tired, and I couldn't sleep, so I told her to get some rest."

"I don't know how you do it," Yvaine said, "but you've never needed much sleep. In the future, though, let me take some shifts too."

"I'll be fine. Ye have enough stuff to worry about without adding him to yer list."

"You're wrong. He is my list," Yvaine replied. "Have you figured out what's causing his coma?"

"I've run some tests on the knife and believe his assailant coated it with some unusual toxin because it's not a modern-day poison. Have ye looked closely at the knife?"

Yvaine nodded. "I haven't seen one like it in a long time."

As Jane got up to check Alex's pulse and temperature, she said, "That would make sense because

I sent it out to an expert who believes it's over 700 years old."

Lady Yvaine didn't say anything until Jane had sat back down. "I shouldn't be venting to you, but I'm frustrated. I don't understand how Elizabeth can be so cold towards her grandson – wanting me to declare him a warlock and punish him accordingly."

I guess it's like Einstein said. The person who walks alone is likely to go where no one has ever gone. And that scares people." Jane paused, then added, "I'm sorry, but I didn't tell ye the whole truth the other day. Alex's head wound is from a different incident than the knife attack. Somebody shot at him, but luckily, they just grazed his head."

"What has he gotten involved in now?" Yvaine asked.

Jane put a finger to her lips. "He probably can't hear ye, but I want to keep it quiet. To answer your question, though, I don't know. What's most concerning to me is that I believe his wounds are from different attackers."

"Why do you say that?" Yvaine asked.

"Diana's told me what happened in London. I believe the head wound is related to those instances because whoever attacked him there used modern weapons and techniques – like the head wound. This knife attack, though, is something entirely different – it's something out of the past. But, outside of our order, I can't imagine who would want to kill him."

Yvaine steepled her fingers and leaned her chin on them. "Elizabeth shared something with me about what happened in London that I haven't told anybody yet, so

I expect this to stay between us. That means I don't want Diana to know what I'm about to tell you."

Jane edged forward in her seat. "Understood."

"I'm sure you heard about the police investigation into the death in the London Museum. The inspector in charge believes it was the work of a professional assassin, who is one of the world's most wanted, but elusive criminals. At first, he thought the target in the museum was the dead man, but later told Elizabeth he thought Alex might have been the target. It's the reason they left London so suddenly."

Jane cleared her throat. "I haven't been completely honest about Alex."

Yvaine's eyebrows shot up. "Go on."

"This isn't the first time someone has tried to kill him. Some men were after him in Spain and Romania too. I don't understand who would want to take a hit out on him. The one thing I keep returning to is that this is all about the Maqlû."

"Why didn't you tell me about this before?" Yvaine asked.

"Because I thought it was someone from our order, and I wasn't sure who I could trust."

"Surely you could trust me," Yvaine said.

Jane nodded. "But I wasn't sure who ye would tell."

"I guess we have a ways to go to rebuild our trust. I can assure you, though, that in the future, I will not share with the others what you tell me about Alex. What's his prognosis?" Yvaine asked.

"I'm not sure. Ye know what poisons can do to a person. At the very least, I think it'll be a tough struggle." Jane hesitated, then asked, "If what I hear is true, why do ye want me to go through so much effort to keep him alive?"

A determined look came over Yvaine's face. "My instructions have not changed. Do whatever is necessary to keep him alive. It's my growing conviction that he's far more valuable to us alive than dead, despite what you've heard."

"It sounds like ye have an idea of who might be behind all this. What are ye not telling me?" Jane asked.

"There's a lot about our order that I haven't shared with anyone. Maybe someday, I'll tell you. But, for now, you'll have to trust me."

"I wish ye would share sooner rather than later, no matter what it is," Jane said.

Yvaine hesitated, then said, "You're right. I shouldn't keep my biggest fear to myself." She took a deep breath and added, "I fear he's going to irrevocably change our order. And that scares a lot of people, many of whom are not in our order. But what type of change, I can't say."

"Maybe he's like that Chinese proverb that goes, a crisis is an opportunity riding a dangerous wind," Jane said.

"Maybe. Now get some rest. You need it."

The light was so dim that as Lady Yvaine stepped into the hallway, she didn't see the legs sprawled out from a chair near the door. She tripped and nearly fell.

Startled awake, Diana pulled herself up and said, "Sorry. I fell asleep. How is he?"

"We'll see," Yvaine replied.

"Has Jane figured out what's wrong with him?"

"Yes. Now go, get some rest." Yvaine smiled as she saw Diana climbing the stairs to her room on the fourth floor and marveled at the loyalty the two girls showed to a boy that everyone else in the order thought was a threat.

Yvaine checked on Alex several times a day for the next few days. Each time, she saw Jane watching over Alex.

When Yvaine ordered her to get some rest, Jane responded by saying, "I'm very comfortable on the cot here and feel rested. Besides, it's easier to change his poultice and check on his vitals if I don't have to leave here. Elise brings up food and any other supplies I need while spelling me for showers and walks outside to get some fresh air. And ye know I'm the person best suited for this."

Yvaine shook her head and departed. To her surprise, she also kept finding Diana pacing the hallway during the night. She eventually relented and let Diana enter the room when she checked on him at night.

Whatever poison had gotten into Alex, though, was something they had no means of combatting. The days soon turned into weeks and then into months. When the new school year approached, Yvaine moved Alex and Jane to a small cottage on the grounds where the incoming students wouldn't disturb them. She was under no illusions that there wouldn't be rumors, but she figured it would soon blow over if nobody ever saw him.

CHAPTER 29

FIRST THEY IGNORE YOU

Diana looked around to see if anybody was watching, then knocked on the door to the cottage. Jane was so surprised at seeing her friend when she answered that she stood there letting the cold air in until Diana asked, "Can I come in?"

Jane came to her senses and ushered her to a chair beside a crackling fire. "I'm sorry. I'm surprised, because ye're not supposed to be here. Why did ye come?"

"No one knows I'm here," Diana said. "So, I'd appreciate it if you don't tell anyone."

"My lips are sealed," Jane replied. "So, what brings ye to the outcasts' cottage?"

Diana grimaced. "Please don't say that. It's hard enough hearing things like that at school all day. I'd hoped to get away from that type of talk for at least a couple of hours."

"I'm sorry. Has it been tough on ye?" Jane asked.

"Yes and no. Of course, there are all sorts of rumors going around the school about what happened last summer. Some are hilariously off-track, but most are just mean."

"How bad?" Jane asked.

"I don't want to talk about it," Diana replied. "Why didn't I ever see this bloodthirsty attitude in our order before?"

"Change can be scary. It tends to bring out the worst in people."

"How do you deal with all the hate?" Diana asked.

"I've heard so many rude comments in my life that I'm inured to it – everything from comments about my height, hair, and style to my lack of magical abilities," Jane said. "But people have been especially cruel about my relationship with Lady Yvaine. It's all so petty."

Both lapsed into silence until Jane slapped the arms of her chair and stood up. "How about some extra-thick hot chocolate?"

"With marshmallows?" Diana asked.

"Of course."

Jane returned a few minutes later with two hot chocolates and some freshly baked scones.

Diana ate her first scone in silence, working up the courage to ask a question she feared the answer to. "How is Alex doing?"

"I'm hopeful. His vitals have stabilized, and he's breathing easier."

"When do you think he'll wake up?" Diana asked.

"I don't know," Jane replied. "It could be tonight, tomorrow, next week, or never."

Diana nodded and changed the subject. "How are you holding up? Miss Inglis is almost always at school, and I don't see the staff coming down here very often."

"He's not very hard to take care of. All he does is sleep," Jane said.

"I know that's not a true statement," Diana said. "You have to feed, clean, exercise, and monitor him."

"I have someone who cleans the place and prepares the meals. I'm content."

"You shouldn't be. You're young and have everything to look forward to. I don't want you tied to an invalid for the rest of your life. I know you don't get enough sleep because I've wandered down here to see how you're doing some nights, and you're always awake."

"I'm built for this type of work."

"But why are you doing it?" Diana asked. "Is it because you like him?"

"Of course, I like him – just like ye do. To answer yer question, though, I'm doing it because he needs help and, not to brag, I think he's getting better care here than at some fancy hospital, where it's sterile and busy. I also feel guilty about what happened when I was supposed to be watching him."

"You mean we," Diana said. "You can't put all the blame on yourself."

The two girls lapsed into silence until Diana asked, "How come you never talk about your family? Like, where did you grow up and such?"

"Because nobody ever asks me," Jane replied. "I never knew my parents. All I remember was growing up with three old ladies in Scotland." Seeing Diana's frown, Jane added, "I didn't use the word old in a derogatory sense. I used it because they were old. I mean, really old. If I had to guess, they all looked well over a hundred years old, but surprisingly they were all pretty spry for their age.

"Then, when I was ten, they asked Lady Yvaine to watch over me because they thought I needed to be around people my age and to get a better education than they could give me. And that's how I came here."

"I'm sorry," Diana said.

"Don't be. I've had four great moms and lived a good life. I'm happy." Jane smiled and waved the topic aside. "It's great to see ye again, but I can tell that ye came here for some other reason. Out with it."

"You always seem to understand what people are thinking better than they do themselves. I can't believe I'm going to say this, but I feel restless," Diana said. "Going off on all those adventures with Alex was dangerous – but exciting. And now, he's helping William Wallace find his body parts. He's got to wake up and finish the job because he doesn't leave things unfinished."

Diana was silent for a while, then asked, "Do you think he found the Holy Grail?"

Jane nodded. "I do. His long absence and showing up on death's doorstep yet again tells me he wasn't off having fun. And the attempts on his life suggest that he's making someone awfully nervous. No. Let me correct that. He's making an awful lot of people nervous. Jest look at our order."

"Do you think he should keep helping Wallace?" Diana asked.

"What I think is irrelevant. He's going to do what he's going to do," Jane said.

"What about Deborah?"

"Alex says ghosts don't move on in the afterlife until they finish their business. Since I believe he's found two of the Maqlû and the Grail, I think she's linked to her twin until he's finished his journey. Besides, since we usually can't talk to her, we'll have to leave yer question for them to figure out. But it's getting late, and ye should get back to the manor before anyone figures out where ye went."

CHAPTER 30
THE PERSON YOU DECIDE TO BE

From his perch in the high reaches of the Karakoram Mountains, Chrysophylax looked out over the vast savanna and mentally sighed. Usually, the sight of the teeming wildlife herds far below would have already caused him to swoop down for the hunt, especially since he hadn't eaten in several days. But he couldn't get the boy off his mind.

It had been months since he'd returned from Earth and promised his family he would stay on Berellus. But he was growing restless with the slow pace of dragon society. And for some reason that he couldn't understand, he felt an urgent need to return to Earth.

Thinking a full stomach might help him reason more clearly, he launched into the air and glided down over the savanna. Spotting a lame Merychippus, and knowing it wouldn't last the night in the kill-or-be-killed plains, he swooped down and made a quick, merciful kill. When he was full, he left the remains of the carcass for the scavengers and headed for his uncle's home.

As he neared Nabu's place, he hesitated and decided to find a secluded spot to wait until nightfall before finishing his journey. He wasn't sure why he felt the sudden need for secrecy, but he didn't leave his hiding spot until he was sure no one was watching. Chrysophylax made the final leg of the trip as fast as he could and skidded to a stop on the ledge outside Nabu's home, and quietly called out, *"Uncle? Can I come in?"*

It was several minutes before Nabu unlocked the door to his laboratory and asked, *"Why the secrecy? Usually, you trumpet your arrival."*

Chrysophylax didn't respond immediately. Instead, he began pacing back and forth across the room. At last, he said, *"I want to return to Earth."*

"I was wondering when you'd get to this," Nabu said.

"Why's that?" Chrysophylax replied.

"You've changed since you went to Earth, maturing in a way I never expected. At first, I thought it was about giving you a purpose – finding out what happened to the ankh. But you have got involved in that boy's destiny, and there's no going back. I've never met your human friend, but he reminds me of Sibyl."

Chrysophylax cocked his head and said, *"Huh? I never thought of him as a friend. He was always just someone I was curious about and who needed my help. But I guess you're right – he is my friend. But there's more to why I want to return than just that. I feel needed on Earth. Whereas here, I feel like a child who gets in the way of whatever the elders want. And nothing ever changes. With him, I feel like I can make a difference – I just don't know what that difference is."*

A deep rumbling chuckle from Nabu reverberated through the room. *"You sound like I did when I was your age."*

"And look what you've done," Chrysophylax said. *"You were one of the instructors at the university on*

Irkalla, one of the original dragons that went to Earth to change the human trajectory, and you're still trying to find a way to help. I want to make that type of difference too."

Nabu shook his head and said, *"Don't follow in my footsteps because I haven't accomplished anything of significance. All of my work on both Irkalla and Earth has gone for naught. And here, the High Council treats me as a threat to their schemes. If you want to make a difference, then I encourage you to make real and lasting changes, my boy."*

"Do you think that little Ryujin that used to bother you is trying to change things?" Chrysophylax asked.

"Why do you ask that?"

"Because, in general, her kind seems to be a disorganized mass of dragonets that flit about. But you've told me that she stuck to Sibyl like glue. And now, she's doing the same thing with that boy. Why?"

"That's a good question," Nabu replied. *"And it's one you should go find an answer to."*

"But I thought you and my parents wanted me to stay out of trouble," Chrysophylax said.

"That's still a true statement. But, one way to accomplish that is by not being here."

Chrysophylax's eyes grew wide. *"Are you saying what I think you're saying?"*

"I'm not saying anything. However, theoretically speaking, if one were to decide to leave this planet, then I would suggest they use the portal in the Kunlun Mountains. It's the most remote on the planet and least guarded, although they'd still have to be careful. I'd

also recommend someone wishing to leave that they go about their normal business for the next few days and disappear during the Daeboreum festival."

"You're the best, Uncle."

Chrysophylax was halfway out the door when Nabu called out, *"Good luck, and be safe. May Marduk guide your steps."*

CHAPTER 31
WHERE THE LIGHT ENTERS

Alex woke and tried sitting up but was too weak and sank back onto his pillow with a groan.

A few seconds later, some wisps of hair tickled his nose. He opened his eyes and saw Jane standing above him, pulling her hair back over her shoulder. "What's going on?" he asked in a gravelly voice.

"Thank Gaia, ye're finally awake. How do ye feel?" Jane asked.

"Weak as all get out." Alex felt something tickling his throat and reached up to touch it, but a tube in his arm stopped him. "What's with this?" he asked.

"Do you remember what happened to you?" Jane asked.

"The last thing I recall was visiting Callendar Park with you guys. I was at the lake talking with Wallace when King Edward and some soldiers attacked. I ran but felt something sting me. The next thing I know – I'm here. Which, by the way, where am I?"

"Ye're at Stormhold, our order's headquarters. Ye've been in a coma for some time. And that sting ye felt was a poisoned knife."

"Are you kidding me? My life keeps slipping away, and I don't even get to experience it. This sucks."

"Be thankful ye're getting to experience life. Ye've been so sick that I've had to keep ye on an IV and a feeding tube jest to keep ye alive," Jane said. "Now, calm down if ye want to get better."

"How long have I been out?"

"It's November," Jane replied. She pasted a smile on her face in an attempt to distract him and said, "But look at the bright side. Ye're sixteen now and one year closer to legal driving age."

Alex grumbled and said, "I could've already had my license back home by now. But how could I be out for that long?"

"The poison on the knife was so unusual that I couldn't find any known antidotes. I don't think yer head wound and physical condition after yer missing year did ye any good either."

Alex remembered the ankh and reached for it. When he didn't find it, he asked Jane, "Do you have my necklace?"

Jane nodded. "I have it safely hidden. And may I suggest that I keep it a little longer, at least until ye can move about on your own."

"Thanks." Alex tried sitting up but again didn't have enough energy to make it.

"Here, let me help you," Jane said. She lifted him halfway and propped a couple of pillows behind him. "Would you like something to drink?"

Alex nodded and said, "That would be great. How about something to eat, too?"

"Hold on for a bit, and I'll get ye some food."

Jane returned a few minutes later with a bowl of chicken broth and a glass of water. She placed the tray over his lap and sat down on the bed. Alex eagerly reached for the spoon, but she pushed his hand away.

"What about this tube in my throat?" Alex asked.

"It's designed so ye can eat with it in. It stays there until I know ye're truly on the road to recovery. And for the first few meals, I'll be feeding ye, whether ye like it or not."

Alex groaned but knew he wouldn't get Jane to budge.

He was surprised at how quickly he tired and was soon grateful for her assistance. When he'd finished, he said, "That wasn't very much. What else is there?"

"I'm afraid that's all ye get right now," Jane said. "Let's see how ye handle that before we give ye something else."

Remembering what Jane had done when she'd nursed him before, he lifted his sheets and saw he was only wearing a diaper. Alex gasped and dropped the sheets as his pale face turned red.

Jane chuckled and said, "All the food and liquids I've fed ye had to go somewhere. And remember, this isn't the first time I've seen ye like this."

"Who else has been here?" Alex asked.

"I've been here most of the time, but Lady Yvaine and the school nurse have taken turns watching over you, too – including cleaning you and such. And don't worry. I haven't let Diana help."

He swallowed the phlegm in his throat and said, "Even though you'll probably wave my thanks aside, I want to thank you for saving my life."

She started to wave her hand but stopped herself and said, "I'm jest glad ye're still with us."

Alex looked into Jane's blue-grey eyes and wondered what the older girl truly thought of him. He didn't understand why she kept risking her life to come on his adventures, nor why she'd spend so much time nursing him back to health, again and again. "You know, I can't help but think back to when we first met, and you told me that the other members of your order treated you like an outcast because you were too different. Well, I think it's their loss."

Jane blushed and looked away.

They chatted for a few more minutes before Alex fell asleep in the middle of their conversation.

It was a couple more days before he left his bed for the first time. Jane had to help him into the living room that looked onto one of the lakes on the property. The short journey was so tiring that he gratefully sank into a chair and let Jane read to him for a while. When his eyes started drooping, she put the book down and got up, startling him awake.

"I'm sorry," she said.

"Don't be. I can't believe I'm so tired without doing anything."

"Ye've been through a lot, but ye're making good progress."

"I've got to ask you a question. You said the nurse and Lady Yvaine helped you, but all I ever see is you and whoever brings you supplies at night. What's going on?"

Jane fidgeted with her fingers before sitting back down. "Please don't take this the wrong way, but Lady Yvaine thinks it better that no one in the school sees ye, including Diana. Yer arrival last spring was a big enough shock because no male has ever stayed at the school."

"So, basically, you've been taking care of me full time for…" he counted on his fingers, "five months? By yourself?"

"Ye needed help." There was a lengthy pause before she said, "And don't worry, I've been calling yer grandfather a couple of times a week and kept him updated on yer progress. He and Chipeta have been worried sick about ye. They would have come here, but Lady Yvaine explained the situation, and they reluctantly agreed to let us handle it."

"Which reinforces my point that no one else has been helping you, has there? I can't thank you enough, but why are you willing to do so much? I know what people in the order think of me."

In a slightly husky voice, Jane looked away and said, "Not everybody thinks ye're dangerous."

Alex took pity on her embarrassment and changed the subject. A few days later, he started taking short walks inside the cottage. The first time they headed outside was after a heavy snowfall, making the forest eerily silent and reminding Alex of the home he and his dad had shared in Colorado.

The days soon became routine, with Jane taking him on a walk outside twice a day, going a little further each time. Soon after they'd started that activity, Jane had him taking online courses to make up for all the school he'd missed. It wasn't until March that Alex felt he was finally getting his normal strength back.

Sitting beside a roaring fire one night, Alex said, "It's time I think about going home. I'm thankful for everything, but I'm putting you out, and I can't keep taking up all your time."

Jane didn't look at him. Instead, she stared into the fire and said, "I knew this day would come, and I have to say I'm sad ye're leaving. But I do have one last treat for ye. We're supposed to have good weather this weekend, and Diana wondered if ye'd like to go to Stirling castle."

"Won't she get in trouble if someone sees her with me?" Alex asked.

"Don't worry. We've got it figured out. I'll borrow one of Lady Yvaine's cars, and we'll meet her at a rendezvous spot." She leaned over and said, "And ye can't say no. Diana doesn't seem to be having much fun at school this year because she's missed yer adventures. Ye've spoiled her, so it would be good for ye two to get out of here for a day."

"That sounds fun. Besides, you're probably getting a little bored having to put up with me all the time."

Jane didn't reply. Instead, she abruptly looked away and stared into the fire.

CHAPTER 32
STIRLING

Alex was excited about his first outing in months, but a sudden blast of cold air caused him to shiver, then jump and cry out when Wallace appeared next to him in the car.

Jane looked in her rearview mirror and asked, "What's wrong?"

"I'm sorry. Sir William just joined us," Alex replied.

Jane turned around to look, causing her to swerve. Diana grabbed the wheel and steered the car back into the left lane, narrowly avoiding an oncoming car.

"I'm sorry about that," Jane said as she got her eyes back on the road. "I need to learn how to tune out yer distractions better. What's he want?"

"I don't know yet," Alex replied, "I've been too busy worrying about getting in an accident."

"Hah, hah. Very funny," Jane replied.

Alex wrapped his arms around his body to stay warm and asked, "Where have you been for the last few months?"

Wallace smiled. "We've been watching over ye to ensure Edward and his men didn't harm ye again. But I see I'm making ye cold, so I'll be gone. I wanted to tell ye that the Red Comyn died defending ye in that dastardly attack."

As soon as Wallace had disappeared, Alex told Diana and Jane what he'd said. The discussion soon turned to finding Wallace's other parts and ended only when they arrived at Stirling Castle.

As much as Diana had talked about Edinburgh Castle being part of a UNESCO site, Alex liked Stirling Castle better as it sat high atop a stony crag overlooking the surrounding area. As they toured the historic castle, Alex kept pausing to look out over the rich farmland spreading out below and gaze longingly at the mountains in the distance. They spent the morning wandering around the castle, then headed to the National Wallace Monument after lunch.

After parking near the reception center, they were debating which of the three paths to take when Alex suddenly said, "Hey guys. My dog just appeared at the entrance to the red trail."

Diana asked, grabbing his hand to see what he was talking about. When she didn't see it, she asked, "Where is your dog? I don't see him."

Alex pointed to where Sport was standing, but Diana shook her head and said, "I still don't see anything. Are you sure he's there?"

"He's there. Maybe only I can see him because pets act differently than people in the afterlife. Ixchel told me that ghost pets are very rare."

"So, is his showing up good or bad?" Diana asked.

"I'm hoping good. Whenever he's shown up before, he's led me to something important. Like in Belize, he led me to Ixchel and the Mayan ghosts that took us to the ghost ship. He also got me to cross the Arges River to that enchanted castle."

"Ye can argue whether that last instance was good or not. So, are ye saying we should follow him?" Jane asked.

"He's here to help, but I'm hesitant, because I worry about what's ahead," Alex replied.

"Then I think we should follow him," Jane said.

Diana grabbed Jane's arm and whirled her around. "Are you kidding?" You just spent months nursing Alex back to health. And now, you're suggesting we follow a ghost dog into what can only lead to trouble."

"It seems like we're safer charging into danger than ignoring it. Jest look at what happened in Falkirk and London. And besides, it might not be dangerous."

Diana threw up her hands. "Fine. Have it your way. I thought for once we could have a pleasant day without drama." Resigned to her fate, Diana made a dramatic gesture towards the hill and said, "Lead on."

Alex took the lead, following Sport on the long path up to the monument. After half an hour of going up and downhill, he reached a spot where the trees started to thin.

Sport left the path and walked a short distance towards where two squarish rocks stood near the edge of a steep hillside with stunning long-range views of the River Forth's horseshoe loop and the mountains beyond. Alex had been there only a few seconds when successive blasts of cold air washed over him. A second later, Sport disappeared as Wallace and Kerly appeared, hovering before him and beaming. "Why do you guys look so happy?" Alex asked.

"There's a better view a little further up this path, but this gives you a good overview of the battleground of Stirling Bridge, which we fought in 1297," Wallace replied.

"What's that?"

"It was one of the greatest victories in our country's war for independence from England," Wallace replied. "We waited for the English here on Abbey Crag, then attacked after a couple thousand Englishmen had crossed the river over a narrow bridge. It was a slaughter. The English retreated, and we followed, giving them a taste of their own medicine."

Wallace's and Kerly's faces lit up when two more ghosts appeared. The one in front had long black hair, a wild-eyed look about him, and a grin that stretched from one side of his face to the other. Kerly and Wallace rushed forward and hugged and pounded the backs of the newcomer. "Stephen, ye old dog," Wallace shouted. "It's good to see ye. But why are ye still here?"

"I can't believe ye ask that of me. How could I leave my two best friends in this world? After I died, I appeared here at Stirling to guard something of yours and am glad ye've finally come to claim what is rightfully yers."

"But where are me manners?" Wallace said. "Alex, this is my good friend Stephen of Ireland. He and Kerly were my most trusted aides."

Stephen looked skeptically at Alex and asked, "Can he see us?"

"Aye, but ye can trust him as he's been leading the search for me bones," Wallace said.

Alex cut in on the conversation and asked, "Who is the other man?"

Wallace's smile vanished as he surveyed the fourth spirit. The man was a few inches shorter than Wallace with a rugged build. He had long, wild red hair and a bushy beard. Of the four, he was the only one wearing a suit of armor. "This is Robert the Bruce, a man of endless ambition and no loyalties – except to his own power and wealth."

"How dare ye say that," Bruce responded. "I was able to beat the English and drive them out of Scotland because I was patient, unlike ye."

"I'm pleased ye finally found yer backbone and stood up to Edward," Wallace said. "But why did ye not throw yer lot wholeheartedly onto our side while we lived and fought? Why did ye wait? Edward wouldn't have stood a chance against us if everyone had committed to our cause. Many a Scot died because of yer unbridled ambition."

Bruce hung his head. "The Red Comyn and I have often talked of what might have been if we had been true to Scotland instead of maneuvering for the Scottish Crown. We both know that our ambition is why we're still here. Unfortunately, neither of us ever had the moral courage that ye had. But I regret my failings and am now at yer service." Bruce kneeled and bowed his head to Wallace.

"Ye need to repay yer perfidy the way Comyn did," Kerly replied.

Bruce looked up. "He's dead?"

"Aye," Kerly replied. "He died defending the lad there against an attack by Edward and his hounds."

Wallace turned to Alex and said, "Ye have a cooler head than I do. What do ye counsel I do?"

Alex looked at the humbled Bruce and then at the glaring trio of Kerly, Wallace, and Stephen. After a few moments, he said, "I didn't live through what you did, but I have come to believe that forgiveness is necessary for closure."

With a loud sigh, Wallace flicked his fingers at Bruce and said, "Ye and me. We're good."

Bruce picked up Wallace's hand with both of his and kissed it. "Thank ye, Sir William." Then he disappeared.

Bruce's departure left everyone silent until Stephen grinned and said, "Anybody up for a little grave digging?"

Perplexed, Wallace looked at Stephen and said, "What are ye talking about?"

"Rumor has it that ye would like to find yer left arm," Stephen replied, "Of course, I could be wrong, and ye might prefer to go hobbling around for the rest of eternity as a one-legged, one-armed freak."

Wallace grabbed Stephen's shoulder and shouted, "Ye know where my bones are?"

Stephen nodded. "It was too late to mount a rescue by the time I heard the Sassenach had captured ye. So, when I heard they were displaying yer left quarter hereabouts, I took it and buried it the first chance I got."

"Where?" asked Wallace.

"I thought it fitting that yer bones should enjoy yer finest victory. So, we gave you a spectacular view of the valley and the battle site." He grinned and pointed at one of the two headstone-like rocks standing before them. "I don't know how ye found the spot, but I buried yer bones underneath this stone to ensure no animal or person could get them."

Wallace bear-hugged Stephen with his only arm, then ruffled his wild hair. "Thank ye, but how are we going to move that boulder? Do either ye or Kerly have the ability to move objects that big?"

Both ghosts shook their heads.

"If you guys wait here, I can get Diana," Alex said. "I'm sure she can move it."

He returned to the path and started to run after them but found he didn't have the stamina and slowed to a walk. He finally caught up to them when he got to the monument's base at the top of the hill. As soon as he called out to them, they turned and practically pounced on him.

"Where have ye been?" Jane asked. "One moment ye were with us, and the next ye were gone. We've been looking around for ye ever since then."

"I'm sorry. I followed Sport off the path, and now I need Diana's help for something."

"Oh god. What did you do this time?" Diana said in mock exasperation. "We left you alone for, what, five minutes?"

Alex grinned and said, "I've found another site for Wallace's bones."

"Well, what are you waiting for? Lead on, Macduff," Diana said, motioning him back down the path they'd come up.

A few minutes later, the trio were standing around the rock Stephen had designated as the marker for Wallace's bones. Jane asked, "How are we going to move this rock, especially since it's so close to the trail? People will see us."

"The trail we came up was pretty deserted, but if someone does come along, I figure Diana can come up with a spell to hide us. Remember, she did it in Spain," Alex said. "Or Wallace and his friends can frighten any unwanted people away."

Diana looked up and down the trail and said, "Let me know if anybody comes before my spell can take effect." She then pulled her fire onyx talisman from her pouch, stretched out her arms, and chanted,

> *"Blind from sight*
> *Hidden from light.*
> *I summon now the mists.*
> *Let us walk enshrouded*
> *Hidden from their sight."*

Within seconds, a dense fog started swirling around their feet, growing until Alex could no longer see the path a few feet away. Then Diana pointed her arms at the boulder and chanted,

> *"Stone from the mountain*
> *Stone from the cave*
> *I place a bind*
> *Upon this rock*
> *Listen to me and abide*
> *Move this rock aside."*

A few moments later, the boulder began to wobble. Diana repeated the spell, stopping when the boulder shook free from its resting place for the last seven centuries and toppled.

Alex looked back and saw Stephen making the sign of the cross and grumbling, "She's a witch. This is blasphemy."

Seeing the Irishman striding toward Diana, Alex jumped between the two with his arms spread out and shouted, "Stop! Do you want to help Sir William or not?"

Wallace put his hand on Stephen. "It's all right. I wouldn't be the man I am today if it weren't for her."

Not seeing what was happening, Diana asked, "What's going on now?"

"One of the spirits was upset with what you were doing, so I had to stop him. Go ahead and finish your spells."

Diana closed her eyes and held her arms in front of her, palms upward, and chanted,

> *"Stone from the mountain*
> *Dirt from the land*
> *Move rock and dirt aside*
> *And show the bones to me."*

Alex watched as chunks of grass and dirt started piling up in a circle around where the boulder had been minutes earlier. Diana kept chanting the spell until she saw a dirty canvas bag appear.

As soon as she stopped, everyone moved to the edge of the hole and looked down. Alex jumped in, picked up the bag, and untied the leather string. He reached in and removed one item, looking up with a big grin. A moment later, Wallace's left arm and torso started growing on his ghostly body.

CHAPTER 33
THEY SEEK HIM THERE

Diana looked up and asked, "Did it help?"

Alex stopped tucking Wallace's bones in his pack, grabbed her hand, stuck his other hand out for Jane, and said, "Sorry. I forgot you can't see them."

The three watched with smiles as Wallace and his friends danced a herky-jerky since Wallace had only one leg. It was some time before the ghosts stopped dancing, and Wallace said, "This wouldn't have been possible without yer help. Now, if ye'll forgive me, I'll take yer leave." Wallace and his friends then disappeared into the thick fog swirling around the area.

Jane broke the ensuing silence by saying, "We need to clean this mess up because the mist is starting to dissipate."

As if to reinforce her point, a disembodied voice said, "Where did this blasted fog come from? It's a sunny day."

All three began shoving the loose dirt and rocks back into the hole, then hurried back to the path and up to the monument.

When they were heading back to the car, Alex asked, "Since you're the history buff, Diana, remind me where the English took Wallace's last quarter."

"Perth. But I don't see how we'll ever get there. You'll be going home soon, and my mom's watching me like a hawk. It was lucky I got to come today."

"Why don't we go into town, get some lunch, and discuss how to find his last quarter?" Alex suggested.

Jane tucked her arm through Alex's and said, "That sounds good."

But both girls were silent all through lunch. When they finished, Alex said, "I thought we were going to talk about how to find Wallace's last quarter. What's going on? Did I say something wrong?"

"Na. It's jest that we're feeling a little down, seeing how our time together is ending," Jane replied.

"But we were just talking about finding Wallace's last quarter," Alex argued. "I'm not sure how far Perth is, but maybe we could go there now and look around."

A reflected movement in the window caught Alex's attention and put his senses on high alert. He reflexively reached down to touch the ankh and felt it thumping against his chest. "We've got to get out of here – now," he said, pushing back his chair and heading for the door.

Diana protested, "Wait a minute. You were just talking about wanting to go to Perth. Now you're hightailing it out of here. What's going on?" she asked, scrambling after him.

By the time Diana caught up, Alex was already speed-walking towards the train station, where Jane had parked the car. "Are you ever going to tell us what your hurry is?" she asked.

Without slowing, he replied over his shoulder, "I think someone's following us."

Diana looked to Jane for her thoughts but only got a shrug in return.

The three made their way through downtown Stirling, occasionally stopping in front of a store window long enough for Alex to check if someone was following. After several stops without seeing anything, he was starting to think he was just being paranoid when he saw a man slip into an alleyway across the street.

Alex hesitated, then turned and stared at the spot. It seemed to goad his follower into action as the man stepped out and walked quickly towards him. Recognizing him as the English gentleman he'd seen in London, Alex shouted, "Run."

Diana started to protest, but Jane grabbed her arm and ran after him.

Alex led them a short distance down Murray Place before following the ankh's guidance to turn onto Station Road. Seeing the train station ahead, he ran harder, hoping his pursuer wouldn't follow him into the open. He felt something whizz by his ear an instant before he heard a car's windshield shattering. Alex hesitated for only a second before he followed the ankh's signal to turn left. "Hurry," he yelled. "He just took a shot at us."

Knowing he needed to focus, he pushed worries about his pursuer out of his mind and concentrated on following the ankh's tugs that set him zig-zagging along the sidewalk. He heard more bullets whizzing by and saw bits of concrete and asphalt fly around him several times. With his chest heaving and legs feeling like lead weights, Alex knew he wouldn't last much longer. Seeing a construction site ahead, he led Diana and Jane onto the lot and ducked behind a pile of bricks as another bullet ricocheted off. Alex grabbed a loose brick and chucked it towards the sound of running feet. He heard a cry of pain, and an instant later, the running sound stopped.

"What's going on?" Jane asked in between gasps for air.

"That guy I ran into in the London Museum is after me," Alex replied.

Diana hesitated, then reached into her daypack, pulled out her selfie stick, and mounted her phone.

"What are you doing?" Alex asked. "Instead of fooling around with your phone, we've got to figure out a way to distract him so you two can escape."

"I'm trying to get a picture of where he is and what he's doing," Diana replied as she stuck the phone beyond the bricks. A bullet immediately blasted through it, causing her to groan, "Not another one."

"I'm sorry I got you guys into this new mess," Alex said. "I should have left you back there and led him away. But now that we're here, I'd advise you to grab some of these bricks and be ready to throw them."

Diana shook her head and said, "There's a better way of defending ourselves." She pulled out her talisman and chanted,

> *"Clouds of black, clouds of white.*
> *I summon thee to show thy might.*
> *Bring thy winds and bring thy might,*
> *Hurl these bricks to where I point."*

She jumped up and threw her arms towards where the bullet had come from. Bricks immediately began flying towards their assailant. The first few missed, but Diana threw her arms again at the man, flinging dozens more bricks at him.

Alex poked his head up, saw the Englishman running towards a trackhoe, and hurled a rock at their attacker for good measure, then ducked behind his pile of bricks.

Deborah appeared and said, "You've got to get out of here now. I've tried everything I can to stop him, but I'm not able to move objects very well yet and have run out of options. The longer you stay, the more you endanger Diana and Jane. I learned there's a train leaving in a couple of minutes. If you can get on it, you can get away."

Alex turned to Diana and said, "Keep hurling things at him. I'm going to try and lead him away from you. When you see him leaving, go find the police." He didn't listen to either of the girl's protests. Staying low to the ground, Alex ran behind the construction materials and equipment until he got to the street. Out of the corner of his eye, he saw the attacker following him. He paused for a second at the streetside, took a deep breath, and made a mad dash through the traffic on Goosecroft Road.

He wove through the cars near the entrance, dashed through the open doors, past the ticket machines, and over the footbridge to the far platform where an antique-looking steam engine pulling six old-fashioned passenger cars waited. He jumped into the nearest car just as he heard someone in the distance shouting, "All aboard." A few seconds later, the train started pulling out of the station.

Alex heard his sister beating at the now-closed doors and looked for her. He didn't spot her as his gaze shifted to his attacker, who was pointing a pistol at him. Alex saw a puff of smoke and heard a muffled bang. An instant later, he felt something sting his shoulder.

CHAPTER 34
TIE A KNOT AND HANG ON

Diana watched as Alex lured the assassin away. Hoping to distract their attacker, she conjured a fireball and hurled it at the fleeing man. She didn't hear his cries of pain but knew she'd found her target when flames began licking at the back of their attacker. Diana was conjuring up another fireball when Jane jumped up and ran after the man. She shook the flames out and ran after her friend, not catching up until they were in the middle of the terminal.

In between gasps for air, Diana asked, "Do you see him?"

Jane spotted Alex running down the steps to the far platform and tugged at Diana's sleeve to follow her. But it wasn't until they reached the end of the pedestrian bridge that Diana spotted the Englishman, who was in the process of raising his gun. Her heart sank, figuring the man could not miss at such a close distance. The next instant, though, Alex disappeared.

Diana felt Jane yank her selfie stick out of her hands, then watched as her friend hurled it at the gunman's head. She took great pleasure in seeing the stick clobber the man, sending him to the concrete platform face first.

Spotting a policeman nearby, Diana ran up to him, pointed at the unconscious form of the gunman, and said, "That man has been shooting at my friend and me. You need to arrest him."

The policeman looked at Diana as if she were crazy, then looked over to where she was pointing and saw a man sprawled on the platform with a pistol lying a few feet from his hands. Within minutes, the train station was crawling with police officers.

It was two hours before Jane and Diana gave their last statements and were able to head back to Stormhold. Even though the police had combed the station, they'd found no trace of Alex. He'd just disappeared – again.

Diana looked at Jane and asked, "How are we going to explain this one?"

Jane shook her head and replied, "Our saving grace is that this isn't the first time he's done this type of thing."

Lady Yvaine, Elizabeth, and Sophie were all waiting to meet them at the entrance to the manor and immediately demanded to hear the whole story of what had happened. Jane and Diana took turns trying to explain the events, cutting one another off when the other was close to providing too much information.

After what seemed like an eternity of questions, Lady Yvaine said, "I guess we have to accept the fact that he's disappeared under mysterious circumstances once again."

"I can't say I blame him," Diana said. "If I were him, I'd be freaking out about now because what kid expects a gunman to chase him through the streets of Stirling?"

Her last comment got a short-lived chuckle from Jane. Before she could say anything else, a maid opened the door and introduced Inspector Forrester.

The inspector walked in and looked from one woman to the next before settling his gaze on Elizabeth. "We haven't found any trace of your grandson yet, ma'am. But rest assured. We're doing everything possible to find him. I thought you should know that the man these young ladies took down today was the man I told you about a few months ago. We have finally captured the Quiet Man, aka Richard Cheney."

Elizabeth gasped while Diana and Sophie looked perplexed. Seeing their confusion, the Inspector shared what he'd told Elizabeth in London, then updated them on Scotland Yard's follow-up investigation. He ended by saying, "When we got word this afternoon that someone had tried killing your grandson, it confirmed my thinking that he was after the boy all along. The Parliament member killed last December was an unfortunate accident. I regret to tell you, though, that I still have no idea why he was so intent on getting your grandson, Ms. Adler. But I guarantee you; we will not stop investigating this case until we have an answer.

The inspector turned to where Jane and Diana were sitting on a sofa next to each other and said, "I know it's small consolation, but I have to congratulate these two young women on their capture of Cheney. They have done what Interpol, Scotland Yard, the FBI, and numerous other agencies haven't been able to do. We owe you both a deep debt of gratitude."

CHAPTER 35
THE TAY RIVER EXPRESS

As the train jerked to a start, Alex lost his balance and fell on his wounded shoulder. He cried out in pain and felt a warm, wet liquid trickling down his left arm. He pulled himself onto a nearby wooden bench as the train got up to speed and looked around to see what type of danger he was in. Seeing he was far outside the Stirling station with no sign of pursuit, he sighed in relief, slipped off his pack, and leaned back against the bench to catch his breath.

He didn't relax for long as something felt off. Looking around, he was surprised to see everything inside the train was as old-fashioned as the outside had looked. Even more surprising was there was no broken glass from the gunshot. But neither was the source of his discomfort.

Knowing he had to take care of his well-being before anything else, he dug around in his pack and pulled out some alcohol wipes and bandages. Then, despite being in a public place, he removed his shirt and cleaned the blood oozing down his arm. When he was finally able to see the wound, he sighed in relief that it was only a graze. After letting his skin dry, he applied a large bandage and pulled his shirt back on.

Feeling dizzy, he closed his eyes until his lightheadedness faded. When he thought he could move about without falling, he got up and searched for the conductor. Avoiding looking at the other passengers talking quietly amongst themselves, he rehearsed his lines to explain why he didn't have a ticket. As he passed through car after car, he was surprised at how full they were for such an old, uncomfortable train.

A shiver caused him to notice goosebumps had popped up all over his arms. Surprised that such an old-fashioned train would have air conditioning, he looked around but didn't spot any air vents. His brain was still a little foggy from the shooting, so it took him another minute before it finally dawned on him what the source of his discomfort was – he'd boarded a ghost train.

Alex immediately retreated to his bench, slipped on his pack, and headed for the nearest door, feeling like he needed to get off as soon as possible. He opened the door and was about to jump, but realized that falling several feet at the train's speed was too dangerous. Alex returned to his bench, figuring he'd get out at the next stop.

But the station came and went without the train slowing down. Panic started building inside him, and he decided to ask for help. But he quickly found none of his ghostly companions would look at him. He finally gave up and sat back down, staring out the window at the passing countryside, trying to figure out what to do next.

As the miles went on, Alex became more and more frustrated. The experience was so different from all his other experiences with ghosts that he began wondering if perhaps he was dead. He'd only seen and felt the one wound, but maybe something else had happened to him. A renewed round of shivering put that worry to rest, and despite it not being a warm day outside, he lowered his window to try to warm up.

He stuck his head out the window and instantly regretted the action as he saw a train barreling down the tracks towards them. Out of instinct, he curled up and waited for the crash – but it never happened.

It was several minutes before his heart stopped racing enough that he was able to uncurl. He poked his head out the window again and saw a station come into view. Hoping the train would slow down, Alex grabbed his pack and ran for the door. But they swept past the station so fast that he lost his opportunity.

Alex slumped to the floor, his optimism of getting off fading fast. He was still sitting there when Sadie appeared on his lap. Alex hugged the little dragonet and said, "I've missed you."

The little furry dragon bumped Alex's chin with his head and sent images of a train station flashing through his mind.

He still had difficulty understanding Sadie, but he'd been around her enough times to know that the images were her way of communicating, and she was telling him to get off the train. Alex sidled over to the door and looked out. Buildings were flashing by, but he could see a station fast approaching. The images were coming faster and faster into his head as he saw the edge of the station flash by. Figuring it was now or never, he took a deep breath and jumped.

He landed awkwardly, tumbled, and rolled into a station assistant. By the time he'd righted himself, his ghostly ride had left the station.

The man looked around and asked, "Where did you come from?"

"I just got off the train from Stirling. Where am I?"

The man gave Alex a funny look and pointed at a sign that said Perth. The conductor looked around and said, "That train isn't due for two more hours. Are ye feeling all right? Can I call someone for ye?"

"I'm fine," Alex replied. "It's just been a long day and a bizarre ride on an old-fashioned steam engine train."

The man pushed his cap back and let out a long whistle. "Lad, that sounds like ye're describing the Tay River ghost train. I've heard people say they've seen it, but I've never met anybody who said they'd been on it. If what ye say is true, it's lucky ye got off when you did. Otherwise, ye'd have wound up at the bottom of the river with all those other lost souls."

"What are you talking about?" Alex asked.

"The Tay River Bridge disaster. In the late 1800s, they built a bridge across the Tay River to Dundee. At the time, it was the longest bridge in the world. They considered it such a marvelous engineering feat that they knighted the designer. But on a cold December day, a year and a half after it opened, gale-force winds howled up the river at a right angle to the bridge. It was dark, so nobody knew exactly what happened, but at some point, the bridge collapsed into the river. A train carrying dozens of people crossed the bridge soon after and fell into the river. Everyone died. People say they see the train now and then, riding the tracks until it once again crashes into the River Tay. If you were riding it just now, then thank your lucky stars you got out when you did because there are no stations between here and the Tay River."

CHAPTER 36
SCONE ABBEY

Alex had been in a lot of scrapes before, but nearly drowning with a trainload of ghosts was the most bizarre situation yet. He thanked the attendant, then limped to a nearby bench to figure out what to do next. He'd been there for only a few seconds when Sadie appeared at his feet, then jumped into his lap and curled up. Alex began absent-mindedly stroking the dragonet's fur, wondering what he should do next. His first thought was to head back into the station and take the next train back to Stirling, where Jane and Diana would hopefully be waiting for him. But something nagged at him to stay.

He didn't get to rest long before one of the station attendants shooed him out, telling him he couldn't have cats inside. Since he had a couple of hours before the next train to Stirling, he got up, wandered down to the River Tay, and watched a man fly up and down the river on a jet ski. Just as the man disappeared around the river's bend, a group of motorcyclists roared by, catching his attention. He followed them over the bridge and was climbing the hill on the far side before he realized the ankh was tugging at him to continue.

Reluctantly following his necklace's desire, he kept hoping it would grow quiet, but the city limits were soon far behind, and still, the ankh urged him onward. At first, he wasn't too worried about where he was going, but as time passed and he got further into the countryside, he began wondering if there was some mistake. After over an hour of walking, he came upon a fancy iron and brick entrance to Scone Palace with a road that disappeared into a well-groomed park. Following the ankh's guidance, he turned in.

The driveway seemed to go on forever, but the long-range views were so gorgeous that it wasn't until fifteen minutes later that he realized he'd missed the opportunity to turn back and catch the next train to Stirling. He had no time to worry about it, though, as Wallace, Kerly, and Stephen apparated nearby.

"How did ye know to come here?" Wallace asked.

Alex whirled so fast that he nearly fell. "I didn't. I accidentally jumped onto a train in Stirling and got off in Perth. I was waiting for the next train back but went for a walk and ended up here." He looked around at the park-like setting and asked, "What's so important about here?"

"A little more than a mile up this road is a place once called Scone Abbey," Wallace replied. "When I was alive, they used to crown Scottish kings there on the Stone of Destiny. It was one of the most important locations in Scotland and might be a good place to search for the rest of my body parts."

"Well, since you know where you're going, lead on."

Ten minutes later, they finally arrived at the entrance. After paying for his ticket, Alex followed the three ghosts up the road, but had only gone a short distance when Sir William suddenly grew agitated, clapped his hands to his head, and cried out.

"What's wrong?" Alex asked.

Wallace pointed to a huge building and wailed, "That's not the Abbey. What have they done with my bones?"

Before Alex could calm him down, a deep voice behind them said, "William, my boy. I'm so glad to see ye again. It's been far too long."

Wallace turned and embraced the newcomer. Soon, all four ghosts were slapping backs and talking excitedly. It was some time before the ghosts quieted down, and the newcomer was able to say, "William, aren't ye going to introduce me to yer friend?"

"I apologize," Wallace said. "Alex Scire, this is my good friend, William Lamberton, Bishop of St. Andrews. He was one of my first appointees when I became Guardian. He was also the first cleric to support me and oppose Edward openly. Even when I was no longer Scotland's leader, we worked together on diplomatic missions to try to enlist France's aid for our country's war with England."

Bishop Lamberton bowed and said, "I'm pleased to meet ye, lad."

"I'm surprised to find ye're still here on Earth, Bishop," Wallace said. "Surely ye didn't have some deep dark secret that has kept ye here as punishment."

"I had nothing better to do than wait here until ye pulled yourself together," Lamberton replied. When no one laughed at his joke, he cleared his throat and added, "After the English placed your left leg on display, I waited until they weren't looking, then took it down and buried your remains here."

"Ye know where my bones are?" cried Wallace.

"They're close by, but how did ye know to come here? I've been waiting for some sign of ye but had no idea ye were coming until ye showed up on my doorstep."

Wallace pointed to Alex and said, "He led us here. He and his friends have been helping me find my body parts."

Bishop Lamberton looked hard at Alex for a moment as if trying to divine some secret information. At last, he said, "I've heard about ye."

Alex felt uncomfortable under the bishop's stare and blurted out, "I don't see how. I haven't been in Scotland that long and hardly know anybody."

The bishop shook his head and said, "I can't remember where I've heard of ye, but it doesn't matter. So, William, my boy, are ye ready to recover yer bones?"

"More than ready. Where am I?" Wallace asked.

"I buried yer leg in the old cemetery right over there," Lamberton said, pointing to a stone wall. "Come, I'll show ye."

The bishop led them past a small stone chapel with pointed turrets at each corner, then across a large paved road to an ancient cemetery. He took them almost all the way to the back before he stopped and pointed down to a small unmarked stone sitting flat on the ground. It was nearly covered by moss and grass and lay next to an elaborate headstone with the occupant's coat of arms and skull and crossbones at the bottom. "There they are."

"It's not much to look at," Wallace said. "Are ye sure they're still there?"

"There's only one way to find out," Lamberton replied. "We'll have to dig up yer bones."

Alex groaned, "Not another grave robbing." When all the ghosts looked at him, he said, "At least let's wait till night so no one sees us. Plus, if you need my help, I have to hide until they shut the place down."

"I've got a perfect spot nearby," Lamberton said. He led them back out of the cemetery and to a thick grove of trees nearby. "If ye crawl back into that thicket, ye can wait there. No one will find ye."

"Since I don't have my friend with me for magic, can you scrounge up a shovel so I can dig tonight?" Alex asked.

"Amazing," Lamberton said. "No fuss about a little clandestine work. I like the lad, William."

"Aye. He's a rare find. How about we search for that shovel while it's still light."

"Oh, and could you also rustle up some food and water for me?" Alex asked before crawling underneath some bushes. As soon as the ghosts had left, he lay down and fell asleep. The next thing he knew, a cold hand was shaking him.

It took him a couple of minutes before he was awake enough to sit up and see that darkness had fallen over the grounds. He gobbled down the food they'd brought and, when finished, followed them into the graveyard. With a legion of curious ghosts looking on, he quickly uncovered Wallace's remaining quarter.

As he shoved the last of the bones into his pack, he heard Wallace cry out in joy. He looked up and saw the former Guardian of Scotland caressing his ghostly body in obvious enjoyment of being in one piece again.

When Wallace had finished inspecting his reassembled body, he shuddered in happiness, then turned to Kerly and Stephen and hugged them. When he got to Bishop Lamberton, he knelt and asked, "Will ye give me a final blessing before I cross over?"

The bishop said a quiet prayer, made the sign of the cross, then placed his hand on Wallace's shoulder and said, "Go in peace."

Alex kept his gaze on Wallace, thinking his moving on would be even more impressive than others he'd seen since there'd been a blessing. But as the seconds turned to minutes and nothing happened, all the spirits started getting restless. Wallace, who'd remained kneeling, furtively looked around to see if anything had changed. Finally, he looked up and said, "I don't understand. Why am I still here?"

"Just because a person believes they're ready, doesn't mean they don't have unfinished business. What else might be holding you back?" Alex asked.

"I don't know. I'm whole once again, and except for freeing Scotland from England's yoke, I don't have any other business left on Earth," Wallace replied.

"There's got to be something.

"I don't know. Unless it's…."

Alex stepped closer to Wallace. "Unless what?"

Wallace waved off the question. "It's silly, but it couldn't be what I'm thinking." Seeing everyone looking at him expectantly, he said, "I still feel guilty about losing the Stone of Destiny to that thief, Edward."

Lamberton chuckled, "It's a good thing I didn't wait for ye to protect it. I had a duplicate made and hid it a year before the English stole it. If you think that's what's holding you back, then we've got a wee bit of a journey to make. Follow me," the bishop said before disappearing.

The other ghosts stayed. A few seconds later, Lamberton reappeared and asked, "Why aren't ye coming?"

"Master Alex here started this quest and has gotten me this far," Wallace said. "I've promised to protect him and can't leave him here alone. I want him to come with us wherever we go."

"It's about a hundred miles north of here, and he can't walk all that way," Lamberton said.

Kerly coughed to get everyone's attention. "We can fly him there, though."

CHAPTER 37
A LITTLE HELP FROM MY FRIENDS

Bishop Lamberton's eyes grew wide. "Aye, that would work, but I've never done anything like it. I suppose we can always set down and rest if we get tired."

"Are you guys really able to fly me long distances?" Alex asked. "Nothing against you, but I don't want to end up in your situation quite yet."

"We'll be fine as long as ye're not afraid of heights," Kerly said. "We'll need to fly high enough so no one will see a boy flying through the air without visible means of support."

Alex grinned ruefully. "I guess not. Well, let's get this over with. Let me tighten up my pack straps, though, because I don't want to drop Sir William's bones after all we've been through to get them."

Just as Kerly grabbed his left arm, Alex said, "Hold on. I just realized we need to go to Stirling first and get my friends. I don't know what we'll be facing, and I'd feel a lot more comfortable with them coming."

Lamberton grabbed Alex's other arm, then nodded at Kerly. The two launched into the air, did a half-left turn, and headed southwest, with Wallace and Stephen following them.

The speed at which they launched into the air caught Alex by surprise. But it quickly became the least of his worries. The cold from the spirits, combined with the wind and higher elevations, soon caused his teeth to start chattering. The wind whipping into his eyes was yet another discomfort. He experimented with the best way to hold his head and learned that if he looked straight down, the brim of his Tilley shielded his eyes, and he could keep them open to see what was below. The problem with that idea, though, was how high they were. He'd never understood Diana's fear of heights – until he looked to the ground several thousand feet below him. Knowing he had no parachute or anything else to keep him from falling to his death, he reflexively jerked, causing Lamberton to lose his grip. For what seemed like an eternity but was just a couple of seconds, Alex flew with one arm, flapping wildly until the bishop caught his arm and steadied him.

When he'd finally overcome his nervousness, he began looking around. Except for the lights of Edinburgh off to his left, the countryside was dark, making it impossible to see anything on the ground. He eventually closed his eyes and gave in to the sensation of flying like Superman.

It was long after midnight when they finally approached Stormhold. Only then did Alex realize he didn't know where Diana's room was and had his wingmen fly him slowly around the manor house. They had almost made one complete loop when he heard windows opening above him and Jane calling out, "What are ye doing out there? Get in here, but be quiet about it."

His ghostly companions lifted him to the open window, where he stepped onto the windowsill and into the room. When he was safely on the floor, he turned to Kerly and said, "Give me a while. I'll let you know when we're ready. Besides, it looks like you could use a rest."

"Aye, laddie, that I could," Kerly said before disappearing.

Alex shut the window and turned back to Jane. "Do you have a blanket I could use? I'm freezing."

"Where have ye been?" Jane asked as she went over to her wardrobe, pulled out a down comforter, and wrapped it around Alex. "The police have been looking for ye everywhere."

"It's a long story, but the short version is I accidentally hopped onto a train of ghosts, got out in Perth, went to Scone Palace, and helped find Wallace's left leg, but he still hasn't moved on. So, we're heading north to where a new ghost said he hid the Stone of Destiny. I thought you and Diana could help, so we came here. And by the way, thanks for saving my life today yet again."

"Ye shouldn't get so careless with it. Ye only get one," Jane said. "Now stay here, and I'll get Diana. I doubt if she went to sleep as she's been worried sick about ye."

"Hey, could you bring me some food? I only had a little bit to eat in Scone. And we'll probably need some supplies because I don't know how long we'll be gone."

Jane nodded, then did a double take. "Are those blood stains on yer shirt?"

"It's nothing," Alex replied. "Just a graze. Can you please get Diana now because I don't want to be here when the sun comes up?"

"That can wait. I won't have ye dying on me after all I've done bringing ye back to life. Let me look at it." She came close and said, "Lift your shirt."

Alex was a little embarrassed but did as she asked.

She gently removed his hasty bandage and looked at the wound. "Well, it could be worse. I'll have Diana get the provisions, but while I'm gone, I want ye to go to my bathroom and clean it the best ye can. When I return, I'll do a final cleaning and re-bandage it, and then ye can tell us more of what happened."

She was gone longer than expected, but when she finally opened the door, she had Diana and a couple of stuffed packs. "Okay, now start talking and give us the long version."

In between bites of sandwiches Jane had brought, Alex told the girls everything that had happened since he'd left them. When he finished, he asked, "So, are you willing to come with me to help Sir William move on?"

"Do you see the bags? They aren't just for you. But I'm curious. How are we going to get to wherever we're going?" Diana asked.

Alex slipped his shirt back over his head, wincing a little as he did so, and didn't immediately answer.

"Well?" Diana asked.

"Uh…, well…, uh…, we're going to fly," Alex replied.

"What do you mean we're going to fly?" Diana asked.

"How do you think I got back here so quickly? A couple of the ghosts flew me here. Once you get used to it, it'll be fun, but they'll be flying fairly high, so no one will see us." He looked at Jane and said, "That's the main reason I was so cold when I arrived. Which means both of you will need to dress warmly."

"I'm not surprised," Jane said, "which is why I brought ye a coat and gloves. I've also left notes for yer grandmother and Lady Yvaine saying that ye're alive and we'll be back as soon as possible. I need to brush my hair, but I'll be ready in just a minute."

"I wouldn't worry about your hair. It'll be a waste of time putting it up. Besides, I like it natural looking," Alex said.

Jane blushed. "That seems a little two-faced. Ye usually have yer hair in braids."

"Yeah, but mine's a cultural thing."

"And mine isn't?" Jane ran the brush through her thick hair a few times, then quickly put it into a braid. She turned around, looked at the job she'd done in the mirror, and grimaced. She was about to redo it when Alex said, "It won't help. Besides, we're in a hurry. We have to get this thing done and get back before we get into more trouble."

"Do you have any idea where we're going?" Diana asked.

"No, but I'll ask them when they come get us. A word of caution – when you're up there, relax and don't wiggle. Also, you might want to close your eyes until you get used to it to the feeling. And don't look straight ahead. They go pretty fast and the wind will hurt your eyes. Last chance to back out before I call them."

Jane answered by stepping over to the window and opening it. "Call them," she said.

Wallace was hovering nearby and immediately flew into the room. "We're ready," Alex said.

"Good. I brought a few more men with me. Since it's a long ride north, I figure we'll have to take a few breaks to rest and switch out spirits to balance the workload."

"Well, send the first two in then." Alex turned to the girls and asked, "Who wants to go first?"

To his surprise, Diana stepped forward. "Let's get this over with."

"Remember to relax," Alex said. "And it might help to keep your eyes closed."

"Are you kidding? This is my chance to be Supergirl," Diana replied. "And I'm not about to miss out on that." She pulled out what appeared to be a new cell phone and was texting something when Bishop Lamberton and Wallace grabbed her arms and yanked her out of the window.

Alex heard Diana shriek but didn't give it any thought as he assumed it was from the ghosts whisking her out by surprise.

Kerly and Stephen gripped Jane's arms and flew her out next. Two spirits Alex hadn't seen before grabbed his arms and were passing through the window when the door opened behind him. He turned and saw Sophie rushing into Jane's room. Luckily, he only heard the screams and shouts for a few seconds before he was out of earshot.

CHAPTER 38
LOCH NESS

Seeing her cell phone fluttering to the ground, Diana wondered how she'd explain to her mom that she'd need yet another smartphone, knowing the one she'd just lost was only a few hours old. Grimacing at the thought of what her mother would say, she forgot Alex's warnings and looked down. When she did, she screamed and closed her eyes. She thought she heard someone calling her name, but couldn't hear what they were saying because of the wind whistling around her.

After several minutes, she worked up the courage to open one eye but only saw an occasional pinprick of light on the ground far below. Then, remembering how she'd bragged about being Supergirl in front of Jane and Alex, she chided herself for being scared and slowly opened her other eye. Wanting to make sure she wasn't alone, she turned her head to one side and saw Alex flying parallel to her about ten feet away.

"You okay?" he shouted.

"I am now," Diana shouted back. "But I fear I'm dreaming all this and will wake up soon."

She could see Alex grinning and barely heard his reply. "Nope. You're really flying. It's great, huh?"

Diana was about to retort when she felt something bubbling up inside. It built until she couldn't help herself and screamed wildly in the air, "Wheee!"

Time soon lost all meaning as they flew on through the night. She didn't know where they were going but was pretty sure they were heading north, as there were so few lights. Occasionally, the moon broke through the clouds, and she'd get an occasional glimpse of mountain peaks in the distance.

About an hour and a half into the trip, she felt their speed slowing, followed by a decrease in altitude. A few minutes later, she alighted on a grassy slope, broken only by scattered rocks and a few trees. She could see Alex standing a few feet away and asked, "Is anything wrong?"

"Nope. The spirits were tired and needed a break. They've already disappeared, so it's just the three of us for a while. I'm freezing. Do you mind whipping up one of your fires?"

After Jane and Alex had gathered firewood, Diana started a small fire with her magic, but it had only been going for a few minutes when it started raining. They ran to a nearby Scotch pine, ducked under its branches, and watched the fire die out.

Diana started talking animatedly about the flight but soon noticed that Alex wasn't saying anything. "Are you all right?" she asked.

"I'm fine. I'm just exhausted from everything that's happened today," he replied.

"Diana sat on the ground with her back against the tree and said, "Sit down next to me. We can share some heat until this storm passes, and I can build a fire out in the open. You too, Jane. We need as much heat as possible."

She didn't know how long it rained as she fell asleep as soon as Alex sat beside her. Before she knew it, the sky was starting to lighten in the east. She tried sitting up, but Alex's head was on her shoulder, pinning her down.

Her movement woke him, causing him to jump up and say, "I'm sorry. I didn't mean to use you as a pillow."

"Relax. All of us needed some rest," Jane said. Standing in the middle of the clearing, she asked, "How soon do ye think yer spirit friends will be here?"

Alex blinked a few times and rubbed the sleepers out of his eyes. When he could focus, he said, "They're waiting for us."

"Ye take it easy for a bit," Jane said. "Wallace has waited for centuries; he can wait a little longer. Right now, we're going to get a fire going and warm ye up, then have some breakfast."

As soon as they'd finished, Diana jumped up and said, "I'm ready. Let's get going."

They packed up and were soon on their way. Diana enjoyed the second leg more than the first because she was more relaxed, and the dawn's early light allowed her to see more of the landscape far below. It wasn't long until a ribbon of dark blue water appeared on the northern horizon. They soon crossed over the narrow lake and landed a few hundred yards away from some crumbling castle ruins overlooking the water.

Diana gazed up and down the lake, taking deep breaths of the clean, cool air. Without taking her eyes off the scenery, she asked, "Where are we? All the Scottish lakes look the same to me – narrow, with high hills on both sides."

"This is Urquhart Castle on the north shore of Loch Ness," Jane said. "I used to play around these ruins when I was a kid. Centuries ago, though, it was one of the most important castles in Scotland." She turned to Alex and asked, "The real question is, why are we here."

239

CHAPTER 39
ONE THORN OF EXPERIENCE

Making sure his glamour spell was still in place, Chrysophylax dipped a shoulder and turned to make a loop around the lake while sending his thoughts out, *"Apalāla, are you there?"*

"You don't need to shout. What do you want?" Apalāla replied.

"I need to ask you for a favor, but I prefer to talk on one of the surrounding hills as I'm not keen on diving into those dark, frigid waters you call home."

"Which is precisely why I live down here. No human or dragon, until now, has ever bothered me. It's a perfect hiding place."

Chrysophylax grumbled at the thought of going into the cold waters but steeled himself and dove. He entered with nary a splash and plunged several hundred feet deep. It wasn't hard to find the cave entrance, for all he had to do was track Apalāla's thoughts. He popped up inside her lair tucked under one of the southern hills surrounding the lake and shook the water from his hide. Then he strode across the cavern towards where an Elasmosaurus-like creature, half again as big as he was, lay stretched out on the stone floor.

At his entrance, Apalāla raised her head and said, *"What brings you here? I haven't had any visitors for hundreds of Earth years."*

"I wanted to tell you that I believe a human is on his way here and to ask you to help him," Chrysophylax said.

"Why should I care about one lowly human?"

"Remember when many of our kind came to Earth centuries ago to find my mother?" Chrysophylax asked. *"They searched for years, to no avail, and eventually gave up. I'm not sure how he did it, but the boy I'm expecting found my mother and freed her from a space-time vortex. He also managed to restore her ka after another human had cut out her heart stone."*

"That's impossible!" Apalāla said. Despite her desire to separate herself from human and dragon affairs, she rose to her feet, leaned in, and asked, *How'd he do it?"*

"I'm embarrassed to share my mother's explanation, because it sounds like religious hoodoo."

"Go on. Your story intrigues me."

"She said that he poured holy water over her wounds, including her heart stone."

"Your mother is no fool, but that makes no sense. But that's neither here nor there. If you've already found Abraxas, why are you here?"

"Finding her was an unexpected benefit to my main mission. I originally came to Earth to help my Uncle Nabu with a plan he'd devised to find and bring all the Maqlû back to Berellus."

Apalāla cut in. *"I always liked your uncle. He was one of the few dragons on the high council who said the humans weren't ready for us to expand here. But I still don't understand how that affects me."*

"I'm getting to that," Chrysophylax said. *"Nabu was planning on using an Irkallan device to manipulate one of the humans to find and retrieve the Maqlû when he suddenly lost control of it. Unfortunately, his backup plan, whatever it was, also failed at about the same time, so he sent me to investigate a couple of years ago. I discovered that his device, an ankh, had fallen into the hands of the wrong person – the boy I've told you about."*

"I'm not sure I want to hear anymore. What's this person like? Is he like Gilgamesh and his bunch – running amok over the world, trying to gain power?"

If dragons could grin, Chrysophylax would have had one that split his face. *"Quite the contrary. As far as I know, the boy has already found and destroyed two of the Maqlû because he thinks they're evil and corrupt people."*

"I'm growing more interested in this person," Apalāla said. *"But why would he be coming here?"*

"I don't know if he is, but he was over 100 miles south of here yesterday afternoon. I figure that since there are only a few dragons still here on earth, and each of you has chosen to live near one of the Maqlû, it can't be a coincidence that he's so close. I would guess he'll be here sometime in the next few days. If I'm right, he'll probably need the help of someone who knows the area and everything that goes on around here, which leads me to you."

"I still don't understand why I should help one of their kind," Apalāla said. *"The ungrateful wretches have done nothing but ignore our advice or hunt us down."*

"Yet, you've stayed here," Chrysophylax said. *"And despite your obvious disdain for their species, which I sympathize with, I believe you still have concern for them. Look, all I'm asking you to do is keep an eye out for him and help him as best you can. Oh, and I should warn you about two other things. One, he can talk to us, just like some of the humanoids on Irkalla could."*

"Interesting. And the second thing I should know about him?"

Chrysophylax cleared his throat and said, *"Usually, I can track where he is because he has an unusual aura. But he can also talk to the dead. And when he's with them, he often disappears from my sight."*

"Why would he hang around with the dead?"

"That's not the right question. I believe you should have asked why the dead hang around him. To the best of my knowledge, it's because he helps them, just like he helped my mother."

"Even more interesting," Apalāla said.

CHAPTER 40
THE CHINTAMANI

Bishop Lamberton motioned towards the ancient castle and said, "Come this way."

The ghosts headed off, but Alex didn't follow as he caught a glimpse of a large greyish-green creature briefly surfacing before diving back into the water. As he watched the ripples spread across the lake, he thought he felt something tickling his brain. Thinking he was imagining it, he shoved the thought aside but jumped when Jane cried out.

"Are you all right?" Diana asked.

Jane ignored the question and turned towards Alex. "What was that?"

He pretended to be ignorant and looked away. "I don't know what you mean," he said.

"Yes, ye do. It felt like someone was inside my mind messing with it," Jane said.

Alex thought about continuing to profess his ignorance but knew Jane would see through him. "I'm not sure," he replied.

Jane stepped closer. "I can tell that ye have an idea what it might be, though."

"Maybe, but it's a crazy idea…." He was grateful not to have to explain more as he saw Wallace motioning for them. "Come on," he said. "The ghosts are heading towards that crumbling tower."

When they arrived at the tower, Bishop Lamberton pointed to the base and said, "Figuring the English would take everything of value, I stole the Stone of Destiny and hid it here."

"But Diana said that the Stone of Destiny used to sit inside the throne in Westminster Abbey and is now mostly in Edinburgh Castle," Alex said as Jane and Diana linked arms so they could hear what was said.

"That's what people are supposed to believe," Lamberton replied. "I found another stone at the bottom of a privy and had some men carve it to look like the original. Then I swapped the two. So, for the last seven centuries, all the English kings and queens who have sat on their Coronation Chair have sat on a completely different type of throne – if you know what I mean."

"Ye didn't?" Wallace said. "Why ye old scoundrel, I didn't think ye had it in ye."

"You keep mentioning this Stone of Destiny. What is it?" Alex asked.

"The Stone of Scone, or as some call it, the Stone of Destiny, is a symbol of Scottish national pride, but it has religious and political significance as well," Diana said. "For instance, legend has it that it was Jacob's pillow." Seeing the puzzled look on Alex's face, she added, "You know, the Old Testament character Jacob. He tricked his older and stronger brother out of his birthright and riches but had to leave home fearing for his life. One night, he slept on the stone out in the desert and wrestled with an angel all night. In the morning, the angel renamed him Israel. Supposedly, the stone made its way to Ireland, where St. Patrick blessed it. Then, it came to Scotland, where they crowned Scottish kings on it for centuries."

"I'm glad ye saved the stone from the English, but how's that going to help me move on?" Wallace asked.

"Since ye gave so much to Scotland, I thought that burying ye next to the Stone would help ye move on," Lamberton said. "Plus, there's something else here. Do you remember the Chintamani – the stone ye used to carry with ye everywhere and attributed your successes to?" the bishop asked.

"I lost that during my invasion of England," Wallace replied.

"Well, one of my men found it right before the Battle of Falkirk. I tried rushing it to ye, but it was too late. I never managed to give it to ye after that debacle, so I hid it underneath the stone when we placed it here."

Alex heard Jane and Diana gasp and saw Wallace lift Lamberton into the air. Unsure what everyone was so excited about, he asked, "What's the Chintamani?"

"That's one of the Maqlû and is supposed to be one of the two best-kept secrets in our order," Jane said. "I can't believe ye found it."

"Hey, no one's found anything," Alex replied. "Remember, all Bishop Lamberton said was that he buried it here underneath the Stone of Destiny. There's a big difference."

"All this is starting to make sense," Jane said. "Otherwise, why else would we be out in the middle of nowhere standing in the ruins of a castle?"

"But it can't be here," Diana said. "The Chintamani is one of the most powerful magical objects in the world, as it's supposed to control the earth element. Some people liken it to the Philosopher's Stone, which is why it's supposed to be in some highly protected place that nobody knows where it is except those guarding it."

"Well, it must not be that well protected because Wallace said he used it as a good luck charm before he lost it," Alex said.

"None of this makes sense. Our history says that it's been in our possession for over a millennium, which means Sir William couldn't have had the stone."

"I don't much care about it because all I'm here to do is help him move on," Alex said. "The real question is how we should bury his bones?"

Diana placed her hands on her hips, looking at the base of the tower. After an agonizingly long silence, she said, "I might be able to do this, but I'm not positive."

"What do you mean?" Alex asked.

"Well, you've seen me move dirt and rocks around, light fires, and manipulate wind and water. Essentially, I was asking some of nature's elements to do my bidding. I can do the same thing to dig a hole, and then you could manually insert the bones, but I'm worried about causing the wall to cave in." At last, she turned to Jane and said, "What do you think? Can I do it safely?"

Jane nodded and said, "Jest go easy. If ye have to, move small amounts and test yer way forward."

Diana walked to the corner of the castle, and pulled out her talisman. She then waved everyone back and said, "Now be quiet. I need to concentrate." A moment later, she chanted,

> *"Rocks from the mountain*
> *Dirt from the land*
> *Shift aside*
> *And bring the stone to light."*

Alex jumped when he heard a loud grating noise. He looked around to see where it came from and saw pebbles shaking around the tower's base. Loose dirt started bubbling up as if something was tunneling underneath the building. The soil kept spilling out onto the grass until a hole appeared.

Diana dropped her arms and asked, "Is it there?"

Alex got down on his belly, stuck his arm into the hole, and called out, "I can feel a big stone and…. Wait a minute. There's something else here." He pulled his arm out a moment later and lifted a bag in the air.

Lamberton rushed forward, grabbed the bag from Alex's hands, and pulled out a small gold cross. He rummaged around the bag for a few more seconds before turning it upside down to empty the remaining contents. "It's not here. The Chintamani is gone."

"Where could it have gone?" Wallace asked. "We have to get it back."

"I understand why my friends want it back, but why are you so adamant about it?" Alex asked.

"When I was a young man, the English threw me in jail, where I got so sick that they thought I was as good as dead. So, they threw me onto a garbage heap and let me rot. An old female physician drug me away and nursed me back to health using that stone, which had some other-worldly power emanating from it.

"When I finally recovered, she lent me the stone and told me to always keep it with me. After that, as long as I had it with me, I was incredibly lucky and successful. But, as I said earlier, I lost it during our invasion of England. By then, I'd become too conceited and believed my good fortune was due to my smarts and not the stone. Which is why it cannae fall into the wrong hands.”

Alex heard a car pull into the parking lot above them and said, “We need to get out of here. People are starting to arrive, and we’ll get in trouble if someone catches us here.”

Jane looked at him in surprise. “I can’t believe ye jest said that. Ye, who makes getting into trouble a national pastime, are worried about a little trespassing. The worst that would happen is they make us pay whatever admittance fee they charge and apologize for coming here before opening time.”

“I agree with Alex,” Diana said. “We should bury Sir William’s bones sooner rather than later. That is if he wishes that. Otherwise, why did we come all this way?”

“I don’t think I’m worthy of the honor of being buried with the Stone of Destiny,” Wallace said.

“Who better?” Kerly asked. “Besides, ye’ll not get better views.”

Wallace looked at each of the three spirits, then nodded at Alex. “Aye. It’ll do. Thank ye kindly, everyone.”

Alex knelt and pulled Wallace’s bones out of his pack and placed them in the hole, arranging them so that Wallace’s skull was on top. When he finished, he stepped back, turned to Diana, and asked, “Will you do the honors of filling it in?”

Diana nodded, then sang a spell so softly that Alex couldn’t hear the words. A minute later, it looked like they’d never been there.

Wallace turned towards Kerly and Stephen and hugged them as they went through a second round of farewells. When he got to Bishop Lamberton, he knelt and asked, "Will you give me a final blessing before I move on?"

The bishop said a quiet prayer, made the sign of the cross, then placed his hand on Wallace's shoulder and said, "Go in peace."

Alex kept his gaze on Wallace, thinking his moving on would be even more impressive than the others he'd seen since there'd been a burial and a blessing. As the seconds turned to minutes, and nothing happened, all the ghosts started getting restless. Wallace, who'd remained on his knee with head bowed, started furtively looking around to see if anything had changed.

"I know I haven't seen much of the afterlife, but it can't be this simple. Can it?" Diana asked.

"What are ye getting at?"

"Think about it. We've gone through all this trouble to find Wallace's bones and bury them here. And since the other spirits haven't moved on, it would seem that burying his bones might not be the answer either. I'm sure it will help, but it's not essential."

"Maybe Sir William can't move on until we find the Chintamani and ensure it's safe again," Jane said.

Diana brushed some wind-blown hair off her face and looked at the burial site. "That makes sense, but how would we find it?"

Jane smiled. "Are ye kidding? We have our own bloodhound with us. All we have to do is set Alex loose."

"I'd be willing to help if I could, but I have no idea what this stone you're talking about looks like, much less where it's located," Alex replied.

"Has that ever stopped you before?" Diana asked.

Bishop Lamberton interrupted their discussion, saying, "There's nothing more to do here now, so we're going to take off and rest now. We'll be back soon to take ye to Stirling."

After the spirits disappeared, Diana inserted an arm into Alex's and said, "Let's walk down to the lake and wait until the café opens. I could use a cup of hot chocolate before we return."

"I know just the spot," Jane said. "Follow me. There's a nice boat landing in that little grove of trees down there."

"What about the stone?" Alex asked. "A minute ago, you were talking about finding the Chintamani. Now you're discussing hot chocolate. What's with that?"

Diana smiled and patted Alex on the arm. "We're just giving you time to do your thing. Now, come on. Let's enjoy the time we have before all hell breaks loose."

They reached the spot Jane had mentioned and were about to sit on the grass near the water's edge when Alex felt a bump on his legs. He looked down and saw a green cat. It took him a few seconds before he recognized the little dragon. "Sadie!" he exclaimed. "What are you doing here?"

Images of a huge greyish-green creature flooded his mind. He picked her up and softly said, "Calm down. I can't understand you."

"What's with you and cats?" Diana asked. "They're always rubbing on you in the most bizarre locations."

Jane came closer and peered at Sadie. "Where did ye find a green cat?" she asked.

Not wanting to get into what he was sure would be an uncomfortable discussion on dragons, Alex said, "It's become a thing recently. But instead of cats, we need to focus on the issue at hand. We only have a little while before the ghosts return and take us back to Stirling. And if you think it's important we find this Chintamani stone, then there's only one thing I can think of that might work."

"What's that?" Diana asked.

"Well, it seems like things tend to happen when I'm alone," Alex said. "Which means maybe nothing will happen unless you guys return on your own. That way, you can blame me for everything, and you won't get in as much trouble."

"No, no, no. Don't even think about it," Jane said. "We're not going to leave ye alone. Not with everything that's...."

Alex didn't hear what else she said as Sadie suddenly jumped out of his arms and ran up the hill towards the old castle. He turned to watch her run away and didn't notice the water bubbling below him. An instant later, something wet nudged him so hard that he flew backwards.

He landed with a thud, briefly knocking the air out of him. When he'd caught his breath, he sat up and looked for what had hit him. Two enormous eyes peered back at him while a voice boomed inside his head, "*Are you Alex Scire?*"

CHAPTER 41
NESSIE

Alex gazed in awe at what could only be the famous Loch Ness Monster.

"You're not what I expected," Nessie said.

Keeping an eye on the water dragon, Alex shouted over his shoulder at the girls, "Close your eyes." Hearing Diana about to say something, he cut her off and said, "Please don't argue with me; just do it."

"I've got my eyes closed, but what's happening?" Diana asked.

"We've got a little situation here where you might get hurt if you open your eyes," Alex replied. He heard Diana groan but tuned her out and focused on Nessie. "What…what do you want?"

"My name is Apalāla. I want to understand why you're here."

"We were helping a friend move on in the afterlife and are waiting for him and his friends to take us home."

"So, you're not here for it?"

"Here for what?" Alex replied.

"Maybe Chrysophylax was right." Apalāla shifted around until her body was parallel to the shore. *"Come, I've got something to show you."*

"Wait, you know Chrys? Where is he?"

"Interesting. I've never known a human to give one of us a nickname before."

"I can only hear one side of a conversation, so I'm assuming you're talking to another ghost," Diana said.

"But why do we have to close our eyes? Who are you talking to, Alex?

"I don't think it's a ghost," Jane said, "because I can hear the entire conversation. He's talking with someone named Apalāla about someone else named Chrysophylax."

Diana stomped her foot on the ground. "It's not fair. Why can you guys hear and I can't?"

"I don't know, but whoever he's talking to is communicating with him via telepathy. I want to hear what's going on, so hold off for a minute."

"Who are your companions, and why are they here with you?" Apalāla asked.

"They're good friends who try to stop me from doing stupid stuff, and when that doesn't work, help me out of jams. Would you mind closing your eyes so they can look at you? They looked into Chrys' eyes once and fainted."

"Of course."

When her eyes were closed, Alex turned to the girls and said, "You can open them now, but don't freak out."

Jane and Diana squealed in delight when they saw who Alex had been talking to and came running up. Diana grabbed Alex's arm and swung him around to face her. "Is this Nessie? Do you know her?"

"I've never met her before. Her name is Apalāla. She's a water dragon who's been hiding here in Loch Ness for a while," Alex said.

"Nessie's a dragon? How do you know that? Are you saying you've talked to dragons before? When were you going to tell us?" Diana asked without pausing for answers.

Alex thought back to when Abraxas had adopted him into her weyr and shifted his feet, wondering how to avoid the questions he knew would come if he'd let the girls keep asking them. Knowing he had to tell them something to satisfy their curiosity, he said, "Both of you have seen two dragons before. You don't remember the first one because you looked into Chrys' eyes down in the cenote in Lamanai and blacked out. You've seen the second one quite a few times, but you keep thinking she's a cat. Sadie is a Ryujin dragon that can blend in with her surroundings. But can you hold off with the interrogation for now? Apalāla was talking about something, and we're being rude by interrupting her."

"I'm okay with their questions. It's a good way of finding out who I'm dealing with." Apalāla poked her head towards Jane and sniffed. *"There's something familiar about you. Do I know you?"*

"I used to live across the lake with my three mothers. I'm Jane Roland, and this is my friend Diana Bennet."

Diana stepped closer to the creature the world knew as Nessie and ran her hands along Apalāla's neck. "I wish the girls at school could see me now." Hearing Jane clear her throat, Diana hastily added, "Don't worry. I won't tell anybody about this. But this is so cool."

Alex looked at Jane and said, "Apalāla wants to show me something. What do you think? Do I go with her?"

Jane looked down at the brown water and replied, "I don't know. Loch Ness is very deep and very cold. And once again, we'd be charging off into who knows what."

"Wait. You're not thinking about going down into that lake with her, are you? We'd die," Diana said.

"She's not here so we can take pictures of her," Jane replied. "I'm not sure exactly what she's thinking, but we should assume the worst could happen."

Alex's hand reflexively went up to where the ankh lay. He'd been so distracted by all that had happened that he hadn't noticed it was practically jumping around on his chest. Shaking his head at his folly, he stripped off his jacket and gloves and laid them on the ground. Then he tightened the chin strap on his Tilley, shouldered his pack, and said, "We could argue about this all day and talk ourselves out of whatever is ahead. But I've decided I'm going with her – wherever that is. I'll understand if you don't want to come." Without waiting for a response, he clambered onto the dragon's smooth, wet back, then turned and stretched out a hand. "Are you coming?"

"You're not going to catch me on that thing," Diana said. "We'll freeze to death or, even worse, drown."

Jane pulled off her coat and placed it on the bag of supplies she'd brought for the trip. Then she grabbed Alex's hand and clambered up behind him. "Come on, Diana. Ye didn't want to come at first last night either, but ye've got to admit it was fun. Besides, how many people in the world have seen Nessie, I mean Apalāla, much less get a ride on her."

Despite her misgivings, Diana laid her bag down and took her coat off. Then she crawled up behind Jane. As soon as she was on, Apalāla turned and swam southeast across Loch Ness, heading towards a cliff face on the other side of the lake.

When they were only fifty yards from the cliff face, Alex asked, "Where are we headed, Apalāla, because all I see are steep hillsides and water?"

"I'm sorry. I've been alone for so long that I've forgotten I need to communicate with others. But because you helped my good friend Abraxas, I've decided to follow my instincts. I hope you don't disappoint me as so many other humans have. Now take a deep breath and hold it, because I'm about to dive."

Alex looked over his shoulder and shouted, "I'm sorry, guys, but we're going to get a little wet. So, hold tight and take a big breath."

He could feel Jane's arms tighten around his chest and hoped Diana was doing the same to Jane. When he saw Apalāla's head dip into the water, he took a big gulp of air and held it. He'd swum in lakes high in the Rockies, but they were nothing compared to the frigid waters of Loch Ness.

They dove so deep that he had to pop his ears twice before they leveled out. He eventually opened his eyes to see where they were going, but the water was so dark that he couldn't see more than a few inches ahead. Then, just when he didn't think he could hold his breath any longer, he felt Apalāla ascending. A second later, they broke the surface of the water, but it was so dark that Alex couldn't see his hand in front of his face.

Apalāla came to a halt and said, *"I know you didn't ask for this, but I believe Tiamat has led you here. As such, I will tell you that the next step in your journey lies beyond this chamber. Good luck."* She started sliding into the lake, forcing Alex, Jane, and Diana to jump off and wade onto a rocky shore.

With his teeth chattering, Alex managed to say, "Do…do…do you think you… you can conjure up a li… light, Diana?" Before he could finish his sentence, Diana started chanting her light spell. She was so cold, though, that it took her several attempts before she could speak the words clearly enough to summon a ball of flames.

"You need to look for firewood because I can't sustain these flames for long," Diana said. "And even if I could, they're not hot enough to do us any good."

When she spotted some driftwood, Diana threw the flames on the dried wood. A second later, she had a small crackling fire that gave off a bit of heat and light.

After the three had found enough driftwood to keep the fire going, Jane started pulling off her shirt.

Alex barely managed to squeak, "What are you doing?"

"I'm trying to warm up," Jane said as she wrung the water from her shirt. "Ye two need to do the same thing, or ye'll get hypothermia."

"I can't," Diana said. "He'll see me."

"Ye need to get over yer reservations," Jane said, "Take yer shirt off and dry it."

"I'll go look for some more wood," Alex said. "Let me know when I can come back. Besides, it's so dark in here that all I have to do is step away from the fire, and I can't see you."

Diana waved him away and said, "Don't stand here talking. Go."

Alex went to the furthest edge of the flickering light, gathered another armload of wood that had washed up on the underground shoreline, and called out he was returning. When he got back, Diana and Jane were standing so close to the fire with their shirts out in front of them that they were practically over the flames. He put a few more pieces of wood on, then sat down and took his pants off. He squeezed them out and started rotating in front of the fire, with his wet shirt still on to hide the ankh.

When she'd stopped shivering, Diana asked, "Why did Nessie bring us here?"

"She said something about Tiamat, whoever that is, and our journey lying beyond the chamber, whatever that means," Alex said.

Jane cleared her throat. "My theory is that Apalāla brought us to the Chintamani's hiding place."

"Why would she do that?" Diana asked. "And why here?"

Jane put her shirt back on and rotated so she faced the fire. "Alex has already found and destroyed both the Palantir and the object at the heart of The Fountain of Youth. And I'd bet almost anything he found the Holy Grail." She looked at Alex and said, "Am I right?"

Alex didn't respond.

"I'll take that for a yes," Jane said. "If I'm right, it stands to reason that he's here for the Chintamani."

"That's not true," Alex retorted. "I only came here to help Wallace move on."

"Tomatoes, tomatos," Jane replied. "It doesn't matter why ye came here. The fact is ye're here."

"But why do you think the object is here?" Diana asked.

"I grew up not far from here, raised by three women who were part of the order. I always wondered why they lived so remotely," Jane said. "And now, Alex happens to bring us here. And he happens to run into the most famous creature in all the world – Nessie. It can't be a coincidence."

Alex was still so cold that he didn't feel the breeze blowing over him as Deborah and Wallace apparated.

"I've sent Kerly, Stephen, and the other men to scout out this cave. But what happened?" Wallace asked. "How did ye end up on this side of the lake?"

"We got a ride from one of the locals," Alex replied. "Can you guys move back a little ways? I'll be warmer, and the girls will be more comfortable while they dress."

"Ah, so the ghosts have reappeared," Jane said.

"My sister and Sir William are here. The others have gone to scout this place."

It was several minutes before Stephen returned and said, "Kerly and the others are still scouting this cave, but it's enormous. There's a path winding through a bunch of giant boulders scattered about in the next chamber, but it ends at a rock door we couldn't pass beyond."

Even though they were still damp, Alex pulled his pants back on and was tying his bootlaces when he noticed the ankh was pulling him into the cave. After he finished dressing, he grabbed one of the sticks in the fire and, using it as an improvised torch, asked, "Are you guys ready to get going?"

"That sounds like a ready or not type question," Diana said as she finished buttoning her shirt.

Once Jane had kicked the fire out, Diana conjured a ball of flames and said, "As much as I dread what's ahead, lead on, Alex."

They passed through the first chamber but had to crawl through a short tunnel to reach a much larger chamber. When he was through it, Alex could see the path Stephen had mentioned, weaving in and out of boulders varying in size from a soccer ball to a small room.

As soon as Diana had exited the tunnel, she saw torches lining the walls. She went to the nearest one and used her magical flames to light it. After extinguishing her hand-held flames, she took the torch to a second and third one and lit them. When all three torches were burning steadily, she handed them out then motioned Alex onward.

A hundred yards in, the cave narrowed down, gradually turning into a large tunnel with walls and a floor that were so smooth it looked like someone had carved the tunnel out of the rock.

Noticing a doorway on the far wall, Alex walked over to it and ran his hand along what he thought was the edge. Unable to feel or see any crack that would confirm it was a doorway, he mumbled, "I don't get this. It looks like someone went to a lot of trouble making this place, but it seems to be a dead end. There's got to be something ...." He never finished his sentence as the ankh yanked him to the side a split second before an arrow smashed into the wall where his head had been a second before.

The door suddenly slid open. Without any support, Alex fell through, hitting the stone floor so hard that his torch and burning stick went out. The door closed, sealing him off from the others.

CHAPTER 42
VENGEANCE NEED NOT BE FEARED

King Edward had thought Pythia was being overly cautious when she'd told him to learn about the boy before he did anything. But it had never been in his nature to be patient, as he'd always found it better to act decisively, so his enemies didn't have the chance to grow stronger. Thus, it came as a shock when not only did Wallace show up with his warrior friends to drive him off during his first attempt on Alex's life, but witches had also come to the boy's aid. Despite his frustration with Wallace constantly hovering about the boy, he'd learned his lesson and had been gathering forces ever since, waiting for the right opportunity.

Pythia hadn't been clear what magical object Wallace had lost, but Edward knew, whatever it was, that he was close. Why else would the boy have led him to such a remote place and summoned a primordial beast from the lake? He waited for a minute to see what the boy would do next and was glad he did when he saw Wallace and his men follow Alex into the lake.

Edward called his men out of the woods and motioned for them to follow him. He passed the monster as it swam away without the kids and shuddered, glad he didn't have to deal with it. When he finally popped up inside the cavern, he saw everyone gathered around a fire. Wanting to attack in darkness, he held his men in the water until the kids put out the fire and headed deeper into the cave.

He couldn't believe his luck when the group hit a dead end in the second chamber. Knowing he had them trapped, he motioned for his men to spread out, then watched as the two girls left the group and began exploring the inner cavern.

Edward kept his best archer beside him, pointed out the boy, and watched intently as his archer pulled the string back, pausing only briefly before letting the arrow fly – the signal for his men to attack. He saw the arrow strike just above the boy's head, then caught a brief glimpse of light as a door slid open, and his target dropped out of sight.

Edward wanted to follow, but the battle raging around him made it too dangerous to move from behind the safety of his boulder. He heard the screams of the spirits on both sides dying around him but didn't care about the losses.

The fighting lessened as the casualties quickly mounted. He saw the two girls still wandering around the cavern despite the ghostly battle waging on all around them and knew they weren't a threat. When the fight shifted off to one side of the chamber, he flew towards where he'd seen the boy disappear and threw himself at the door, assuming he would easily pass through it. Instead, he hit hard and rebounded.

Edward studied the door, looking for some mechanism to open it, but found nothing. He then pulled out the sword Pythia had given him and called upon its powers. When the sword started glowing as brightly as the sun, he thrust it into the door. It slid through like a hot knife in butter. After carving out an opening, he flew in.

CHAPTER 43
WITCHES BREW AND
CAULDRON TROUBLE

Alex lay on the cold, damp stone for a few seconds before he groaned and pulled himself up. Unable to see anything in the darkness, he stuck his hands out and felt along the wall, trying to figure out what he'd fallen into. He'd only taken a few steps when a wall torch flickered to life.

Grateful for the light, he looked around the opening, searching for a way to get back to Diana and Jane. When, once again, he couldn't find the slightest crack in the wall, he gave up and turned to see what was beyond. The flickering torch gave off only a tiny amount of light, so he couldn't see very far, but he felt the ankh tugging him forward. Reluctantly he stepped towards the unknown darkness. He'd just reached the edge of the first torch's light when another one flamed to life a few feet away, showing him that he was in another tunnel.

With each step, he could feel the ankh tugging him forward. He finally reached a wooden door where a tiny sliver of light peeked out from the bottom, but just as he was about to grab the latch, a familiar voice came out of the darkness. "It's been a long time since we talked, but I'm happy to see your encounters with the Maqlû weren't chance. What's your plan?"

Despite figuring he wouldn't see her, Alex looked around the dimly lit tunnel. "It's Sibyl, right?" Without waiting for an answer, he asked, "Why are you here?"

"I've been watching your progress and am pleased you've come so far."

"If you knew what I was getting into, why didn't you say something?"

"I didn't know what lay ahead of you. All of this is as new to me as it is to you," Sibyl replied.

"Any advice?" Alex asked.

"I have but one suggestion – embrace your destiny. Right now, you are half-heartedly stumbling into these situations instead of attacking them on your terms."

"That's easy for you to say. Would you be charging into all this if you were in my shoes?" Alex asked.

"I was in your situation a long, long time ago and faced similar challenges. The main difference between us is that you're doing what I could not," Sibyl said.

"What's that?" Alex asked.

"Neutralizing the Maqlû. But I delay you. Go, and remember, you have friends who have shown they're willing to face death to support you. Trust them, and may Marduk always be with you."

Alex hesitated, then grabbed the rusted latch. An electrical shock caused him to jerk his hand away. Knowing his destiny lay in front of him, he waited until the stinging stopped, then tried again. This time, he forced himself to keep his hand on the handle. He was grateful he did, for it was like he completed an electrical circuit. The door silently opened, and Alex stepped in.

He looked around and saw he was inside a small stone room lit by hundreds of candles and filled with a noxious odor. At the back were three women, each with a staff and each standing behind a large black cauldron. All wore floor-length robes with hoods covering their heads. The woman on the left wore a dark red robe, the one in the middle a greenish-brown robe, and the one on the right a yellowish-brown.

The woman in the middle held up a wrinkled, bony hand and said, "We wondered when you'd find us. Come forward."

"You have the advantage of me. Who are you?" he asked.

All three women pulled back their hoods, allowing Alex to get a good look at them. They were so old that they reminded Alex of crones he'd seen in horror movies. The one in the middle was slightly taller than the other two. With her reddish-brown skin and silver hair braided in the same style as his, Alex thought she looked like she could have been a member of his tribe. "I'm Aruru, but most people call me Hellwain nowadays." She pointed to the woman to her left, who had darker skin and shorter hair. "This is my sister, Ninsun, or Hecate, depending on her mood." She turned to the Polynesian-looking woman on her right and said, "And this is my other sister, Mammet, or Puckle to her friends. I must know, though – why have you come in search of the Chintamani?"

"I'm not looking for it, although Bishop Lamberton thought it might be in the area."

"How could you possibly know him?" Ninsun asked. "He's been dead for centuries."

"My friends and I are trying to help William Wallace move on. But I'm here because of Apalāla."

Hellwain's eyes narrowed as she tried figuring out who Alex was talking about. At last, she gasped. "You mean Nessie? But she doesn't like humans."

"Can you blame her?" Alex asked.

Hellwain nodded in agreement.

Mammet spoke up, saying, "People have searched for this place for centuries, but none have ever managed to break through our defenses. Yet you don't seem very excited. Why did you go through all that effort if you didn't want to come here?"

"That's a question I'm still trying to figure out." Alex spotted one of the *Sibylline Books* sitting on a pedestal behind them just then. Pointing at it, he said, "Why do you have that thing out in the open? It's dangerous. You should keep it locked up. Better yet, you should destroy it and whatever else you have like it before it harms other people. From what I've seen, the Maqlû and stuff like it only cause death and destruction."

The women were so surprised at his outburst that, at first, all they could do was look from one to the other. Then they huddled around Hellwain. Alex tried to hear their whispered conversation but couldn't make out anything.

It was several minutes before they returned to their cauldrons. "Clearly, there are forces in play that we don't understand," Aruru said. "The fact that you found us means we're in danger of losing everything we've ever strived for. So, despite your avowed disinterest in the Maqlû, we have no choice but to force you to take our test."

"What if I don't want to take it?" Alex asked.

"Then, we'll kill you," Mammet replied. "We must keep our location and the stone's existence a secret. But, since you've come this far, we'll give you a chance and let Gaia decide your fate. All you have to do to live is correctly choose which cauldron has the Chintamani and retrieve it. You have a one in three chance of having more power than you could imagine. If one could master the Chintamani, one could move mountains and turn deserts into paradises. They could easily extract gold, silver, and precious gems to buy whatever their hearts desire. It can be yours if you choose wisely."

"I'm pretty good with math," Alex said. "And your offer means there's an even better chance you'll kill me. Please let me go. You keep the blasted thing because I don't want it. All those objects do is corrupt whoever has them or wants them."

When he saw the three crones were unmoved by his plea, he said, "Since you still have the object, I'm assuming everyone else has failed your test and died. How many people have you made that offer to before?"

"None. We used to lend the stone out for what we believed were good causes, but it corrupted everyone who held it, just as you said," Ninsun replied. "The last time was to help Sir William fight the invading English. We took it back after he abused its power and invaded England. That is why we've hidden it here. But somehow, you found us, which makes us wonder if Gaia is guiding your hand. Therefore, our consciences dictate we offer you an opportunity to save yourself."

"Can't you see how messed up this is?" He shook his head and, in a weary tone, said, "This is the type of thing that caused me to stop trying to find magical objects to help my sister move on."

"Nothing you say will change our minds," Hellwain replied. "We've seen too much of life to trust you. Now stop dallying and take the test. We must know whether Gaia sent you or not. In one of these cauldrons lies the Chintamani. Find it, and as long as you stay on a righteous path, you'll have riches and power beyond your imagination. Stray, and you'll die." She snapped her finger, and magical fires sprang to life under each cauldron.

Every fiber in his body told Alex to run away, but the ankh kept him firmly planted. Hoping it would help him choose wisely, he stepped over to Ninsun's cauldron and looked in. A horrible stench wafted from the bubbling dark-red-colored ooze inside. Steam rose from the pot in waves so thick that he could hardly see the woman behind it.

Ninsun reached into a small pouch hanging by her side and pulled out a pinch of red crystals. She sprinkled them in and said, "Don't be deceived by looks. Good and bad often look the same on the outside." Then she stuck her staff into the contents and stirred. Dark clouds tinged with fiery orange streaks hovered over the surface while little energy bolts shot through the clouds like lightning in a storm. The clouds dispersed, uncovering a surface that looked like it had been brushed with the colors from a spectacular sunset and giving off a delightful rose fragrance. "Choose my cauldron," Ninsun said, "and fame and fortune can be yours. But know that with great rewards comes great risk."

Unsure how to respond, Alex turned to his left, briefly stopped at Hellwain's cauldron, then proceeded to Mammet's. He looked down at the simmering bile-colored liquid, giving off an even more putrid smell than Ninsun's. And just like the first pot, it changed colors when Mammet added her blue crystals. As she stirred the liquid, it turned to a lush spring meadow green and then to purple, giving off a sweet lilac smell that wafted through the room, overcoming the earlier stench. "Pay no attention to my sister," Mammet said. "For my brew will bring you everlasting peace and tranquility. But beware. There are no choices in life that don't come without consequence."

Alex looked from Ninsun to Mammet, then stepped back to Hellwain's cauldron in the center. Even though there was no smell coming from it, the site of the greenish-brown brew in the pot caused him to screw up his face in disgust. The liquid didn't bubble, nor did she add crystals to it as her sisters did. Instead, she stuck her staff into the mixture and sent streaks of gold and silver shooting across the surface. As she stirred, the liquid gradually turned into a pearlescent-colored mix, giving off the intoxicating sweet scent of gardenias, which overpowered the other scents in the room. "My sisters make a good case for choosing their brews, but you should choose mine instead. Inside my pot is something everyone has dreamed of. Choose mine, and you'll have everlasting life, never having to worry about dying. Be careful, though, as it might be too much of a good thing."

Everything seemed so surreal that Alex considered pinching himself to see if it was all a dream. He touched his shirt where the ankh lay, hoping it would give him guidance, but it had gone quiet and sat cold against his skin.

Ninsun broke the silence that had descended on the room. "Come. Make your decision, but choose wisely, for immortality, fame, fortune, peace, and death are all possibilities."

He tried to read each woman's expression but could barely see them through the steam that was thicker than ever. At last, he took a deep breath and said, "You must take me for a fool. You said up front that you wanted me dead. Then you make me amazing offers. Mammet, you offered me everlasting peace. But that only comes after you die with no unfinished business. Ninsun, you offer me fame and fortune, but that comes with too high of a price. I've met a lot of ghosts who had both when they were living, and none were happy with their lot. Even while alive, they had to watch out for others who wanted what they had and were too often willing to do whatever it took to get them. And Hellwain, you offered me everlasting life. What a terrible gift – to live forever and see everyone you care about die. Nature intends for all creatures to live a normal life. So, no thank you to all of you. Your way only leads to self-destruction in the end."

"So, you choose death," Hellwain said.

"Isn't that what I said would happen at the beginning?" Alex replied.

Hellwain stared at Alex for a few moments before a smile creased the corners of her mouth. Before she could say anything, a muffled crashing sound caused everyone to jump.

Alex whirled around and saw Edward flying into the room, holding a brightly glowing sword. He pulled up and hovered a few feet in front of Alex, panting to recover his breath. "Pythia was right about you," the king growled. "She told me you would lead me to the secret of Wallace's success. My men and I have already killed most of your friends out there, so hand me this Philosopher's Stone, and I'll kill you quickly and painlessly so you can go see them in the afterlife."

Alex rolled his eyes. "Why does everyone keep talking about killing? I don't have this stone you're looking for, but these women say it's in one of their cauldrons." Alex stepped back and swept a hand towards the vessels. "Be my guest. Take it. I've already told them I don't want it."

Edward cautiously moved forward and peered into each pot. "What type of trick is this?"

"No trick." Alex heard banging at the door and Jane's muffled voice asking if he was there, but he didn't answer as he turned his attention back to the king.

"Don't count me such a fool," Edward said. "This has to be a trick. That stone is priceless."

"What's going on, Alex?" Hellwain asked. "Who are you talking to?"

Alex sighed. "King Edward's spirit is here; he wants the stone and will kill me for it."

"Then do what he wants," Hellwain replied. "Give him the stone."

Alex turned around, confused by what she was saying. He studied her face, searching for a hidden meaning, but couldn't figure out what she was getting at. A sharp pain caused Alex to look back. He nearly fainted when he saw the point of a flaming sword sticking into his back.

"Go on," the king said. "Get it for me, and I'll make your death painless."

Alex looked from Edward to the women and was surprised that all three crones were smiling at him. He felt the ankh tugging him towards Ninsun's cauldron, where the liquid inside had turned back to the bubbling lava he'd initially seen.

"But I don't know where it's at," Alex said.

"You're lying, boy," Edward said with a growl. "I saw you glance to the right."

Alex looked at the other cauldrons, wondering if the ankh was misleading him for some purpose. To his surprise, he saw Hellwain imperceptibly nod her head. Reluctantly, he stepped in front of Ninsun.

Another poke in his back caused Alex to close his eyes and thrust his arm into Ninsun's cauldron, hoping looks were deceiving. He immediately knew it was a horrible decision. Every nerve in his body screamed in agony. His screams echoed so loudly through the chamber that even the king grimaced and turned away.

He was about to pull what he thought was the stump of his arm out of the cauldron when he heard Ninsun whisper, "Trust yourself. See this through to the end."

With the ankh urging him forward, Alex gritted his teeth and closed his eyes even tighter, hoping it would help him shut out the excruciating pain. He thrust his arm further into the bubbling liquid and felt something hard brush his fingertips. Alex tried grabbing it, but the object was just out of his reach. Holding onto the cauldron's rim with his free hand, he stood on his toes and shoved his arm further until his shoulder nearly touched the molten-looking material.

He was in so much agony that he didn't know how his hand could still work, but somehow, he wrapped his fingers around the little stone. As soon as he did, he felt an energy pulsing through his arm, unlike anything he'd ever felt. There was a flash of light, and he fell head-first into an empty cauldron – the pain gone. The pot tipped over, and he wound up on his back, staring at a small, colorful stone in his hand with strange markings all over its surface.

Surprised he'd survived, he scooted out of the pot on his back. As he got to his knees, Edward flew at him, greed written all over his face. Alex reflexively held the stone behind his back, away from the advancing wraith.

The king stopped a few feet in front of Alex and said, "Give me the stone, boy, before I decide to make your death more painful than it need be."

With false bravado, Alex said, "You mentioned that Pythia had warned you about me. Did she tell you how many other ghosts she's sent after me that never returned?"

Edward hesitated. He held up his flaming sword and said, "But none of them had this to help them."

Alex pretended to yawn. "I'll admit a burning sword is different, but they all had magical objects. Have you ever seen what happens to those spirits who've lived bad lives when they move on?" He shuddered, then added, "I have. And I still get nightmares about them."

Edward took a step back. "You're bluffing, boy."

"Am I? Do you want to risk going to Hell if you're wrong? If you change your behavior, you still have the chance to move on to a better place than where you're headed for now." Alex glanced over at Hellwain's cauldron and noticed her pot had changed to a fiery liquid, reminding him of a molten lava pool.

"You tire me, boy. Give it to me now, or the only thing I'll promise you is that I'll squash you and your friends – as I've done with everyone who gets in my way – as I did with your friend Wallace."

The smell of burning sulfur started wafting through the room. Hoping he was doing the right thing, Alex suddenly swung around and tossed the stone into Hellwain's cauldron. Then he looked pointedly from Hellwain, to the book, and then the pot. With a smile on her face, she grabbed the *Sibylline Book* and tossed it in with the Chintamani.

For a long second, the colored rock and book sat on top of the liquid, causing Alex's heart to sink as he thought he'd made a terrible miscalculation.

Edward screamed in horror and started reaching for the Chintamani but stopped when a war cry from behind caused him to turn and see what the disturbance was.

Wallace burst into the room, flew forward, and thrust his sword through Edward's heart. The king looked down in disbelief at the long piece of ghostly metal sticking through his chest. He stumbled backwards, then fell on his knees. A second later, he'd turned to dust.

Seeing the burning sword lying on the floor, Alex reached down and grabbed it, then tossed it into Hellwain's cauldron. He watched, with a sense of relief spreading through his body, as the three magical objects burst into flames then slowly sank into the bubbling liquid.

A cry of pain off to his side caused Alex to spin around just in time to see Mammet collapse onto the floor. Ninsun groaned, clutched her chest, and fell forward onto her cauldron.

Alex was too stunned at the rapid change of events to do anything other than ask, "What's going on?"

Hellwain, who suddenly looked pale, waved her hand and mumbled something, causing the fires to go out and all three cauldrons to disappear. With a wan smile, she said, "You have destroyed our life force."

"I'm sorry. I didn't mean to, but I couldn't let him have the stone."

Hellwain smiled and held up her hand. "It is we who are sorry we tested you like that. Please understand that we've seen so many people misuse magical objects that we've become distrustful of humanity. We're grateful for what you've done, for you have released us from a terrible burden."

"What will happen to you?" Alex asked.

"What happens to all living creatures – we will die soon. But don't feel sorry for us. We have lived unnaturally long and full lives. Farewell, Alex Scire. May Gaia always be with you."

Hellwain went over to Mammet, helped her to her feet, and together, the three women shuffled towards a door in the back of the room.

CHAPTER 44
THE AFTERMATH OF WAR

Alex was so stunned by the sudden turn of events that he completely forgot about the ghosts in the room until Deborah grabbed his arm, and asked, "Are you all right?"

The cold from his sister's touch shocked him out of his stupor. "I'm fine, but what are you doing here?" he asked.

"Trying to save your skin again, but it looks like we're a little late. I lost you in Stirling and have been tracking your aura ever since. I arrived this morning just in time to see Nessie taking you three down into the lake with her. Luckily, Wallace and his friends returned when they did, for King Edward's forces attacked when you were at the outer door. I'm so glad you're safe, but what happened here?"

Alex waved the question aside and asked, "Where are Diana and Jane? Are they all right?"

"They were fine when I left them a minute ago," Deborah replied. "I'm not sure how you got through the outer door, but Edward had to cut a hole through the door with his magical sword before he could slip in. We followed him as soon as it was safe, but...." A loud explosion interrupted Deborah's explanation. When the sound had stopped reverberating in the chamber, she added, "It looks like Diana has managed to blast her way in."

Jane came rushing up but pulled up and stared at Hellwain, who was still standing in the doorway. "Mom?"

Hellwain smiled, then closed the door behind her.

"That was your mom?" Alex asked. "You should go after her and make sure she's all right. I think I did something that might have hurt her."

Jane touched his arm and said, "In a minute. I want to make sure ye're not hurt first."

"I'm fine, but…."

"Tell me, were there two other old women here too?" Jane asked.

"Yeah. I think their names were Ninsun and Mam…something," Alex replied.

"Mammet. They are my adoptive mothers that I told you about," Jane said.

Diana stumbled up, her face covered in dust and her hair sticking out in all directions, grabbed Alex's hand, and asked, "What have we missed?"

"I'll tell you later," Alex replied. "Where are Stephen and the others?"

"They dinnae make it," Wallace said in a soft voice. He paused, then slammed a fist against the wall. "Damn. I should've known we were heading into a trap. We should've been better prepared. Now, some good men don't have the chance to move on to heaven."

"It's not your fault," Alex said. "If anyone's, it's mine. I've had enough experience with these situations that I shouldn't have gone off half-cocked like usual. I knew there would be trouble – I just didn't know what type."

Bishop Lamberton joined the group. He saw Alex's and Wallace's dejected looks and said, "Come now, what are ye looking so glum for?"

Wallace threw his arms into the air and said, "It's all been for naught. I'm in one piece, but most of my friends have died. And I still haven't moved on. What more must I endure?"

The bishop smiled. "Nothing. Look."

Wallace looked down and saw his feet were shimmering. Astonished, he looked over to Kerly and saw the same thing happening to his former aide.

"Go in peace, my friends," Lamberton said, but he spoke to thin air as both Wallace and Kerly had disappeared."

The bishop smiled and said, "I, too, must go because I have more to do here on Earth. May God bless you."

"What's happening?" Diana asked.

Alex told the girls a highly edited version of what had happened since he'd fallen through the door, but when no one said anything after he'd finished, he thought they were mad at him for destroying the Chintamani. Wanting to defend himself from their recriminations, he said, "I couldn't let it fall into the hands of someone like Edward. And besides, the three women in there seemed relieved they didn't have to guard it anymore."

"I think you made the right choice, brother. The more I see of the Maqlû, the more convinced I am they're dangerous objects. But right now, I'm afraid I must leave. I'm exhausted trying to keep up with you. Please tell Diana and Jane that I miss them."

"I will."

"May Gaia be with you, brother."

"And you, sis."

"I take it that Deborah jest left," Jane said.

Alex nodded. "I know you two must have questions, but do you mind holding off until we get outside? I've had enough of this place and don't want to be here any longer than I have to." Before either girl could reply, he took one of the torches down from the wall and moved to the back of the room. "The women who were in here left by this route. Since I don't think we could survive leaving the way we came in, I'd rather use their exit. And we better get going because I didn't see much besides trees on this side of the lake when we came in this morning."

Diana walked to Alex's side and studied what appeared to be a blank wall for a minute. "Jane, you've got to look at this."

Her fellow Druid came up and kneeled to see what Diana was pointing to. After studying the marks for a minute, she let out a long, low whistle. "I never thought I'd see those in a place like this?"

"What are you talking about?" Alex asked.

Diana smiled. "How does it feel to be on the other foot for once – that we know something you don't?" She took pity on him and said, "They're special runes to protect this place."

"Do ye think how to crack them, Diana?" Jane asked. "I thought I knew runes pretty well, but I've never seen half of these symbols. They looked like a mixture of runes and some ancient foreign language, although they looked familiar. I jest can't remember where I've seen them before."

Diana handed Jane her torch and pulled out her talisman. "I think so," she replied.

Curious that both girls were stumped, Alex bent down to look at the markings. He gasped when he realized that many of the symbols on the wall were similar to those on his ankh.

Jane was about to say something to him but got distracted when Diana spread her arms and chanted,

"Stone from the mountain
Stone from the cave
Listen to me and abide
Move this rock aside."

A few seconds later, Alex felt a rush of air as the door slid silently open.

Jane rushed through, followed by Diana, who grabbed Alex's hand and said, "Hurry. You need to get through before it closes."

He followed them into another tunnel, barely getting in before the door clipped his heels.

Jane gave Diana's torch back, then held hers up to provide enough light for the others to see, while leading them up a gently sloping tunnel. A couple of minutes later, they encountered a second stone door.

Diana chanted the same opening spell and stepped outside.

Alex followed and was nearly blinded by the bright Scottish sunshine. Pulling his Tilley down for shade, he let his eyes adjust, then looked around. But all he saw were the forested hills surrounding Loch Ness. "How do we get out of here?" he asked.

"That's a good question because ye picked one of the more remote places in Scotland to come to," Jane said.

She pushed some of her still-damp hair out of her face and added, "I'm pretty sure we're still on the eastern side of the lake, so I'd suggest we head up the hill and take a left when we get to the road. We're much closer to Inverness than Fort Augustus, and I'm hoping there'll be more traffic headed that way."

They were silent as they worked their way up the hillside until Diana stopped for a break and said, "You gave us the Cliff Notes version of what happened back there. What haven't you told us?"

"I can add one thing," Jane said. "Alex met my moms back there." She turned to him and asked, "What were they like?"

"Not very inviting. It was like that Shakespeare story you made me read last winter with three crones standing behind cauldrons, with the stone in one of them," Alex said. "They were pretty upset when I first showed up and threatened to kill me. But then they changed their mind and said that if I chose wisely, they'd let me have the Chintamani. Even then, I wasn't going to pick it until King Edward busted in and threatened to torture me if I didn't give him the stone. That's when it got really weird. All of a sudden, Hellwain seemed to want me to find it. With Edward's sword at my back, I happened to pick the right cauldron and had the object in my hand when Wallace burst into the room and killed the king."

"It wasn't happenstance," Jane mumbled.

Not hearing her friend, Diana said, "I can't believe you found the Chintamani. So, what did you do with it?"

Alex cringed when he replied, "I tossed it in one of the pots and burned it, along with the *Sibylline Book* they had and the king's magical sword. Then they left, and you guys came in."

"I don't understand how you can talk so casually about finding and destroying one of the Maqlû," Diana said.

"I couldn't let Edward, or anyone else, take it. It's too dangerous," Alex replied.

"How did my mothers react to what ye did?" Jane asked.

Alex thought about the look of relief on Hellwain's face after he'd destroyed the stone. "They seemed relieved – almost like I did them a favor. Although…."

"Although what?" Jane asked.

"They're dying," Alex said. "That object was keeping them alive."

It took Jane a moment to digest the news. At last, she said, "Don't feel bad. I think ye did do them a favor. Hellwain smiled at me when she was leaving, something she rarely did when I lived with them. In fact, none of them ever seemed happy as they always had a weary look to them."

Sibyl's last words of advice suddenly came to mind, driving Alex to say, "I want to apologize to you two, especially you, Diana."

"You have nothing to apologize for. I was just doing my usual grumbling," Diana said.

Alex shook his head. "It's not about what happened today." He reached into his shirt and was about to pull the ankh out when Jane said, "Are ye sure? Ye don't have to."

"It's overdue." He pulled his necklace out and showed it to Diana. "This is the cause of all your questions about me. My father meant to give this to my sister, but I accidentally took it the day she died. I don't know how it works, but it enables me to see ghosts, talk to dragons, and, importantly, acts like a compass to the Maqlû."

Fearing how Diana would react, he took a deep breath and blurted out, "I don't know how I'm going to do it, but I've decided I'm going after the other Maqlû. Since you're both sworn to protect them, I'll understand if you never want to speak to me again."

Diana's answer was to rush forward and engulf him in a hug. A second later, Alex could feel Jane's arms wrapping around him.

The three stayed that way for some time, with Alex growing increasingly uncomfortable at the display of affection. At last, his growing rigidity signaled to the girls that the group hug was over. Blushing, he couldn't help but ask, "What was that for? I thought you'd be mad."

"We've been waiting so long for ye to finally let yer defenses down," Jane said. "So, what are ye thinking yer next step is?"

He grinned and replied, "First of all, finding a way back to civilization."

They resumed their climb and soon reached the road. None of them spoke for some time as they trudged along. A few cars passed, but none stopped. Their talk drifted to more mundane stuff for the next couple of hours until they stopped for a break just as the sun started touching the top of the steep hills overlooking the lake.

"How long will it take us to get to Inverness?" Alex asked.

"I'm hoping somebody takes pity on us and gives us a lift," Jane replied. "Otherwise, it'll take another day. I wish we'd ended up on the other side of the lake where our jackets and supplies are because if we don't get a lift soon, it's going to be a long, cold, hungry night."

As if on command, a large black SUV with heavily tinted windows, coming from the Inverness direction, passed by, then braked and started backing up, eventually coming to a stop beside them. The three teenagers froze, unsure if the car was stopping to help them.

All four doors opened a second later, and women began piling out. Sophie emerged from the front passenger seat, pointed at Alex, and shouted, "Get him!"

***

Enjoyed *The Chintamani*?

If you enjoyed this story and have a moment to spare, I'd appreciate a short review on Goodreads or the site where you bought this book. Your help spreading the word is greatly appreciated, as reviews make a huge difference in helping new readers find the series. Thank you!

ALSO BY THE AUTHOR
The Maqlû Series

After mistakenly taking his dad's magical ankh, Alex Scire suddenly sees ghosts everywhere, including his sister, who's stuck in the afterlife. To help her move on, he joins an expedition headed to the ancient Mayan city of Lamanai to search for a magical object. But to succeed he has to battle a tyrannical ghost king's army and survive assassination attempts by those who killed his family.

After destroying the Palantir, Alex Scire vows to find another magical object that will help his sister move on in the afterlife. He sets out on a ghost ship, along with his Druid friends Jane and Diana, to find the Fountain of Youth. To succeed, though, they'll have to find a place that might not exist, battle pirates, and survive an eerie hurricane in the Bermuda Triangle.

After destroying The Fountain of Youth, Alex Scire finds himself adrift on the ocean, until he stumbles upon a ghost who holds the secret to the Holy Grail. Thinking he has one last chance to help his sister move on, Alex embarks on a quest that takes him from the dungeons of the Spanish Inquisition to Dracula's haunts in Transylvania to find the Grail.

AUTHOR'S NOTE

Historical accuracy of *The Chintamani*

The Chintamani is a book of fiction originally inspired by the movie *Braveheart*. But, as I discovered in writing the other books in this series, **'Truth is stranger than fiction,'** and William Wallace's life was much more incredible than the movie. So, I've tried honoring his memory by drawing inspiration for the rest of the story from real places, people, and events. For instance:

Although I have taken literary license to portray their **characters**, many of the ghosts were inspired by real people.

- William Wallace was a giant of a man, standing almost 6' 7" tall. He lived during a turbulent time in Scotland's history when many Scottish nobles were vying for the crown. Despite that, he rose to become the Guardian of Scotland due to his many amazing, almost unbelievable, military exploits (I've only included a smattering of them in the book). The story of the English pulling him out of jail and throwing him on a refuse heap, expecting him to die, only to be rescued by a local woman, is supposedly true. (Note: much of what we know of Wallace's history was written over a century after his death and, therefore, subject to questioning.)
- Bishop Lamberton, Kerly, Stephen, Robert the Bruce, and the Red Comyn were all contemporaries

of Wallace. Their roles in the fight against England, especially Bruce and Comyn, are subject to debate.
- Wallace's main adversary, King Edward I, also known as 'Longshanks,' was a giant for his day, standing about 6' 3" tall. Interestingly, although both men spent much of their adult lives fighting in wars, both were reformers who, in many ways, were ahead of their times in their philosophies.
- Sir John Seagrave's role in Wallace's trial and execution is based on historical records.

Most of the **locations** in the book are based on places I've visited, including;
- Porlock is a small town on the southwest coast of England. It was cold, windy, and rainy when we were there (the only bad weather day of the entire trip), but I was thrilled by the miserable weather because it inspired me to include it in my story.
- If you ever get to Stonehenge, I encourage you to walk to the monument from the Visitor Center, like Alex did. It gives you a much better perspective of the UNESCO site than taking the shuttle bus.
- London was overwhelming because there was so much history and things to see and do, especially Kew Gardens and The British Museum.
- Of all the cities where Seagrave hung Wallace's quarters, I especially liked Berwick upon Tweed. It had everything – a cute train station, an old castle, a fort, a huge river, the North Sea, a cute downtown, and a fascinating cemetery that I used as inspiration for one of the grave-digging scenes.

- Scotland (Edinburgh, Stirling, Loch Ness, the Highlands) had a totally different feel than England – it was much more wild, beautiful, and peaceful, in my opinion.

Some of the **backstories** in the book are based on historical events or local legends, including;
- The Poppy Girl at Castle Keep in Newcastle – the castle's most famous ghost.
- The Tay River Bridge Disaster gives me goosebumps just thinking about what happened that terrible night.
- If you ever go to Wallace's Monument in Stirling, I recommend you take the same trail Alex did up the mountain. Even though it's longer, it's still an easy climb but has fantastic views.
- If I ever go back to Britain, I'd go at the same time of year we did – mid to late May. Rhododendron Dell in Kew Gardens was fabulous, as were the Bluebells in Stirling, and the Gorse in Scotland.
- To make my wormholes and dragon world as realistic as possible, I've had to do some research on quantum physics. One of the fascinating things I learned in this research is that some of the smartest people in the world (e.g., Stephen Hawking) believe that parallel universes and space-time vortexes are possible.

For more information on the historical places, events, and characters included in this book, go to my web page, where I have posted a glossary.

ABOUT THE AUTHOR

JC Holmberg is the author of the Young Adult Fantasy Adventure series – *The Maqlû*. He and his wife, Mari, live in *The Kentucky Wildlands*. John splits his time between working on his forestland in the mornings, writing in the afternoon, and continuing his travels to research settings for future books.

The picture below is of the author at the Traitor's Gate in the Tower of London, where Alex finds William Wallace's skull.

FOLLOW THE AUTHOR

Although *The Maqlû* is a fantasy series that includes ghosts and magic, the books are set in the amazing real world with fascinating historical characters. To learn more about the author, the background of each story, and some fascinating fun facts included in the books, go to,

www.jcholmberg.com

www.ingramcontent.com/pod-product-compliance
Lightning Source LLC
Chambersburg PA
CBHW050801190726
48285CB00005B/1745